KNOCK DOWN GINGER

John Swinfield

PEACH PUBLISHING

By the Same Author

Legless in Polperro

ISBN 978-1-78036-330-1

Published by
Peach Publishing

Dedication

For Bridgit and my family. For those who have suffered and still are. For those of courage who labour in adverse circumstances around the world. They know who they are.

Acknowledgement

My thanks to police sources and friends and contacts in south-east Asia and South America. They must remain anonymous. I am also very grateful for the help and counsel given to me by the distinguished literary agent, Sonia Land, and her colleagues in Sheil Land Associates.

PART 1

He was on the cracked leather chesterfield in the Admiral Keppel snooker room. A cue rammed so hard into his mouth it poked out through the back of his neck. Dark suit, white shirt, regimental tie. At *The Imperial* he was known as the Captain. Down from Norfolk on Britain's east coast for a night in London. Scissors had been jabbed in his left eye. His right popped and bulged. He was tied hand and foot. Before the cue had been rammed into his mouth he had been gagged with black duct tape. The spinal cord had dislocated the atlantoaxial joint connecting the head to the neck. Usual procedures. Forensics, pathology, DNA sampling. Inch by inch searches. The club closed. Rooms taped off. Members and servants quizzed.

***

Detective Inspector Jack Raven would lead the investigation. Known for his cold eyes and hot temper. He sat on the Captain's bed in the chamber in the eaves. The club roof and cupola were being refurbished. Forgotten attics turned into more chambers. The club façade on Pall Mall in London was clad in scaffolding. The dead man was Frank Arthur Gleeson. Formerly of the Royal Engineers. Latterly an executive with Cathedral Insurance. The porter said Gleeson had arrived in the middle of the afternoon. He had taken tea and toast on the balcony overlooking the atrium with its black and white floor and busts of dead members. From there he had gone to his room in the roof. At some point he had visited the snooker room. To be slaughtered. Raven sat on Gleeson's bed. The chamber was suffocating. The roof-light had jammed. The air conditioning had malfunctioned. Gleeson travelled light. Shaving bag, underclothes, silk tie, shirt.

The choking, gurgling. Gleeson's face running with sweat as he closed in with the scissors. Gleeson told him about Capes. Her part in it. He watched the fish. Round and round it swam. He rolled the ball in his hand. Heavy. Smooth as glass. He'd sealed Gleeson's mouth with duct tape. After stabbing him in his eye he'd torn off the tape. Gleeson's head lolled forward, mouth agape. He'd driven the cue into his mouth.

***

The ancient snooker room looked like an abattoir. Blood which had soaked the chesterfield was splattered over the panelled walls, floor, the green baize of the table and a large, morose oil painting of Admiral Keppel.

***

Rosie Diamond had the mild diffidence of a police officer promoted beyond her experience. To be assigned as Raven's deputy was an important promotion. He had a formidable record. His reputation was that of a moody loner. While other policemen followed football, he kept a small yacht on the River Deben in Suffolk. They said that he had always sailed close to the wind. The nearest Rosie had been to water was fighting off dudes on the muddy banks of the River Quaggy in Lewisham in south London where she had grown up. Old hands said Raven's temper became worse after his wife died. Volcanic they said. They'd spiced it up for Rosie's benefit.

***

Rosie thought there were three reasons she'd been promoted. She was black, a woman and a Cambridge university graduate.

Though flattered by her selection, she was convinced she was too inexperienced. Raven had deliberately requested her. She was quick witted and self-deprecatory. He liked officers who could laugh at themselves. Too many detectives were all swagger and no deduction. He liked strong individuals. In the past he'd led big manhunts. He understood the value of team work. But he also knew its limitations. Teams of detectives could pull in the wrong direction. The less able hiding their shortcomings in a crowd. With murder there were no short cuts. Each needed instinct, tenacity and an iron determination.

***

Raven's bosses were pleased he'd asked for Rosie. But some fretted she'd be tainted by the habits of a detective who could have gone higher if he'd stuck to the rules. He'd been reprimanded about his casual disregard for proprieties as often as he'd been commended for his effectiveness. In the upper echelons of the force Diamond was seen as a flier. Clever, personable, black. The personification of public relations policing at its best. She was the subject of jealousy. More senior officers had been keen to work with Raven. To see if his well-honed *feel* for murder inquiries might rub off on them. Behind her back there was bitchiness. It didn't worry Raven. He wanted brains and instincts. Some senior officers chose to surround themselves with dullards, knowing they would never challenge or usurp them. Raven had confidence in his abilities. In those around him he sought excellence over mediocrity. He saw Diamond's lack of confidence as modesty. It would be better than being with cocky bastards. Refreshing to work with somebody who didn't think they were God's gift.

***

At the police station – the nick – autopsies were called 'canoe trips.' Raven hated them.

"Autopsies. Forensics. Sods in white coats think they can solve everything."

Carter was one of the brightest pathologists. He skinned Gleeson's face. Rolling the skin down. Settling it like a scarf round the chin. He took out the brain, slicing into it, poring over it.

"Touch of dementia," he said.

Holding it closer to the lamp.

"Bit of a way to go before he was barking. We're all mad in the end .."

He stared at Rosie over his mask.

Cutting Gleeson's body open from the neck to the lower belly. Pulling the folds of flesh to one side. Digging his fingers in. Lifting out each organ.

"Good liver. It'd win a rosette."

He delved into Gleeson's abdomen.

"Toast, apricot jam."

When hollowed out the cadaver looked like a canoe.

***

Raven thought back to when he had first joined the force. He was twenty. His first canoe trip. His stomach had churned. Back then when the pathologist had finished he had instructed his assistant to reassemble the corpse. The young apprentice had rolled the facial skin from the chin up and back over the skull. Kneading it this way and that to make it fit as snugly as possible. After smoothing out the crinkles the apprentice had suddenly looked up at the newly-enlisted Raven and shouted 'Boo!' The pathologist had reprimanded the boy. Telling him that the dead deserved as much dignity as the living. He later told Raven: "The lad's a scallywag. But it was very funny. You looked as white as a ghost. As pale as death itself."

Raven had never forgotten. He turned to Rosie.

"You alright?"

She nodded, forcing a smile.

"Ever seen a black girl turn white?"

***

Gleeson had lived in the 18th century Decoy Cottage in the remote village of Stocking Easter in Norfolk's Broadland, an idyllic network of rivers and lagoons called broads or meres. Stocking Easter lay a mile from the sea. Lonely dunes and tufted banks of marram grass offered scant protection from the icy winds and ravages of the North Sea. Gleeson's wife, Vicky, had died years before. She was remembered in the village as a typical army officer's wife. Brisk, organised, verging on the bossy. Blonde hair in a bun. Brown eyes, long legs, a come on look. Some said she was being screwed by Brian Cousins, a local businessman with money in a nursing home with a dubious reputation. Raven stared at her photograph. There was something about her stance. Perhaps she'd been a model? He studied his surroundings. Low ceilings. Beams. The cottage had been cosy. Now it was as chilled as a corpse. Two worn chairs and a sagging sofa at a tiled hearth of old red brick. Horse brasses. The squad had turned the cottage inside out. A picture-book garden. Soon to grow wild. Sweet peas, clematis, honeysuckle. Gleeson had loved his garden.

***

Rosie climbed the narrow, steep and twisting stairs. The small bedrooms had low, sloped ceilings. Ducking her head to avoid the beams, she began sifting cupboards and drawers. On the dressing table were photos of Gleeson and Vicky. Another was of a little girl in a yellow swimming costume on a beach. Bucket and spade, a shy smile. Through the little leaded window she could see a copse on the far side of a ploughed field. The vast Norfolk sky joined as one with the flat landscape. Beyond the trees lay the quiet, dark waters of Easter Mere. The wind cut like a blade. Rattling the panes. Whistling in the fireplace. Norfolk, land of the North Folk. Of marsh and fen. Of biting winds and huge, empty skies. Where Norsemen had arrived centuries before. The Vikings in their long-boats, raping and pillaging.

"Let's go." Raven shouted.

***

Raven always spent as long as he could in a victim's home. Soaking in the mood. When the chaos had subsided. When the clamour had died down. After Pathology and Forensics and the searches were complete. When neighbours and witnesses had been quizzed. It was then that he could begin to wear a victim's skin. Get to *know* them. *Feel* them. *Smell* them. They headed for the copse. The sudden crack of a breaking twig. A fleeing deer. Bolting towards Easter Mere. Fringed by reeds and carr. Police divers had poked about in its black and glutinous ooze. And found nothing. The copse was sunless, dense. Watery fen and tangled undergrowth had been flattened by lines of coppers searching on their hands and knees. An interesting thread had been found. It had been despatched to the labs for analysis.

***

He lay in a ditch in his fatigues. Watching Raven and Rosie pick their way round the edge of the muddy field to the copse. He had his Pentax with the long lens. Rosie's blurred image swam into focus. He reeled off a string of shots. The killing of Gleeson had gone well. But he'd not planned on this. He knew the copse. Before the killing he'd spent time there. Lying silent and still on the damp ground. Binoculars trained on the cottage. He'd wanted to know everything about him. He could have killed him at the cottage. But it would have been inappropriate. He'd returned to Norfolk to have a last look at Gleeson's place. He'd have trashed and fired it. But the police were there. Did they know he'd come back? He swapped the camera for binoculars. Pressing so hard they left a pale ring round his eyes. No, they didn't know anything. It was just bad luck. They were only scratching around. They didn't have a clue. He'd return when they'd gone. He'd go back to Alexander in London. The fish would need food.

***

Before they left the village they had a drink in the Nelson pub. Locals regaled them with their woes. No post office or buses. Unexplained screams from the nursing home. Second-homers pushing up prices. Turning it into a ghost village. Smug bird-watchers in camouflage. Genuine Broadsmen knew each murmur of the sedge-filled dykes. The hollow whoop of the shy Bittern. The slow beat of a Heron's wings. The rainbow flash of a Swallowtail butterfly skimming over patches of milk parsley.

***

That night they stayed at the Wherry Hotel. On the river Wensum. Opposite the railway station in Norwich, the capital city in East Anglia. From where Gleeson had made his final journey. The next day they went to Cathedral Insurance, Gleeson's former employer. For years it had been an international conglomerate. But the recession had taken its toll. Cathedral had been hit hard. It had been subject to several takeovers. Its parent company was now based in Eindhoven in Holland. Gleeson's boss had been Henke Reinfeldt, a Dutchman. His manner as smooth as his skin. A high-flier. Flaxen-hair, bleached highlights. Grey-green eyes, frameless glasses. Late twenties.

"Gleeson had been here years," he said. "A veteran. Always going on about the old days. How everything had been so much better. When Cathedral ruled the world. We had meetings about what to do with him. How to get rid of him. But with his long pension it was cheaper to let him come to the end of his time than to pay him off. The old company had a thing about army types. Loved them. Polished shoes, stiff upper-lip. You know the type. We're much more relaxed. More modern."

***

Raven had fixed him with one of his deep-freeze stares. He disliked anybody who talked about being 'modern.' Reinfeldt's elbows were on the desk, hands making a steeple. Finger tip-to-tip, manicured nails. Perfect cuffs, an easy-press suit. Living in hotel rooms. A suitcase man. Stateless, hiring and firing. Unhindered by sentiment or loyalty. Raven hated Reinfeldt's fixed smile, the shiny teeth, the blonde streaks in his hair, his moisturised skin. Above all he loathed his permanent, smiling *pleasantness*. Nobody could be that pleasant *all* the time; unctuous, so eager-to-please. He probably ate babies for a hobby. Or on moonless nights strangled kittens and chucked them in the Wensum. Olivia used to tell Raven he had become too cynical. *Realistic*, he'd say. Reminding her of all the apparent innocents he'd met over the years who turned out to be blood-drenched freaks.

***

Reinfeldt had astonishingly pearly teeth. Glinting like a toothpaste advert. Raven used a favourite ploy. He would ask something bizarre. It shook up an interviewee. Threw them off balance. He suddenly asked Reinfeldt:

"Are your teeth whitened?"

"I'm sorry ..?"

"They're so white."

"What's that got to do with Gleeson?"

8

"Nothing. They just look so perfect."

Reinfeldt tried to compose himself. "Well, anyway ..Gleeson was old school. We're more jeans and dress down .."

"Are they whitened?"

"Please .. Inspector .. well, yes, if you must know .. capped and whitened."

"Expensive?"

"Very. They were done in Holland."

"Why?"

"A university friend .. went into dentistry."

"But why have them whitened ..?"

".. I don't know .."

"Was there something wrong with them?"

"There was nothing wrong .."

"Cosmetic then ..?"

Rosie suppressed a giggle.

***

Rosie smiled at Reinfeldt, her manner warm and friendly. "You said dressed down .. but you're in a suit."

"I'm senior management."

Raven: "Wasn't Gleeson?"

Reinfeldt made notes with his Mont Blanc fountain pen. "*Thought* he was."

"Are you saying Gleeson was too old .. that he thought himself more important than he was?"

Once more, as though answering their questions was too much trouble, Reinfeldt had started scribbling on his pad.

"Mr. Reinfeldt," said Raven, his eyes icy. "Answer when you're asked."

"I'm sorry .. we're not allowed to say *too old*. But .. I s'pose so, yes. He was the face of the company. If newspapers wanted anything or somebody had to go on television he was the one we always wheeled out. We laughed about it. He was a bit of a pain."

Rosie: "Sounds as if you couldn't stand him?"

Reinfeldt got up from his desk, moving to a window. Crumbling offices, once part of Cathedral, were being converted into townhouses and apartments.

"That's putting it a bit strong .. but he didn't like me being his boss. I was much younger than him. That can be difficult. And there was something else .. he always seemed to be so rich."

A bulldozer was at work on the site. Clouds of dust in its wake.

"Rich?" Raven stared at him.

"One day, when he was going to London .. I asked him why his jacket was bulging. It looked like a gun. But it was a wad of money, notes. Hundreds of pounds."

"For what?"

"God knows. I didn't ask."

"Why not?"

"We weren't like that. He wasn't easy to get close to."

"Your fault or his?" Rosie asked.

He returned her smile, a flash of white teeth. "I'm quite easy .. so people tell me."

Afterwards she told Raven : "Self-regarding little creep."

***

At *The Imperial* the surveillance cameras were of no use. They'd gone wrong weeks before when the wiring was cut by a roofer. The porters at the main Pall Mall entrance seemed vigilant. Tradesmen had to use a side door which let on to a vast, subterranean kitchen. It was possible to enter the kitchen and leave by the gloomy, stone-flagged basement, past a photo-gallery of deceased members. From there a staircase led up to a lobby next to the main saloon. Or the killer could have used steps which led to the dining room from a tree-fringed lawn at the rear of the club.

***

On the afternoon of the slaughter there were few people in *The Imperial*. It was busier at night when servants laid a table as a temporary bar in the atrium. A place for members to meet guests for a drink before supper in the dining room with its marble pillars decorated in gold leaf. Forensics were hampered by builders' dust. There were a thousand fingerprints and footmarks. The club had been invaded by strangers. As well as builders creating more bedrooms – the chambers in the roof as the club called them – there had been a stream of heritage big-wigs ensuring that nothing untoward was being done which contravened the club's listing as a building of merit. *The Imperial* was an architectural masterpiece. The most elegant club in London. Its membership was small if compared to neighbouring clubs. But over the years it had become a money-pit. In constant need of repair. Subscriptions had started to rise and members had begun to grumble. Instead of upping the fees or widening the membership – the latter would have made it more like a hotel than an exclusive club – the members had agreed, somewhat reluctantly, to let in outsiders. For a handsome fee they could hold cocktail parties, book launches and wedding receptions in the club's gilded library. It meant countless strangers had passed through, exacerbating the difficulties which confronted Raven and the squad.

***

At the time of the killing two members were in the small study room where silence was enforced with such rigour that if a member so much as coughed he risked being reported to the club secretary. Each had vouched for the others' presence. In any case, they were too frail and elderly to have exerted the level of violence used on Gleeson. A third member was asleep in a winged chair in the smoking room. His presence endorsed to the police by servants anxious that his snores would disturb a fourth member, Sir Alistair Dilke. Dilke was a retired judge. He had been busily crafting his notes for a lecture at *The Imperial's* legal society, his tall, lean frame,

11

hunched over an ormolu writing desk. With his usual courtliness he smiled when a servant, newly-arrived from Portugal, whispered of his concern.

"Don't worry." Dilke laid down his pen. "It's the club port at lunch that's the real miscreant."

Phil Leach was the number three in the squad. He interviewed Dilke. He had given evidence in court cases in which Dilke had presided. He liked him. In court he had a droll humour and, unlike many of his peers, a command of the minutiae. Leach had hoped Dilke would offer a fresh insight. They had tea in the smoking room. But the interview disclosed little. "I've dealt with many a murder," Dilke told him. "But it's still a Hell of a shock when it happens on your own doorstep, so to speak."

***

Charlie Samuels, a journalist famed for his wit and erudition, was in *The Imperial* at the time of the killing. He'd returned from a posting in Buenos Aires, in south America, twenty years before, and had lived permanently in the club ever since. He'd been working in the committee room. The only room where laptops and mobiles were allowed. *The Imperial* rules had been established two centuries before, and had barely altered since. Jackets and ties were compulsory. Briefcases had to be left at the porter's desk. The club chairman was a retired Marxist academic. Renowned for his intellect and waspishness. He told one hapless new member who had the temerity to complain about having to wear a tie: "If you don't like the rules why did you join? Nobody asked you to. *The Imperial's* been here a long time. It will survive without you." The committee room was miniscule. Servants had seen Samuels through its half-glass door. As he typed they had brought him a decanter of *Imperial* claret. Rosie interviewed him. He said it was a tragedy such a scoop had occurred under his nose and he'd had to ignore it; club rules forbade members from airing its business in public. "They'd have chucked me out. Not worth it for a few bob in Fleet Street. Love the club. All its shadows. When everybody's gone home and the lights are turned down low you can hear it breathing. It's all the ghosts. Ghosts are insomniacs. They get restless. We've had all sorts of members here. Cabinet ministers, soldiers, spies, poets and painters." He noted Rosie's charms, wishing he was thirty years younger. He had enjoyed a distinguished career. A wide circle of friends drawn by his unassuming nature and self-mockery would join him for supper, enjoying a decanter of the famed *Imperial* claret, followed by a frame of snooker.

"Had a drink with Gleeson once. He went on about insurance. Absolutely riveting!" Blue eyes twinkling, raising his eyebrows, running a hand through his grey hair.

"We've a snooker society here. But he didn't join. The servants tell me he was always practising though. If I was one of your lot I might find that a bit odd."

Two elderly members left the dining room, walking slowly, arm-in-arm. One heavily dependent on a silver-topped stick. The other with a mane of silvery-white hair and a wing collar.

"The chap with the cane was a distinguished submariner .. commander somebody or other. Got a VC. Look at him now. You could hardly credit it. Comes to all of us, of course. Poor old blighter. Don't know the chappie with the collar. Probably keeps his head on."

He looked round, taking in the marble pillars entwined with gold leaf, the black and white floor, the blazing fire on the far side of the atrium, the wide, sweeping staircase up to the library and the ornate smoking room.

"Tell you what .. one thing's for sure .. we'll need a new cover on the table. Balls won't run true if they're bouncing over dried blood. And we'll have to get rid of the chesterfield. Even if you could clean it up it'll have too many connotations. That poor devil being impaled on a cue. Up go the subscriptions again. C'est la vie."

***

The squad combed the records of club servants. Some curriculum vitae were over blown. It was not unusual. Everybody exaggerated their credentials. The club seemed a fair employer. Members had to treat servants with dignity. If they had a complaint about servants they had to channel them through the secretary.

"But they're *servants*," Rosie said. "Victorian patronage. If they bow and scrape they're looked after. But step out of line .. well, it's hard luck *old chap* .. curtains."

***

They were in Raven's car in St. James' Square opposite the club. He flashed his warrant card at a traffic warden. She'd allow him a few minutes on a double yellow.

"We all need patronage," he said, gently closing the door. It was an old Alfa Romeo. It ran well but he'd seen oily smoke. Olivia had bought it unseen off the Net. She had fallen in love with the badge. He'd been sceptical. But he liked its deep-throated noise and dark-blue, elegant lines. Olivia wasn't sure about the colour. "It's Italian .. hot-blooded, sloe-eyed .. it should be red," she'd laughed. Raven had teased her that it wouldn't last, it would fall apart. When they drove it off the forecourt they went for a celebratory lunch in Marlow. The restaurant was an Italian, like the car. They'd strolled by the river, arm in arm. The Thames tumbling over the weir. The day was special. It shone in his memory. He could remember every detail. The red and white check tablecloths, what she wore. They had talked about having children. He'd wanted four. She'd settle for two. They'd sipped Barolo. Laughing, smiling. He'd been wrong about the Alfa. It was reliable, though there was a hint of rust on a wheel arch and it needed careful coddling. He couldn't really afford the maintenance. But Olivia chose it and he couldn't bear to sell it.

Rosie looked at him: He was his customary immaculate self.
"Do you think a roofer might have killed Gleeson?" she asked.
But he was lost in thought, head down, pacing across the square.
His clothes were another of Olivia's influences. She liked him in a
suit. Dark blue, well-cut, understated; a white cotton Oxford, the
classic button-down shirt by Brooks Brothers of Madison Avenue
in New York. At one time she'd taught in America.
"You can't beat Brooks Brothers," she used to smile. "I can't be
seen around with some scruffy Plod!"
"You'll make me a dandy .." he'd laugh.
"Jack Raven," she'd tell him, nestling into him, feeling his
muscled arm.
"There's no way anybody could mistake you for a dandy."

***

Raven stared across the Mall at *The Imperial*. Trying to block out
Olivia's face. *That* smile; always laughing. A blur of black taxis
and chauffeured limousines rushed by. Decanting occupants at
expense-account eateries in the West End. *The Imperial's* white-
stone façade was imposing. Guarded by tall black iron torches.
Now it was besmirched by scaffolding and sheets of flapping
polythene. Before the building work it looked elegant, especially
at night, its salons brilliant with light from Bohemian chandeliers.
Each of its high-ceilinged rooms dressed for a soiree. It was then
that the servants lit the flambé, gas flames hissing and leaping
into the night, shadows dancing on the white stone. He turned
to Rosie. She thought he'd forgotten her question. Or that he had
failed to hear it in the din of the traffic. "Why would a roofer kill
him? There's no motive. It wasn't robbery. He'd got four hundred
pounds on him. And why would a roofer torture him?"

***

The builders were Poles, Lithuanians, Russians. No employment records were kept. Some were illegals. They knew nothing. Kept themselves to themselves. Safer that way. The roof was stifling. The air fetid. Dust danced in a sliver of sun peeking through a broken tile. Sloping rafters. Workers scurrying in a sideways gait over bare wires and rusted nails. Backs bent, heads down. Crouched like goblins.

***

The noise hammered in Raven's head. Stefan Padowski was the gangmaster. A wife and three children in Warsaw. The job was behind schedule. The club secretary had got at him. His boss from Camden had given him a hard time. Now the police were delaying him. He had to get on. Keep the job moving. Yes, he'd had to fire workers. Everybody hated him. The last one he'd had to sack was a pot-smoking Estonian. He'd nearly set the roof alight.

"Off his bloody head," Padowski grinned. Teeth studded with gold.

"Booze and weed."

A Cypriot plumber had caused a bathroom ceiling to collapse.

"No member in bath or secretary go ape shit." The gold grin. There had been others. He didn't know who they were. Where they came from. Where they went.

"I am not daddy. This good job. All they have do is work hard. Keep head down. Take money."

He remembered somebody who he thought was English.

"But darker skin. We pay him cash first week. He not come again."

He ran his fingers through his hair. Powdered in dust.

"Most sparkies not rewire soddin' plug without big bang. He good sparks. But one day here. Next day gone."

16

***

Padowski's fingers were as thick as Polish sausages. Soiled and calloused.

Raven stared at him. "Who cut the wiring for the CCTV cameras?"

"It was accident. Somali man. I give him sack. He didn't mean do it. He upset. He got big shock from wire. Not real electrician. No way tell sometime. He hopeless."

"Where did he go?"

"Don't know. Take off."

"He wasn't the good sparks? The other man? You're sure?"

Padowski shook his head. "No .. different man."

Raven watched him. "This is a murder. You'll be in trouble if you're lying."

Padowski remembered the old days. His mother in a headscarf. Grey, lined-face, weeping. In the still of the night the lorries with canvas sides that had pulled up at his home. Police jumping out. Banging at the door. His father being bundled away. Rain on wet cobbles. For sure, he promised. He'd tell the truth. The man he remembered as a good sparks looked as if he'd been in the army.

"Old clothes. Brown and green. We said it funny for man who spoke like British man to be poor as Polish. He don't come back. So we not pay him. He work hard, good work. But he not come back for money."

He pointed a sausage finger at his head.

"What wrong with him? He must go mad up here."

***

As they left Rosie glanced back at the scaffolding.

"Twitchers wear camouflage."

They ran across the Mall, dodging taxis. A courier on a racing bike – green Lycra, goggles, helmet – swerved round Rosie, giving her a V-sign.

"Mad bastard!" she yelled after him.

Raven had a parking ticket.

"Bugger."

She laughed.

"They could have towed it away. We've been here hours."

The square was flanked by Georgian houses, now offices. Discreet brass plates at every door. Accountants, solicitors, investment banks.

"Leeches always get the best addresses," he said.

Pigeons flapped round an old woman feeding them bread from a Tesco bag.

"West End birds. Choosy where they roost."

He looked at her, opening the door of the Alfa.

"Camouflage? Bird-watchers? Twitchers? Why not?"

***

Clipper Quay. A Docklands apartment. She was in the bath. Bludgeoned with what might have been a claw hammer. It had smashed deep into her brain. Ross from Pathology said a depressed skull fracture caused an intracranial bleed. Raven said Ross was a miserable sod but it went with the territory. Ross tried to blind him with science. Blood had built up in the brain. There was coning. The brain had been forced through the foramen magnum causing compression of the lower part of the brain, the medulla and pons. It had triggered cardiovascular and respiratory arrest. Raven repeated his mantra to Rosie about coppers playing second fiddle to pointy heads.

"What he's trying to say is that she was bashed to death with a hammer. She was also strangled with the belt of her dressing gown, just to make sure."

Hands and ankles tied. The loops drawn together in a way they recognised. Black sticky marks round her mouth. The killer appeared to have pounced in the small kitchen. Taped and tied her. Dragged her to the bathroom. She'd been scalded by the water.

Cigarette burns on her right shoulder. A clump of hair cut off.

***

He'd got her name by torturing Gleeson. Gleeson had been quick to squeal when he picked up the scissors. He'd given him her address. Who she worked for. Her job. Gleeson told him she was called Capes. That she was 'special' to him. But he'd betrayed her quickly enough. Anything to save his neck. Or his eye. He'd followed Capes. Where she lived, worked, played. He recognised her friends. They drank in 'The Broker' in Canary Wharf. Champagne. Lanson Black Label. He knew her habits. Everything about her. Each detail. She often had a drink before catching the Docklands Light Railway. Assured, elegant. Sunglasses pushed up into lustrous black hair.

***

"How many more?"

Raven was at the French windows. They let on to a tiny terrace overlooking the Thames far below. A silver thread in the evening sun. Beyond it lay the Isle of Dogs. Canary Wharf tower. Financial skyscrapers. Citadels of usury. The capital of Britain's banking industry.

"Each one reaching up to Mammon," he muttered. "Estate agents call these terraces Romeo and Juliet balconies. It's all bollocks."

He looked at Global across the river. The porter said the woman worked there. Its logo flashed on and off. A pink and yellow rainbow.

"Money grabbing bastards. Let's go and see what they know."

He turned from the view. But Rosie had fled. She'd run down the stairs and vomited by the bins in the underground car park. Her stomach had cart-wheeled when she and Raven had minutely examined the corpse. The twisted frame, the gouged head crooked to one side. Mouth open, as if frozen mid-scream. Trickles of dried blood on the white tiles, the bath water cold and scarlet.

***

Rosie was waiting for him by the Alfa.

"You look terrible, "he said. "Go home or go back to the office. I'll do Global."The corpse was that of Sylvia Capes. An American divorcee. She'd joined Global Finance from Stratton Hyde in New York. The Head of Human Resources at Global, Sally Peters, told Raven that when Capes joined the company she had been seeking new horizons. She had wanted a fresh start after a painful divorce. Peters said Capes had been popular with a wide circle of friends. She was a regular in the Global gym on the ground floor. Her job took her round the world. She was keen, motivated, fluent in Spanish.

***

Raven told Sally Peters that Human Resources was called Personnel when he was a young policeman.

"Really?" she said. As if scolding an errant child. "You're behind the times. It's a science. No big company could operate without HR. There's more to HR than unwanted pregnancies and heart to hearts. We leave that to vicars."

She breathed authority. Tall, thin, long blonde hair framing delicate features, high cheek-bones. A power-dresser in a dark Dior suit. He remembered the photograph of Vicky, Gleeson's late wife, in which she looked like an ex-model. In Peters' office there was a trace of Chanel's *Chance*. Raven knew the different smells. Perfume had been one of Olivia's pleasures. She had a weakness for it. A photo on a shelf behind Peters caught his eye. A dark-haired, older woman, in sun-glasses. He was coming to the opinion that

Peters was a harridan, bossy and calculating.

"Capes didn't come to you with any problems?"

"No. We don't know every *personal* detail. International finance is competitive. There's tension at the highest level. The downturn hasn't been easy. Bankers aren't popular. HR doesn't go into *personal* things."

She made *personal* sound poisonous.

***

Sally Peters' office was on the eleventh floor. From his chair at her desk Raven could see only sky and grey, scudding clouds.

"You've fired a lot of people .. was Capes up for the chop?"

"It's a recession. We have no control over world markets."

"That wasn't my question."

"Not as far as I know .. she was good at her job. The reports were excellent."

"Reports?"

"Staff reviews every six months .."

"Did she have any enemies?"

"I wouldn't know. We're not the Stasi."

"Have you?"

"What?"

"Enemies."

She hesitated.

"What have I to do with this?"

"You knew her."

"So?"

He'd rattled her.

"Your world sounds exciting." His sarcasm creeping in.

"We have our moments." She felt his distaste, turning back to her computer.

"You've sacked a lot," he said.

She was arrogant. And he was winding her up.

"If we have to let people go it's done with dignity."

Balls, he thought. Human Resources knew the back doubles of employment law. How to fire people on the cheap. She irritated him. She was too high and mighty. Lost in hubris. He'd bring her down a notch. Pursue a different line.

***

"Do you have children Ms. Peters?"

She was taken aback.

"What's that got to do with it?"

"Nothing. How do you combine a family with a career?" He smiled. Eyes cold.

"We don't have children."

"You're married ..?"

"I have a partner .."

"A banker?"

"I don't see .."

"Sorry .. didn't mean to annoy you?"

"You're not .."

"So he's a banker ..?"

"Did I say *he*?"

"Sorry .. apologies .."

"My personal life is none of your business."

"Ms. Peters .. this is a murder hunt .. everything's my business. Was Capes a lesbian?"

"Not as far as I know .."

"I have to ask."

"Why?"

"There might be a sexual element."

She looked at her watch. Patek Phillipe. She'd had enough. She turned and read aloud from the computer.

"Capes grew up in Texas. Went to university. Spent time in Latin America before joining Stratton Hyde. You've heard of Stratton ..?"

Raven nodded. Patronising cow.

"Mother a therapist. Father a lawyer. The right sort for Global."

"Why?"

"Global's international. We like sophisticates. People who've travelled. Seen the world. People who know their way around."

"I thought it was just oil and cowboys in Texas." His smile was as cold as frost. "You won't be leaving the country Ms. Peters?"

"No. Why?"

"I might come back."

"This is outrageous. Am I a suspect."

"We need to find the killer."

He got up. Trying not to look at her legs. The high hem of her dark skirt beneath the glass-topped desk.

"Must go. I know how busy Personnel gets. Sorry .. my mistake .. HR."

The lift was at the end of a marble corridor. Past the faux Kandinsky's.

***

He lit a Player's. Mama used to say smoking was a bad habit. Mama and Papa had been good to him. House, money, wine. Grandpa loved his wine. He'd kept it in the garage. Where he had his motorbikes. The Velocette, the Matchless, the 1979 Triumph Bonneville. The Norton built before the war. Mama said Che Guevera used a Norton to tour Latin America. He'd called it The Mighty One. La Ponderosa. He sipped a Burgundy. La Tache 1991. Grandpa kept only the best. He blew smoke rings. Capes had not liked the cigarette. She'd flinched. Water slopping over the side of the bath. He'd sat on the bathroom stool. Blowing smoke rings. Watching them drift, losing their shape. In the bath she'd looked vulnerable. Gagged and tied. Gleeson had told him she worked out every lunch time in the Global gym in Canary Wharf. He'd been there. Watching her through the big window on the ground floor. He recognised her from Gleeson's description. On an exercise bike. Black leotard, hair bunched up. Yellow bandana, yellow wrist bands. Then she'd disappeared. Back to her computer. As he walked away he'd felt lonely. Insignificant. Staring up at the skyscrapers. The giant screen with its running share prices. People jostled him. In dark suits like Gleeson's. Papa always said the smarter the suit the bigger the crook. Everybody had newspapers, heads down. Standards and Metros. Pushing and rushing for the Jubilee Line and the Docklands Light Railway. Brash groups drinking at tables by the waters' edge.

***

"How was Global?" They were in The Feathers. Rosie had lined up a gin.

"Spin and gloss." He poured the tonic.

"Hard piece in HR."

"I thought Personnel was all sweetness and light."

"So did I."

He looked at her. Dark trouser suit. Shiny hair plaited into a bun. Tiny silver ear-rings. Immaculate.

"We've got to find the link between Gleeson and Capes."

The ice clinked in his glass.

"Get into every nook and cranny."

She showed him the *Standard*. 'Woman Banker Slain.'

***

In the Admiral Keppel snooker room Raven set up the balls. Each colour on its spot. Filling the triangle with reds.

"Ever played?"

Gleeson's blood stained the cloth. It was an old Riley table with a heavy slate bed. Massive and confident. Fat bevelled legs. Polished top-sides gathering dust. The room gloomy, airless. Sealed off since the killing. Smelling of dust and chalk. He put a coin in the meter. The green baize was suddenly awash with light.

24

Rosie remembered her dad in Lewisham snooker hall. Her mother giving him Hell when he got home late, speech slurred, stinking of Guinness.

"Dad taught me."

"Fuck it!"

Raven hurled the black along the table. So hard it bounced over a cushion, clattering across the floor.

"There's a red missing. How could we miss that? I bet our boy took it."

An hour later he lambasted the squad.

"And you're not the only ones. It's my fuck up. I'm leading this circus."

***

The thread from the Norfolk copse was of a natural dye the labs couldn't identify. Once coarse it had worn thin. Washed in a powerful detergent.

"Who makes the detergent? Who's it flogged to?"

Rosie was in Raven's tiny office. Battered desk. High window. Grey filing cabinet. Chipped mug. 'I prefer gin' stamped on it. A gift from the squad when he left Leeds. A strip-light made him feel like a battery hen. The bulb in his desk lamp had blown. Some idiot said it had to be fitted by a specialist. He'd sworn at a clerk who'd lectured him about health and safety. One day he'd change it himself. He told Rosie everybody in the nick had their bums stuck in glue pots. She was half out of the door which let on to the squad room.

"Tell 'em to get their bloody fingers out."

She knew she'd face a barrage of sarcasm. Standard stuff. A slip of a girl. Didn't know her backside from her elbow. Giving them orders. Chucking her weight around. He rummaged in a drawer. A bottle of Tanqueray, half empty. Old notepads, dry biros, dead batteries. More corpses, he thought. Boat keys, sailing shackles, a creased passport photo of Olivia. He shoved a pile of papers off his desk on to the floor. They cascaded in a small cloud of dust. Head in hands he stared down at the brown thread in its plastic sachet.

***

The squad took each builder aside. It delayed the work and antagonised Padowski. The same question in myriad ways. Who was it in camouflage? Nobody knew. The club had employed a reputable building firm. In reality it was two accountants who farmed out the work to gang-masters. They supplied freelance sparks, plumbers and roofers. Most of them immigrants. They liked to be paid in cash. If anybody inquired they flourished official-looking documents in an unknown language. The paper work was largely forged. For a murder squad in a hurry dubious documents and bogus identities caused delay. The squad had neither the time or inclination to navigate the immigration labyrinth. For gang-masters the uncertain status of workers was a useful bonus. The terror of exposure guaranteed that workers kept their heads down and their mouths shut. It was a closed and itinerant world. Nosy strangers were not welcome. Especially the police. The gang-masters drove Range Rovers, all black glass and bull bars. They wore gold necklaces and gold Rolexes and carried wads of twenty-pound notes. A hard-eyed coterie which had grown fat out of the immigration chaos. Unemployment was running high. They could pick and choose their workers. Set the conditions. What they paid. Their message was clear. Step out of line and we'll turn you in. Fear of exposure was a powerful whip.

***

Raven perched on Capes's bed. Cameras at the block had caught an image the porter couldn't identify. The time fitted. Whoever it was had kept their head down. Face hidden in a hood. Dark jacket. Sneakers. The labs tweaked it. Without success. The porter had not stayed at his desk. He'd wandered around picking up litter. Blown into the gardens from the Thames path. He'd been in a flat repairing a tap. And been well-tipped for his trouble. He'd tidied round the bins. Checked on the Porsche and Bentley cars in the garage. Canary Wharf high-rollers. Capes and her pals liked their toys. She didn't own a car. She spent long periods overseas. She had money. She used taxis. Or the Tube. In London a car was an encumbrance. Raven opened a wardrobe. Deep in thought he flicked at the rails of clothes. Valentino and Dior. Less expensive stuff. Hobbs and Zara. The muted hues of a discreet lady banker. A trace of perfume. *Joy*. Why did he hate you and Gleeson? Why kill you in the bath? You weren't raped. It wasn't robbery. The squad had taken the flat apart. They'd found twenty thousand pounds in sterling. Some in the cooker filter. The cooker was unused. Capes would generally have dined out. There was more cash behind a tile at the back of the bidet. Two thousand in a plastic bag in the fridge. Five hundred in a bedside cabinet. Where was it from? And for what? Her bank account was healthy. Chunky salary each month. Usual deductions. She appeared to own the flat. There was no indication of a mortgage. International bankers had overseas accounts. Tax havens. In her world everybody played those games. With a fat salary and hefty bonuses a Docklands flat with a Romeo and Juliet balcony would have been easily within her grasp. He moved to the hall. He ties and gags you. Drags you to the bath. Scalding water. Burns you with a cigarette. Hammers you to death. Strangles you. What did he want from you? Or is he just a sicko who gets his kicks out of hurting people? On the terrace he looked across to Canary Wharf. His stomach was knotted. Change your lifestyle his doctor had told him. Stop living on frozen food. The pains came when he couldn't crack a case. He knew he had the ability. But he also knew he didn't have the temperament. He worried too much. He could never switch off. Murder played on his mind. His dreams were violent. He felt the familiar clenching in his guts. The nagging pain in his lower back. He knew in his heart there'd be more killings. The bastard was enjoying it. He was on a roll. He wouldn't stop at two. Two wouldn't satisfy him.

Rosie joined him in Capes' flat. She'd been at Global with the squad.

"Did you find anything?" she asked.

He shook his head. Holding his back.

"No. You?"

"Damn all."

The squad had crawled over Capes's work station. Computers seized. IT department turned inside out. Friends quizzed. Rivals grilled. Nothing. Raven was edgy. There *must* be something?

"We interviewed everybody for hours," she said.

"You'll have to do it again."

"Everybody'll be up in arms."

"I don't give a toss?"

He had his back to her. Staring down at the Thames. A sailboat with a brown sail was heading out to sea. He turned to her.

"I don't care who we upset. This is a maniac. There'll be more killings."

Outside his car had been booked again. He threw the ticket in the back with the others. The Alfa's throaty roar. His 'phone rang. The Nick. Somebody had been on from Global about harassment. Saying his officers had been too aggressive.

"Tell Global to go fuck itself." He switched off.

***

He didn't go back to the Nick. Cursing the traffic he made his way to Greenwich. Parking at the Playhouse. Walking quickly. Cutting through the market. Heading for a terraced house with a black front door. In a Georgian street facing Greenwich Park. Near the National Maritime Museum. Lovers sprawled on benches in the cool of its white colonnades. Miriam had long auburn hair. Long legs. High cheekbones. Eyes darkish blue. He'd known her before Olivia. One of the hookers he'd let off with a warning.

Working her patch on the cobbles at Chapeltown in Leeds. Later she'd moved to the Mustang club in Soho's Frith Street. Working the door. Not the punters. She'd taken him seriously. He'd been explicit. Telling her she'd end up like all the other addled old tarts. Thin arms pocked by needles. She later got into what she called management. A job with Blue Star. Porn publishers. He'd lost touch with her years before. But soon after Olivia's death he had met her again. By chance. She'd given him one of her coy smiles. Sashaying around. He couldn't keep his pale eyes off her. Her jeans so tight they looked painted on.

"I'm a stylist now. Show the girls what to wear. It's not much so it doesn't take long."

She'd laughed. The familiar smile. He remembered it from the old days, before he was married.

"I book the girls. Get the costumes. Set up the shoots. Sort out locations. Jack .." She had sidled up close. Pressing against him.

"Let's not go there. I don't do any naughty stuff. I don't have any customers. I don't do drugs. There's no pimp beating me up. I owe you. I went straight. Just as you told me. I'm a white collar worker now .. good as gold."

***

She had teased and provoked him and they'd fallen into bed. Tearing at each others' clothes. Olivia was not long dead. Afterwards he was consumed with guilt. But lust and loneliness are a powerful aphrodisiac. And the relationship had grown. On this occasion their love-making was over quickly. Her athleticism matching his urgency.

"You're under pressure," she said. "You're an animal when you're tense. Your eyes get even paler. Like blue diamonds. It's how I like you. My animal."

From her bed they watched tourists meandering round the boating lake in Greenwich park. He told her about the case. She'd read about it in the papers. She nuzzled into him, feeling

29

his warmth. In the morning she reluctantly, finally, let him pull away from her. When he left her eyes had filled with tears. He walked away. Not turning back. Fighting the guilt. In his dreams that night he was back with Olivia. *That* smile. Her limbs wrapped round him. He woke with a start in the early hours. Lathered in sweat. Sheets and pillows drenched. By 4am he'd showered and mixed himself a large gin and tonic. Mainly gin. By 5.30 am he was back at his desk.

※※※

Analysis of hard drives and footage from surveillance cameras had revealed little. Exhaustive interviews wasted time. Produced no real leads.

"This is where we're at."

Raven had a list. He was addressing the squad.

"He ties knots in an odd way. Gags them with electricians' tape. Padowski said the man worked as a sparks. It ties in. At the *Imperial* he wore brown and green clothes like military stuff. Twitchers wear camouflage. We know he'd been in the copse. We found DNA which matched that in the snooker room and in Capes's flat. So it's irrefutable. It's the same person. But we have a problem. We don't know who the Hell it belongs to. We can assume he watched Gleeson's cottage. But why kill him at the club instead of at the cottage? The thread's important. What's the delay?"

His gaze roved across the squad. Every copper in the room was red-eyed with tiredness.

Leach said: "The detergent's all over the country. The maker flogs it to half a dozen wholesalers and then it's farmed out to hundreds of businesses and industrial outlets here and overseas. It's a job trying to track it down. Takes time."

Leach was one of Raven's favourites. Seasoned and intuitive. He'd worked with him before.

"We're doing our best Guv."

Raven nodded. "I know you are Phil. Keep pressing."

In the past Raven had laid into his chiefs about being overwhelmed by paperwork. He'd banged the desk at a strategy meeting.

"We need less forms and clerks and red-tape and more bloody coppers."

He'd lost his temper. Storming out. Slamming doors.

"I know you're all knackered," he told the squad. "But this nutter will kill again. We haven't got all the results in. The labs are still working their balls off."

He looked at his list.

"Scissors in Gleeson's eye. Cigarette burns on Capes. Why does he hate them? They're like props in a play. Why kill Capes in the bath? Why torture her? Just for the Hell of it? Or did he want something from her? If he'd done Gleeson at the cottage it was quiet and remote? He could have taken his time. If it had to be at the club why the snooker room and not in his bedroom at *The Imperial* where it would have been easier? With less risk of being interrupted."

A resigned titter ran round the room.

"OK. Have it your own way. Chamber."

***

A grey dawn. A cool wind. The threat of rain. Mrs. Charlotte Clarkson drew back the curtains. The bloodied head of her husband Charles stared up at her. Mounted on the bird table. His torso was in the lily pond. Bound hand and foot in the usual way. Blood blackened the water. Staining the pink and white lilies. The blade had severed the cricoid cartilage. Slicing through the trachea, spinal cord and carotid arteries. The killer had used an axe from the woodshed at the back of the summer house at the bottom of the Clarkson's garden. Forensics, pathology, DNA. Inch by inch searches. Interviews with friends, neighbours, colleagues.

***

Clarkson had been an optician. He'd built up a string of shops and sold out to a larger chain. The squad pieced together the minutiae of his life. He'd played an average game of golf. His wife played bridge. When younger they'd been fanatical about tennis. Rogue weeds on their private court now tested the patience of the gardener. Posts and netting were neatly wrapped in the old summer house behind which Clarkson had been beheaded. The triple garage had a snooker room above. The garage housed Clarkson's Lexus and Charlotte's VW Golf. Clarkson liked a drink at the golf club with a small group of friends. He drank *Famous Grouse*. His handicap was sixteen. He wore Church's dark brown suede brogues. His favourite food was Gnocchi Siciliana at *Umberto's* off the Strand. He'd been a regular at *Bianchi's* in Frith Street. And disappointed when it closed down. He thought Lewin's city shirts were good value. Such was the detail the squad accumulated.

***

The Clarkson's lived in de Freville Drive on the Fitzgerald Estate. A tree-lined oasis in Blackheath in south London. From the heath there were distant views of Canary Wharf. At the entrance to the Fitzgerald enclave a white sign with black lettering warned visitors that it was a private unadopted road. Which is why its tree-lined avenues were pot-holed and open only to residents. The houses represented an architectural melange. Grand mock Tudors with shades of Lutyen. Carefully trimmed greensward. High hedges of copper beech.

***

The Clarkson's had two children. Adrian was a software engineer in an office in Charlotte Street in London's West End. He spent time at a science park in the Cherry Hinton suburb of Cambridge where his company had its laboratories. His sister Andrea taught at a comprehensive school in Attercliffe, an industrial suburb in the north east of Sheffield. Her Leftish and environmental creed was at variance with that of her parents. The Clarkson's diaries listed Conservative party meetings. Bridge dates, golf fixtures, charity coffee mornings. Details of a Swan Hellenic cruise. They had been looking forward to a forthcoming cultural odyssey to St. Petersburg in Russia, visiting the Hermitage Museum. An ornithologist had been booked by the cruise company as the key speaker.

***

Raven's boss Joe Wragg had run out of patience. The press office had been deluged. Newspapers and TV ran lurid stories about a serial killer. His Nibs, the Chief Constable, was in a rage. The chairman of the police authority, Albert Henshaw, went public in the *Standard*. Henshaw had an OBE for services to steel fabrication. He had been looking forward to his knighthood with no hiccups en route. Henshaw loathed Raven. It was mutual. The previous year Raven and Olivia had enjoyed a gin too many at a Christmas police shindig. Olivia had told Henshaw that in her book an OBE, the Order of the British Empire, usually meant Other Buggers Efforts. She had also told him to remove his sweaty hand from her knee. Too loudly. She and Raven had laughed about it later that evening when they finally fell into a cab. He told her she'd probably blown his career. Over the years it was inevitable that Wragg would be dubbed Toe Rag. Wragg suggested more seemly behaviour was expected of a senior officer and his wife. Raven never mentioned it to Olivia for fear she'd turn violent. Commander Wragg had had a successful front-line career. He was said to be unhappy in management. With Raven he had not minced his words.

"I won't have my officers or their wives fucking up people like Henshaw. Get out."

Now Wragg was on Raven's tail again.

"Three killings. When's it going to stop? I can give you more officers. If you're not up to the job you just have to say so. Everybody knows you were knocked sideways when Olivia passed on. We can easily draft somebody else in. It's no reflection on you. I've got 'His Nibs' on my back."

He was at his large desk in his black leather chair.

"And Henshaw's playing up again."

At Henshaw's name Raven let rip.

"Screw Henshaw. I've enough on my plate without worrying about that little prat." His eyes were as pale as water. He stared down at Wragg. Clenching and unclenching his fists.

"It doesn't seem like yesterday you were in my shoes. Doing a real job. Not playing politics. I haven't got time for this."

With that he turned and left. Wragg tried to compose himself. Raven's outburst had stung. What he'd said was true. But Wragg was ambitious. As he climbed the ladder desk-stuff increased. It went with the job. It was inevitable. He'd been a good detective. He and Raven had been close. But Raven had changed. He now seemed to have a disregard for the ordinary constraints of policing. After Olivia died there was a new menace about him. As if he'd stop at nothing.

***

Wragg 'phoned 'His Nibs,' the Chief Constable.

"I've had a word with Raven. It's a complicated inquiry. If I think he's not up to it I'll pull him out. But you know his record. He's a good operator."

The Chief Constable wanted to know how they could pacify Henshaw.

"Don't worry about him. I'll have a word."

Wragg had learned the management game.

34

"I'll make Henshaw feel included. Let him in on a couple of strategy meetings. Nothing crucial. But it'll make him feel important. Let him think he's on the inside track." The Chief relaxed. Toe Rag was right. Raven was effective even if he was tricky. But it wouldn't be good management to tell him. He wouldn't want him getting above himself.

*****

Raven climbed the outside wooden staircase to the Clarkson snooker room over the garage. It had fake beams in keeping with the mock Tudor house. A cushioned-seat in a bow-window gave a view down the garden towards the summer house. The table was laid for a game. Reds in a triangle. Each colour on its spot. They were all there. This time there was no missing souvenir. Psychos like to build up collections. So what else had he taken? Charlotte Clarkson told Rosie her husband played snooker with a friend who'd since died. He sometimes played with his son Adrian. But it was rare for Adrian to forsake the smart pleasures of his flat in Primrose Hill in north London for a weekend in Blackheath. Adrian had laughed that his pals wouldn't dare venture across the Thames into the jungles of south London. On his last weekend visit he'd thrown a bundle of washing at his mother. On the Saturday he'd disappeared with friends that he'd known since childhood. He complained at breakfast on the Sunday about a splitting headache. His father said it was only a hangover. It led to a row. Andrea visited infrequently. Sheffield to Blackheath was a slog. And on a teacher's stipend the train fare was costly. When she did visit she usually had a man in tow. Charles Clarkson said the house had become a cross between a knocking-shop and a bed and breakfast.

*****

Charlotte Clarkson was used to her husband retiring late. On the night he was killed she'd taken sleeping pills. It was only in the morning that she realised he had not joined her. She and Charles had similar tastes. Classical music, historic houses, bird-watching. They belonged to the National Trust and the Royal Society for Birds. The previous weekend they'd visited a bird of prey centre in Dedham Vale on the Essex-Suffolk border. They'd spent the night at the Three Chimneys hotel on the river Stour. On the journey home, Liszt playing in the Lexus, Clarkson told her about the different species he'd seen. She told Rosie she didn't like birds of prey. While her husband visited the centre she'd explored Constable country. Black and white cottages. Pin-tile roofs. Beautiful villages. She liked Nayland, the church with its Constable painting. On the drive back she'd told Charles that if ever they decided to leave London she wouldn't mind the idea of living in Nayland.

**

Raven sat in the bay window of the Clarkson snooker room. Lost in concentration. He knew the squad laughed about his thoughtfulness. But he was not offended by his reputation as a thinking man. It was better than being known only for his quick temper. As he stared down the garden he could just make out the colonial-style summer house. Wooden, white-painted, almost hidden by the swaying fronds of a giant willow. Raven had spent time in the summer house. Poring over it, getting to *know* it, and through it, by some strange alchemy, getting that much closer to the victim. A veranda ran its length, with two old Lloyd Loom chairs, the cane painted dark green. Inside there was a small sofa, an easy chair and a desk. A telescope on its tripod. Binoculars. There was a gap in a shelf full of bird books, as if one was missing. Charlotte was unsure. There were too many books for her to remember.

**

The walls of the summer house were of knotted pine, stained a dark brown. There was a smell of linseed. Clarkson had maintained an ornithological log. Noting the location, time and date of each sighting. It was dotted with references to mantles, scapulars, upper and lower mandibles. He visited the pavilion every night. His nocturnal forays had become a family joke. From his notes it seemed that he had been surveying a Little Owl. A minor bird of prey best known for its sad, almost melancholic cry. It frequented an ivy-clad stump in a thicket which divided the Clarkson's garden from that of a neighbouring mock Tudor. He would watch it for minutes at a time. Quietly studying it through his binoculars. Raven was a town boy. He thought there was something creepy about twitchers. Something of the night.

***

Rosie ran up the outside stairs to the snooker room. She was breathless, animated. "We've had a break. An old lady up the road said she saw somebody hanging around. Said he looked like a soldier."

Raven rolled the black gently down the baize. Watching it come slowly back to his fingers. Bouncing softly off the cushion.

"Sounds good."

"They're old. Frightened."

He scooped up his coat. "Don't blame 'em."

***

Mrs. Emily Lawrence was insistent. She'd seen the man in camouflage before. She couldn't think where but it would come to her.

"He was looking into our garden."

She wore a flowered pinafore. The house had been spruce at one time. Now it was as tired as its owner. An Ideal boiler on its last legs, old ply units painted cream, a Formica-top table, crazed and chipped. Utility furniture, from the post-war era. Her husband had served under Montgomery in the Second World War.

"Desert Rat," she said. "That's when Ted's hearing went. All those bangs. I was on ambulances. Driving around through all the rubble and the fires. Middle of the night. You've never seen anything like it. Everywhere ablaze. It was the ships and the docks they were after. Night after night they kept coming back. Bombing us to pieces. That's why I noticed this boy. He was in army stuff. Made me remember the war."

Raven thought what a thankless world she'd fought for.

"The thing is .." her voice a whisper, "Ted says if we cause trouble they'll put us in a home. They can split us up you know .."

She had a small, creased face. As if it had lived a thousand lives. Raven thought of his long-dead parents. Of Olivia. Of Capes, her mangled corpse. Damn all the stuck-up HR cows. All the liars and cheats and mad-eyed psychos.

***

Two days later Mrs. Lawrence remembered. He was an electrician. The Cook's down the road had used him. Old man Cook had a workshop in his garage. He'd had it rewired. The Cook's were known on the Fitzgerald estate as a miserable pair.

"Chippy Northerners," she said. "Bit mean. They think we're all softies. Ted says it's because they don't know any Cockneys. Ted's a Cockney alright."

***

Leach and Forensics descended on Cook's garage. Ron and Elsie Cook had moved south to be near their daughter and grandchildren. He'd sold his garage in Huddersfield. The electrician had knocked on his door asking for work. He'd been about to shut it in his face.

"There've been burglaries, immigrants hanging around. I'm not

38

racist. But you know what I mean."

He said the man had darkish skin but spoke good English.

"Our Elsie said he was alright. Said he had a nice smile. Anyway, he said he'd do it for a few quid."

Leach studied him. Tartan slippers. Stained pullover. Ex-car dealer. He could imagine him shouting the odds. Homing in on the mugs. Cook said the man had dark hair, broad-shoulders, he was strongly-built.

"Nice enough lad. Did a good job."

He shifted from foot to foot. Picking at his sweater. Never looking Leach in the eye.

"He had a dark jacket, trousers .. brown and green .. sort of swirls. What do you call 'em? Fatigues. That's what they were. Like army fatigues."

"Car?"

"No .. motorbike. Big and noisy. Made a bloody racket."

"Catch the make?"

"No .. Japanese probably. Aren't they all?"

"Ever on his own?"

"There was a night we had to go out. He was a good lad, never stopped. But we didn't know anything about him. Anyway, we finally left him to it. Locked the place up. Got the alarm on. When we got back he'd buggered off. Never came back for the rest of his money."

Cook had sharp, foxy eyes. Thin lips curling into a sly smile.

"That's how I like it. Not complaining mate. Best ruddy deal ever."

**

Rosie and Raven were at his flat on the first-floor of a white-fronted house in Lansdowne Road, Holland Park. One of London's leafier parts. He'd invited her for a fish supper. Burnt fish fingers. Bread and butter. They talked about each piece of evidence. Why was Gleeson in London? The murders had been widely publicised. If Gleeson was meeting somebody why hadn't they come forward? The rail ticket in his blood soaked suit showed he caught the seven-thirty express from Norwich due in London at nine-twenty-five. It was seven minutes late. He was on CCTV parking his blue Peugeot at Norwich station. Cameras caught him boarding the train. Commuters saw him reading The Daily Telegraph. At Liverpool Street he was on camera queuing for the Circle Line. He got off at Baker Street and set off towards Regent's Park. And disappeared. Did Gleeson meet somebody in the time between Baker Street and his arrival at *The Imperial* at around two fifty?

***

Raven's road was lined with London Plane trees. Bark peeling like paper. Rosie was at the window. A car was trying to squeeze into a space.

"Nice place."

The car's bumper gently nudged a tree.

He looked up from the sofa.

"We liked it. Olivia was at the comprehensive school down the road. Cost a bomb. We had orange boxes. Bloody great mortgage."

He was looking down at sheets of paper snaking across the floor. On each he had detailed the killings. Names, times, places.

"You build up a narrative."

"Like a jigsaw," she said, kneeling down to join him.

He nodded. "If something comes up you add it in."

"Wouldn't it be easier on a computer?"

"You can walk round this. Seems to help. You keep adding bits in. I've had them running into the hall. Little things can strike you. Not working this time."

***

The Chamberlain at *The Imperial* was the Russian-born Ivan

Mikelov. He said Gleeson was a creature of habit, always taking the same tea and toast and apricot jam at the same table on the gallery which overlooked the atrium. The one which gave the best view of the Mall entrance. Later he would practise in the snooker room. Sometimes he wanted a video player brought to his chamber. "Housekeeping always complain. Video brought all way up from store room in basement. Lift not good. Always breaking. Secretary says club can't afford to keep repair lift. So housekeeping carry it all way up to chambers. From basement. When Captain leave they carry all way down again. Complaints, complaints. Housekeeping not Russian. They Portuguese, Spanish. No other member want one. I ask Captain what he play on it. He say old films. Hobby he say. Black and white. He like old film. Like *Brief Encounter*."

Raven had the machine stripped. A smear of finger-prints. Gleeson's, the servants, dozens more. Mikelov said Gleeson usually stayed on Wednesday's and rarely dined in. Sometimes he stayed out all night. Returning in the early morning to bathe and change into fresh clothes.

"He must be rich man to pay for room and not use it."

A half smile threatened to illuminate his features. Tall, burly, his face sad and jowelled. Eyes mournful, hooded. His barrel-chest squeezed into a black butler's jacket. Pin-stripe trousers, knife-edge creases. A Carpathian Bear; his slow, deep tones as sombre as the snows in the forests of Georgia where he played as a boy. His bulk was at odds with the finesse he brought to *The Imperial's* corridors each day as dawn broke over London. Great feet stepping softly, as light as a feather, on thick burgundy carpets. Gently tapping at the doors of the chambers, carefully drawing back the curtains for bleary-eyed members. Delivering *The Times* and the trays of breakfast tea, each piece of white china bearing *The Imperial's* red and gold motif.

"As good as Czar's china," his huge, hirsute hands, pressed against his chest.

"Maybe Captain wants matter of heart stay private. Keep things dark."

As night fell over the de Freville estate he had tortured another name out of Clarkson. As Clarkson knelt on the ground behind the pavilion, head bowed, hands and wrists tied, his killer tore the gaffer tape from his victim's mouth, hovering above him with the axe. He had whispered that he would decapitate him if he screamed. He would free him if he gave him more names and addresses and details. Clarkson had nodded, quietly crying, chest imploding ,fighting for breath, trembling like the Willow.

***

Clarkson's garden in Blackheath was near Lewisham where Rosie had grown up.

"We used to cycle round here. It was another country. They were snooty about it being a private estate. Scruffy black kids tearing around on bikes? Wonder what that did to house prices?"

Raven laughed. It was academic. Britain was in recession. Property had slumped.

"Not round here," she said. "Oligarchs get richer. Houses get bigger."

"Probably don't pay tax."

"My home's near here. You know how it is .."

She laughed, touching his arm, affecting an estuary dialect.

"We Sarf London girls never move far. Hivver Green Guv. Down the road. Near Lewichum."

He teased her about going to Cambridge.

"It seemed like the moon. There are some Blacks there .. but it's hardly Lewisham. Lewichum if you're a local."

***

They walked across the weed-strewn tennis court. Raven's mobile.

The labs had found the killer's prints and DNA in Capes's flat. And Gleeson's.

"It was everywhere. Kitchen, bathroom. And this is neat. In Capes's bed. Looks as if Gleeson and Capes were screwing."

Rosie smiled: "So that's where he stayed. Our randy little insurance man was having Capes away."

***

Through the fronds of the Willow, looking back up the garden, she could just see the snooker room over the garage.

"Why didn't our guy kill Clarkson there?"

"This one's not about snooker .. it's about twitching, or whatever they call it."

"Birds not balls ?"

"It's all balls." He pressed his hand to his side.

"You alright?"

"Fine." His face was drawn.

"You're such a liar .. do something about it."

"Stop going on .."

"I'm not .. anyway, what was I saying? Three dead and two of 'em played snooker. Maybe Capes played? As well as working out in the gym. A sporty type."

He kicked at the stump where Clarkson's owl would perch.

"Horizontal jogging with Gleeson. Bar bells in the gym. I still can't see why Gleeson was done in the club and not at his cottage. Our boy could have taken his time. Gleeson in the snooker room. Scissors and cue. Clarkson's head on a bird table. Capes in the bath. There's a symbolism .."

At the thicket dividing Clarkson's house from its neighbour she said: "Maybe he spied on Clarkson from here? Like he watched Gleeson. He liked to get the lie of the land. He must be good at spying. Doing a recce? Hiding himself away. He knew where the woodshed was and that there was an axe in it."

Forensics had scoured the thicket and examined the woodshed, a lean-to at the back of the summer house. The killer had left the axe where he'd beheaded Clarkson, smeared in blood, traces of his victim's skin and hair on the blade.

Raven winced, holding his side.

"See a doctor."

"It's just a twinge. Need a gin."

"That's what dad said. He liked vodka."

"What happened to him?"

"Snuffed it. Cirrhosis of the liver."

"Job's bloody comforter."

His mobile again. Leach. Gleeson's cottage had been fired.

He looked at Clarkson's house, the garage and the snooker room.

"Let's hope this doesn't end up in a blaze"

***

He'd gone back to Norfolk. This time he was alone. No police. The blaze lit up the sky. By the time the brigade reached it the cottage was a shell. Forensics found a melted clock, the timer. He'd allowed himself an hour to escape, returning to the vantage point he'd found earlier. The cottage erupted. Flames bursting from its thatch.

He'd lit a Player's and watched through his binoculars, astride the motorbike, parked in the dark and rutted track he'd used before. Fountains of fire and sparks in the blackness. He remembered Bonfire Night as a kid. Mama worrying about the hedge. Papa with a bucket of water just in case. Tonight there were bells, sirens, shouts on the wind. The white beam of a searchlight raked the sky. Flames and sparks burst from the roof. Red, orange, blue and yellow. Like the fireworks on Bonfire Night. When he had been happy. He used the key to the cottage he'd taken off Gleeson at The Imperial. Trampling the sweet peas into the earth. Hurling pots to the ground. Stabbing at chairs and paintings. Furniture smashed to splinters, photos shredded.

***

Leach thought Rosie a dish. He told Raven he didn't want to tell her because she'd report him for sexism.

"Bollocks," Raven laughed. "She's not like that."

"Get real Jack. They're all like it. Ambition coming out of every pore."

"You're a cynic. And while we're on the subject tell the others to lay off the catty comments. The women are worse than the men. They can't stand looks *and* brains. This is my playground and I won't have bullies in it."

He was standing at his office door looking into the squad room. It was a tip. Used tea mugs, old files, piles of newspapers. Maps with pins marking murder locations. Photos of tortured victims. Detectives on 'phones, feet on desks.

"I want her treated properly. And I don't want her knowing I said so. Sort it."

"What's she said?"

"Nothing. But I'm not deaf or blind. I know what she's been going through."

"Sounds as if you've fallen for her."

"Balls. Just get it fixed."

***

Raven, Rosie and Leach returned to Norfolk. A copper was keeping gawpers and looters at bay.

"The wind cuts across here," he said. "It's like the soddin' Arctic."

Raven looked at him. He was about nineteen. His helmet looked too big for his head. "Any bother?"

"Not really. Round here they'd pinch anything and flog it on ebay."

"Not much left to sell." Leach was poking about in the ash and rubble.

The young copper told them an old crone had come across the fields

45

"All in black she was. Black teeth, black hat. Said she was a psychic. Said it was the Devil's work. Satan's inferno."

"Goes from bad to worse," Raven said. "Now we've got bloody witches."

The cottage was a shell. The thatched roof and beams had fallen in. The acrid stench of smoke and fire hung in the air. Its destroyer had gone on the rampage.

"Frenzied," Raven said, bending down, flicking at cremated books, pictures, a twisted photo frame.

***

A man in the tap room of the Nelson slipped quietly away when Raven and the others dropped by. Jim Ringer, a poacher. When the cottage exploded he was pursuing his trade. A motorbike had unexpectedly turned down a track where he was setting a trap. Headlight flaring. He'd hurled himself into a ditch. Thinking the law was on to him. But the rider doused his light. His face hidden by helmet and goggles. Ringer had crept off into the blackness. Keeping to the shadows of a bramble hedge.

***

Back in London at The Feathers Raven said: "It wasn't brain surgery. Clarkson's head was hacked off. He was butchered."

"Why the bird table?" Rosie ordered two gin and tonics.

"Hell alone knows. How long had Gleeson been screwing Capes ? How did they know each other? Why go to the club? Why not go straight to Capes's flat and wait for her to return from Global?"

"He went back to the club in the mornings," she said. "After they'd shagged. Had a shower, change of clothes. Then he'd catch the train back to Norfolk."

"Doesn't make sense. After he'd slept with her he'd have bathed at her place. She'd have gone to work and he'd have left for his train."

"Whoever it is has a thing about snooker and twitchers."

He looked at her. "You ever seen these birdie types?"

She shook her head, laughing.

"I grew up in Lewisham .."

"They're smug bastards. Barbours and green wellies. Maps and binoculars. Tear- arsing about in four-wheel drives."

"You're a cynical bugger Jack."

"All Yashicas and binoculars. They're supposed to be Green. Environmentally aware. But sometimes they move around en masse. Squadrons of 'em. Every twitcher-car must have its own little hole in the ozone layer. I don't know why they can't leave the poor bloody tits in peace."

She smiled, touching his arm. "You're a miserable sod .."

"You're right. And it's getting worse. I'll have to put an armed bloody guard on every twitcher."

***

Raven was at home. Exhausted. Bags under his eyes. Stomach clenched. A lousy back. He was worrying. The killer would strike again. He was certain. Another frozen supper. Listlessly shifting it round the plate. Frozen, pre-packed. Since Olivia it was all he'd known. He put on Miles Davis's *Kind of Blue*. Inside the CD was a small card. *Happy birthday J. Forever O.* She'd drawn a tiny flower with a smiley face. Forever was a bloody short time he thought. His head was spinning. Facts and names and jumbled evidence coursing like a river. All the users of industrial detergent had been checked. That bloody thread! Burns. Scalding water. Souvenirs. A clump of hair. The lost bird book. The missing red. The charred fragments of the timing device at Gleeson's cottage. The boffins said it was ingenious. And yes, a good electrician could have made it. But there was too little of it left to be of any use.

***

He was obsessed. On a murder it always happened. You're my prey he thought. I've got to find you. You're a freak. You burned Capes. Tortured her. Ash in the water. The labs said it was a Player's cigarette. Clever bastards know everything. Where did you buy them? No stub. Just ash in the bath. Capes's killer had waited for the porter to take a break. The porter said he'd only been out a minute. Crossed the road to the river, watching the Thames. But he'd been in and out all day. Pottering around. Doing repairs. In the garage. Down at the bins. You couldn't believe a word the porter said. He'd have had his back to the flats watching the river. Day-dreaming. Somebody had slipped in. The man in the hooded jacket. The porter was a sulky bastard. They'd checked him out. A year suspended for an affray at a boozer in New Cross. Nothing since. Said he'd heard a motor-bike. Big, powerful. Said he knew about bikes. But he still couldn't tell what make it was.

***

Kinda Blue had finished. Where was Olivia's other favourite? *Girl from Ipanema*. Stan Getz's mellow tones filled the flat. Astrud Gilberto's fragile murmurings. Keep the volume down. Nocturnal habits upset the neighbours. On a big case he lost track of time. Creeping home in the early hours. What did that cold cow in Global say about Capes? She'd worked for Stratton in New York? She said something else? Yes, that was it. She said before Global Capes had worked in Latin America.

***

He rang Rosie, waking her. She promised she'd look into it first thing in the morning. The squad had been all over Capes she told him. Her office, home, colleagues, competitors. They'd turned over every facet of her life. Poked into every aspect. Gone into every nook and cranny. Just as he'd asked.

"Go deeper," he said. "Right back to her pram. Every little detail."

Rosie yawned, finding her watch on the bedside table.

"Capes spent so much time abroad it makes checking out where she'd been and what she'd been up to that much more difficult and slow."

She'd grown used to Raven's demands and his calls in the middle of the night. But this time she'd badly misjudged his mood.

"So?" he snapped. "Life's difficult. It's how it is."

***

He'd slammed the phone down. And instantly regretted it. She'd been diligent. Conscientious. She'd worked herself into the ground. She'd taken endless stick without any complaint. He immediately rang her back.

"It's just me. I'm sorry. I'm whacked."

"Forget it," she said, relieved he'd called.

"How's the back?"

"Fine. I'm just tired."

"You're lying again. You've got to get that back fixed."

It was 3.20 a.m. While she fell back into a fitful sleep, Raven paced his flat. Bleary-eyed, agitated. Crawling round on hands and knees shuffling the paper narrative. It wound across the floor out into the hall.

***

Leach asked a friend who knew about motorbikes.

"Haven't a clue," he told him. "Could be anything. Japanese most likely."

Rosie said she'd once been on a big Italian motorbike. She told

Leach about a student who'd taken her punting in Cambridge. Afterwards they'd set off for Grantchester on his motorbike. Tea at The Orchard. Rupert Brooke country.

"But we never made it. We turned off the Barton Road and a van shot out of nowhere. We took a Hell of a flyer. We were alright but it put me off bikes."

"Put you off him?"

"'S'pose so. He was in Addenbrooke's hospital with a bad ankle. I took him grapes and flowers. But I couldn't hang around. What's a girl s'posed to do?"

She looked at him. Brown eyes, huge and friendly.

"Only kidding," she smiled. "Nice bloke. Petered out. Always does."

***

Sometimes it's the obvious which gets buried or overlooked. Every member of the squad had seen the club lockers a hundred times. But for some reason they'd failed to register. In the squad room Raven went mad. How could something so blindingly obvious be overlooked? He'd have 'em all back in Panda cars. He gave Rosie a bollocking. But his real fury he saved for himself. He was the boss. His lapse was unforgiveable. The pain in his lower back stabbed at him. Was he losing his touch? He was riddled with doubt. The case was eating into him.

***

At *The Imperial* he'd stormed into the secretary's office. Why did nobody mention the lockers? He knew it wasn't the secretary's fault. He just wanted somebody to yell at. There were clusters of lockers in each corridor. A different key for every member. They were unnumbered. Each member's name was on a small plaque *inside* the locker. For security, the secretary said.

"For what? For Fuck's sake!" Raven shouted.

To add to the confusion the records about the lockers had been lost.

The secretary said: "It started going wrong when the builders moved in."

"Bloody Hell. So nobody knows which member has which locker?"

Raven's anger oozed from every pore.

The secretary's soft pink features creased into an apologetic smile.

"I'm afraid so."

"In that case I'll have to force each locker."

A glance at Raven's pale eyes convinced the secretary he meant it.

"That would be tragic. They're of carved walnut. Lovely bow fronts."

Raven was not in the mood.

"I want Gleeson's locker. If you don't find it I'll have to smash each one to pieces. I don't give a toss about your bow fronts."

Rosie told the squad she was going to Global. Instead she went home. She'd built a rapport with Raven. The squad had warmed to her. But she'd known all along that she wasn't ready. Raven's outburst confirmed her fears. What little confidence she had built up had suddenly drained away. And Raven was right. It was a fundamental error. The lockers were so bloody obvious. There had been two big cock-ups. The missing snooker ball and now this. Perhaps she should pack it in? Walk away? She looked in the mirror. Don't be so pathetic she told herself. Pull yourself together you silly tart. What did Crozier say? The randy old Classicist at King's College who'd fancied the pants off her? Learn from your mistakes. Move on. Stop feeling sorry for yourself. Grow up. That's what he'd told her. Twenty minutes later she'd showered. Fixed her make-up. Was heading back to the Nick. Slamming the front door so hard more of its old green paint flaked off.

***

The Imperial secretary had scurried around to see if anybody knew Gleeson's locker. A cook said he'd seen Gleeson fiddling with one of a batch of lockers which stood in the shadowy basement near the kitchen. Raven rang Lester. After his last stretch Lester had gone legit as a locksmith. He'd been a safe-cracker. Post offices and building societies. He opened three lockers before he found Gleeson's, caressing the brass collar round each lock. He could sense it had recently been opened. It was bare, deep with a single shelf. Even before seeing Gleeson's name on the engraved plate in the locker Raven knew it was the right one. He could *taste* his prey. He gave Lester fifty pounds in tenners.

"Give it to Edna and lay off the nags."

"I'm a new man. Don't do horses or dogs no more."

"How's Edna?"

Raven remembered the small dark-haired woman. Crying when Lester was imprisoned for five years.

"She's OK. And the girls. We was sorry to hear about Mrs. Raven. Really we was."

"Thanks."

Raven turned away.

Forensics took the locker. Wrapped in plastic. In an unmarked van parked discreetly in Carlton House Terrace. Raven's instincts were confirmed. There were DNA traces of Gleeson and his killer.

***

He was thinking of Gleeson. The way he made him betray Capes. It had been the scissors, waving them close to his eyes. Gleeson had looked as if he were having a coronary, heaving this way and that. But he couldn't free himself from the knots. He hadn't expected Gleeson to have kept the things he sought in a locker at the club. He'd imagined that they were at the cottage. He had made Gleeson tell him which key was which. There were four. Two for the cottage, the small brass one for the club locker, the fourth for Sylvia Capes's flat. He sipped at his wine, smoked a Player's, rings of blue curling smoke. Alexander swam round and round. He had made Gleeson admit everything, confessing that he could remember it all and that he was really, really sorry. When he had done with Gleeson he unzipped his overalls and peeled off the yellow rubber gloves streaked with blood and stuffed them into his bag. Beneath the overalls he wore a suit, shirt, a tie. A moment before he had looked like a workman, one of the builders. Now he looked like a member. No servant would dare challenge him, they were too deferential. Worried that if they asked a member to identify himself the member might think it impertinent and complain to the secretary. He had tucked his sneakers in the bag, changing them for the black brogues which had been Papa's. Papa's feet had been slightly larger. He'd stuffed them with paper to make them fit. And pocketed a snooker ball as a keepsake. After killing Gleeson he'd taken the winding back stairs to the basement, crossing the old flagged floor, cracked and uneven. The roof was vaulted, the lighting dim. White distempered walls stained yellow with age, slung with gurgling service pipes and black thick cabling. He'd walked past the cavernous kitchens of burnished brass, the cluttered secretary's office, the studded door to the wine cellar, so extensive it ran out of the club beneath the Mall. The lockers were on the right, a cluster of twenty: four rows, five deep, unnumbered. Bow fronted, burr walnut, brass collars at each keyhole. Gleeson had gasped that his locker was the second from the right, middle row. The key turned easily. Inside there were five of them. He put them in his bag, locked the small door and walked hurriedly back across the flagged floor, up the stairs to the ground level, across the black and white floor of the atrium and out into the Mall. Past Tomas the porter, his head buried in a newspaper. Disappearing into the London traffic.

***

53

Raven had gathered the squad.

"We know he went to the locker. He took something. What was it? If you've just topped somebody you get out fast. You don't hang around. But this was so important he went to look for it."

"Strong nerves." Leach was standing near the back of the room. Rosie turned to him.

"If you're barmy Phil nerves don't come into it. He knew what he was looking for."

Raven said: "Gleeson must have told him. He tortured it out of him. You'd tell anybody anything if somebody was waving scissors around in front of your eye."

"I had a word with the porter," Rosie said. "The fair-haired kid. Tomas from Estonia. He was very frightened. Unduly so. It wasn't just because he was talking to the Law. There was more to it. And I'm not sure why. He's not an illegal. I've checked."

She looked round at the squad.

"Phil, go back to the club and have another go at him. Perhaps I cocked up. Maybe I was too easy on him. We know the club was very quiet. But it was carnage. It was like a butcher's shop. Our boy must have been in a Hell of a mess. Somebody must have seen or heard something."

***

"You've more authority."

They were in The Feathers. Raven was on his second gin.

Rosie smoothed the collar of her trouser suit. "You saying I'm bossy?"

He laughed. "No. Telling people what you want. It's not easy. Phil's older than you. He's been around a while. You've coped with the back-biting."

"Are you firing me?"

"Trying to be agreeable."

"Makes a damn change."

"You were good with the old lady in Blackheath."

54

"I try. It's better now. Everything's calmed down in the office."

"Good. It takes time."

"Bollocks. You warned 'em off."

"No."

"You're such a liar."

He was knocking back the gin.

"You're hitting it .."

A noisy group celebrated in a dark corner. Three Suits, two girls. All tits and tattoos. The pop of a champagne cork, screams of laughter.

"Brayin' triumphalists," he muttered.

He'd seen the Porsche parked half on the pavement.

"You're down," she said.

"It's nothing. Just the case."

She said something, but he cut her off.

"No shop talk .."

He glanced at the party. A Suit trailed his fingers across a girl's breast. They were sprawled on a leather sofa. He thought of the snooker room.

"When did you say you learned to play snooker?"

"No shop talk, you said .." she smiled at him .. ".. When I was growing up. Dad played a lot and got ratted in the boozer. Mam held it all together."

Raven had another gin.

"Sounds bad. You must have been bright."

"Cambridge? Just lucky. Right colour."

"Don't put yourself down."

"It's true. Same with the job. It's politically correct to promote me. I'd never have got this promotion."

"Balls. If you'd been dumb you wouldn't have made it. Black or not."

His eyes were bloodshot.

"If you hadn't got in to Cambridge you'd have said they were prejudiced against you."

"Probably."

She stared into the mirror behind the bar. Seeing her reflection.

"When I was a child I had a secret weapon. Our priest. When the other kids were shooting up and drinking Mam'd send me off to him for extra lessons. Boy, was he educated. He could quote Milton and Proust by the yard. So I became a swot. Mam and the priest. They're the ones to blame for making me what I am."

"Why waste that on being a copper?"

"Mam said I'd get a good pension."

"Not altruism then?"

She laughed.

"Nothing so grand .. Jack, you're two parts to the wind. Let's make a move?"

"You go."

She touched his arm. "What's up?"

The drink had loosened his tongue.

"Olivia died a year ago today." Pale eyes watery.

"It's only the gin. Depressive."

"I'm a good Catholic girl. I'm not leaving you like this. I'll get plastered too. Don't want you punching any bankers."

The crowd in the dark corner guffawed.

"I'll knock their bloody teeth out."

"That'd look nice on the CV."

"So?"

Two doubles arrived.

"I don't even like gin .. well, not this much."

"Grows on you."

In the corner the girl's lipstick was smeared. The Suit had his fingers in her top.

"Thank God she's not my daughter."

"You haven't got children."

"Didn't have time."

She smiled, looking at the group.

"It's Britain today Jack. One of the richest and cleverest nations in the world. Free education for fifty years. And what have we got? Tarts on the lash. Tattoos on tits. And a bunch of rich plonkers driving Porsches."

"And you wonder why I'm cynical."

*****

Leach went in hard. He wanted to hear it all again. If he found a discrepancy in Tomas's story he'd jump on it.

"Tell me the truth or I'll have Immigration crawl all over you. You'd hate to be done for obstructing a murder inquiry. You were on the door. There was no other way Gleeson's killer could have got out."

He knew it wasn't true. There was the garden entrance. The tradesman's door. The builders hoist up and down the scaffolding. Meant for equipment. But roofers used it for illicit lifts.

"Speak slow. I don't understand."

"You know what I'm asking."

In the porter's cubicle with its bulls-eye glass windows in the club's foyer, Tomas had been reading the *Standard*. He usually read it before smoothing out the creases and taking it up to the smoking room as if it had newly arrived. He'd been engrossed in a story about Estonian illegal immigrants. His behaviour had been out of character. He was usually so eager to please some members thought him oily. It took Leach an hour of brow-beating. Yes, OK. He'd been vaguely aware of somebody leaving. He hadn't seen his face. Or if he was carrying anything. Dark clothes. Perhaps a suit. Not sure. He was very sorry. He knew he wasn't paid to read newspapers. He was frightened. He didn't want to lose his job. He didn't want to go back to Estonia. So he'd lied to Rosie. Played her for a fool. Leach had finally got the truth. But it added little.

*****

Forensics. Trapped between the back of the locker and a shelf was a torn fragment. A stamp showing the partial base of a statue. Under a microscope it was identified as the plinth of Cristo Redentor. The giant statue of Christ the Redeemer. Arms outstretched. Embracing humanity and all its weaknesses. Cristo Redentor towered over Rio de Janeiro from the top of Corcovado. The hunchback mountain. A famous tourist trap. One of the best loved sights in Brazil. A wonder of the world.

***

Rosie had difficulty prising details about Gleeson out of the army. Blood out of a stone she said. There were blanks in his background. But she'd still managed to build a useful profile. Raven was impressed. He knew the military liked to clean up its own excrement. It hated outsiders butting in. He had solved the case of a murdered corporal at Aldershot. The commanding officer had insisted it was suicide. But Raven had proved that the victim had been driven to it by bullying. That his tormentors were urging him on at the time he hanged himself.

***

Gleeson had specialised in irrigation. As an army engineer he had been seconded around the world. Offering his expertise. He'd worked in east Africa. At Mpala on Lake Tanganyika. In Egypt at Beni Hassan on the Nile. At Santa Cruz in Bolivia, swept by hot winds, cold when the surazo blew in from the Argentinian pampas. Where typhoid and hepatitis were endemic. He had helped design a desalination plant in Lebu on Chile's long coastline. He had worked in Brazil. In the fly-blown heat of Sao Paolo shanties. And the murderous drug-ridden favelas of Rio de Janeiro.

***

Gleeson's longest secondment had been in Peru. Working in the slums, the pueblos jovenes which ring Lima its capital like a soiled necklace. Where beggars whose ancestors had been proud Inca warriors now scavenged on mountains of rubbish which reeked in the glare. Scrabbling for scraps of wire, zinc, copper. Anything to sell for a fistful of Nuevo Sol on the grubby stalls which lined Lima's litter-strewn and pot-holed highways. Where children wore rags and ran barefoot in the dust. Where the elders talked of once having seen rain. In Lima the rich wore white suits and designer shades. They fled the furnace of the city in black-glassed limousines. Air-con on max. In their wake they left behind the huddled and the dispossessed. Their lives ruled by gangsters and the terrorista bombings of Sendero Luminosa. Gleeson had a grace and favour villa in Lima's Miraflores. Where the wealthy live. He was convivial. Fond of a party. Miraflores' villas face the Pacific. They have air-conditioning, steel-shutters, ice-makers. In a land desperate for water, fountains play on manicured lawns. As night falls well-heeled residents check their intruder alarms and their fortress walls topped with razor wire. Rhodesian Ridgebacks are let off their leashes to prowl the grounds, baying and howling through the night. Householders lie awake listening for the gangsters. For the hooded fanatics of Sendero. For the wild-eyed and the homeless swathed in rags. And for the demented, crazy for a fix.

*****

William and Mary Mews, Knightsbridge, London. In the past it would have smelled of steaming horses hot from their early-morning gallops in Hyde Park. Grooms busy with blankets and brushes. The chink of hooves ringing on cobbles. Today it's an oasis protected from the hoi-polloi behind a high red-brick wall. Its residents enter through a gated arch. Over the generations the stables were converted into mews houses, with garages below and flats above. A hideaway for Russian oligarchs and Chinese entrepreneurs. For oil-rich sheikhs and bankers from the City and

Canary Wharf. The house was small, exquisite. What agents call bijou. Red trailing geraniums in window boxes. Steel-bars at the windows. An alarm high-up winking vigilance. A white front door with a diamond pattern of ornamental black studs.

***

A staircase led from the garage up to the flat. The pied a terre of Mrs. Melody Lockhart from New York. Divorced, aged fifty-one, no children. One of Global's most senior executives. The boss of the slaughtered Sylvia Capes. Melody Lockhart had survived the rolling culls of recession. She commanded a suite of offices at the summit of Global's glass and chrome tower in Canary Wharf. On the far side of London from her home in William and Mary mews. Her office in the sky had Chagall paintings on walls papered in silk. Cream carpets ran ankle-deep. A sanctuary of hushed conversation and coded phone-calls and billion dollar deals. Richly insulated from the frenzy of the trading room twenty floors below. Retainers in dark blue waistcoats with red piping and brass buttons served Earl Grey in thin china. Clouds swirled round the tower's peak. As if the Gods were angry. At her floor to ceiling windows she'd stare down at the fountained piazza thirty floors below. Watching the servants of usury. Milling and scurrying around like a million ants.

***

Melody Lockhart's acolytes would be summoned to her eyrie. Shooting skywards in the mirrored lift. Nervous and expectant. Women patting their hair. Men giving toe-caps a final polish on the backs of their trousers. In her eyrie, the eagles nest, they'd be castigated or congratulated. Fired or promoted. It was to Lockhart that Sylvia Capes would report. Capes was Melody Lockhart's protégé. Through the financial alchemy for which she was both famed and feared Global had paid for Capes' dockland flat. The shareholders knew nothing of its purchase. In Global's grand order it was a tiny consideration. Disguised with ease in the ledgers of a corporation which daily dealt in trillions.

**

Capes had betrayed Lockhart's name to the killer while she lay bound and trembling in her bath. A hopeless barter in which she'd tried to trade her confederates' identities in exchange for her life. In readying himself for the killing of Melody Lockhart he'd watched and waited for her as he had with the others. He'd tracked her down. Stalked her. Familiarising himself with the patterns of her life. She returned to the mews drained with stress. At the wheel of a black Audi-A8. The vehicle of choice for Britain's foremost bankers. She'd been distracted. During the crawl from Canary Wharf to Knightsbridge her mind was elsewhere. The recession had carved into Global's profits. Mergers and acquisitions had dried to a trickle. Thousands of Global employees had been laid off. Revulsion with bankers had swept the globe. They were seen as greedy and immoral. As bad as politicians. Stars of the City had been subject to humiliation by select committees stuffed with politicos keen to jump on a passing bandwagon. Eager to shift public opprobrium from themselves and their expenses' scandal.

**

Melody Lockhart had more on her mind than the travails of banks and politicians. She glanced at a newsagents' billboard. 'Banker hangs himself.' In her mind a blurred picture crystallised. An image of Capes. Contorted, blood-soaked. Tortured to death in her bath. The image terrified her. She had to slam on the brakes to avoid a collision with a car in front as the queue of traffic inched forward.

***

Swinging through the arch into the mews Melody Lockhart barely registered a young man assiduously brushing the cobbles. His eyes averted, head down, toiling over a broom. The wide tyres of the big Audi rumbled across the cobbles. A switch on the dashboard opened electric garage doors. Negotiating the narrowness of the entrance she didn't see the man dart inside, behind the car. The garage doors slid to. As she opened her door, he pounced. Out of the darkness. Stifling her cries. Forcing her upstairs to the flat.

***

He used a similar method to that which he had employed on Capes. A scalding bath. She was transfixed by the razor held close to her skin. Whispering another name to him. Confiding the details of her life. When she finished he'd been overwhelmed by madness. He strangled her with the cord of her dressing gown. Seeing her eyes bulge. Throttling the breath from her. Watching her life ebb away. Letting her slide under the water. He took a souvenir from a bedside cabinet. A small photograph in a silver frame. Lockhart and an unknown man. Arm in arm. Smiling into each others' eyes. Snowy peaks in the background. He left as he had entered. The name she had confessed to him sizzling in his brain like phosphorous.

***

The mews had taken on a bone chill. Bijou charm cast out by slaughter. The squad and Forensics had left their mark. Taking it apart. Each inch dissected. Geraniums torn from window-boxes. Lockhart's mattress sliced open to its springs. Cupboards ransacked, shelves cleared. A destruction disproportionate to the secrets revealed. Nothing had been found. Kitchen, living room, bedroom. The bathroom where savagery had been unleashed. All in ruin. The Audi yielded nothing. Stripped to its chassis. Nor the garage where horses had once been stabled. From whose shadows the killer sprang. The brick floor of a white-walled court-yard had been lifted. The clay beneath forked and analysed.

***

At Lockhart's office in Canary Wharf walls were peeled of silk coverings. Carpets torn up. Masterpieces prised from golden frames. Computers gutted to jigsaw fragments. After Raven had lacerated himself and the squad about the snooker ball and the locker there must be no more oversights. They found no correspondence between Capes and Lockhart. Analysis of landlines, mobiles, diaries in handbags and on computers betrayed no relationship. Nothing. Capes answered to Lockhart. She'd appointed her. But there was not a scribbled note. No everyday e-mail. Nothing. No mention of Capes' itinerary. Or her work-schedule which Lockhart sanctioned. Yet they had spent long periods together. The platinum-haired PA with sharp eyes who ran Lockhart's secretariat in the outer office had said so. Capes had been a frequent visitor. Sipping Lockhart's Earl Grey in the thinnest bone china.

***

Raven looked haggard. Skin pale and stubbled, black shadows under his eyes. He wasn't alone. The stress was telling on Rosie. Her composure had wilted. In its place, a resigned tetchiness. Her thousand-watt smile rarely seen. They were in Lockhart's living room. Sash windows faced the cobbled mews. Raven perched on the arm of a wounded settee. Its back agape. Ripped apart by the squad. Apart from the muted hum of Knightsbridge traffic, the house had taken on a deathly quiet.

"Links," he said, staring into space. "A torn stamp from Brazil in Gleeson's locker. He worked in south America. So did Capes. So did Samuels the journalist. I'm screwed. Four murders and we're still all over the place. We're chasing a phantom."

PART 2

BRAZIL

Maria Rodriguez had been walking at the edge of the river Branco at Caracarai. Five hundred miles north of Manaus in the Amazon near the border with Guyana. Early evening. A molten sun had begun to lose its glare. She'd followed a lonely forest trail. Ducking low beneath a liana hanging across her path in a twisted curtain of fronds. As she crouched, pulling the fronds to one side, she suddenly screamed and ran terrified back down the winding track a mile to the hut in which she lived. Her husband Antonio was in the yard. Chopping wood with his machete to keep the fire alive. She burst into the clearing and threw her arms around him. Gasping for breath she told him what she'd found. He held her to him and told her to calm down while he went to see for himself. He stoked the fire and left her with a steaming mug of bitter black coffee. Maria was so frightened she had not wanted him to leave, not even for a few minutes. But he'd run up the track, machete in hand, and later he'd run another mile, sweat pouring from him. He'd summoned the priest, old Father Niall, who lived in a wooden shack with a grass roof by the river in Aripaita. Old Father Niall had achieved status thereabouts by making a clearing in the forest in which he and the men of the village had built a large hut which he ran as a school. He gave lessons and had trained two of the brighter girls as teachers. The villagers had hung a scrawled sign over its door which proclaimed that the hut with its wooden walls and roof thatched with plaited palm leaves was

'Niall's School.' The torso Maria had found was headless. A little girl, aged six or seven. Captain Jose Manuel Caballero, chief of the police, said she could have been killed anywhere. He thought the body had been washed up into the vegetation at the

65

side of the Branco by the strong currents which had been running for a month or so.

∗∗∗

The pathologist was sweating heavily. Dabbing at his face and neck with a large red handkerchief. Dr. Herman Grunwald had been brought in from Manaus. He was of German extraction. Villagers gathered at the river's edge. Most had never seen a white man. Let alone one in a panama hat and a crumpled cream linen suit stained brown with perspiration. Grunwald was in his sixties. Heavily built. Face red with triple chins, steel-rimmed glasses. He drank from two bottles. The first gin, the second tonic. He poked and fiddled with the body as it lay in the slime at the river's edge. Complaining about the stinking heat and his shoes which had filled with water from the Branco. He told the police chief he drank for medicinal reasons. Quinine in the tonic helped stave off malaria. After some minutes spent prodding and cursing he declared that the little girl had been dead for weeks. She'd probably been killed somewhere else, he said, and that as far as he was concerned the whole wretched business was a complete mystery. He wanted to know who would pay for his damaged brogues and his cream suit to be cleaned.

∗∗∗

Further examination showed the child had been tortured, her body mutilated. Somebody, or several, had had intercourse with her. There were burn marks on her back and arms. Deep scars ran the length of her chest as if she'd been clawed. The police and Grunwald said predators in the river and animals of the forest had inflicted the savagery. Old Father Niall knew they were lying. Either they wanted to protect the killer or killers or they couldn't be bothered. He thought the latter was the most likely. The police were corrupt. They worked with compliant coroners and doctors.

66

Idle, and inept, they lacked both will and resources to investigate a complex killing. Their motto was to keep it simple: the girl had been mauled by wild animals. It was neat and convenient. Signing a case off ensured their superiors did not have to be dragged in.

***

In forty years in Brazil old Father Niall never believed a word the police, army, councillors or politicians said. He had bright blue eyes. Sharp and inquisitive. Thick silver hair fell to his shoulders. But over the years he'd become tired from his labours. Made frail by the ravages of malaria and asthma which had left him rake-thin. At night in his shack he coughed himself to sleep. His slight, bony frame, shook with his convulsions. He coughed so violently he thought his lungs would collapse. Certain that he was dying, and unafraid, had given him a manic energy. He told those who would listen that having the Reaper at his shoulder made him run fast. He had made endless inquiries. But nobody knew who the child was. Or where she came from. Caballero, the police chief, with his pot belly and his gold braid, pledged that there would be a rigorous investigation. But detective work, Caballero said, was more effective if cloaked in secrecy. That being the case the investigation had to be conducted with discretion, so neither he nor his officers would be able to further assist old Father Niall. For months Niall persisted with his questions. The police chief maintained that an arrest was imminent. Old Niall said it was all blether. Nobody was arrested. The girl's head was never found.

***

THE AMAZON
BRAZIL

Father Micheal Flaherty. Frayed shirt. Flapping sandals. Faded shorts scrubbed a thousand times by the band of women who loved him. They made him cakes. Fed the parrot. Swept his hovel. Each day filling the lamp with kerosene. They changed the water in the rusty oil drum which served as his bath on the back porch. Into it he eased his great frame at five each morning when the air was cool and fresh. They walked half a mile and back with buckets of water from the nearest tap. Backs bent. He always protested and said they were too old. It made him feel guilty. He could do it. But they insisted. He would tell himself that if it pleases them who the Hell are you Micheal Francis Flaherty to deprive them of one of their few small pleasures? It was the priest's lot. Women filling the tin drum with water every day was part of it. It was a rusty drum. Slightly jagged at the lip. It scratched at him as he heaved his torso free. Causing him to yell out. Bellowing a string of profanities. Setting dogs barking in the shanties. In the sun his skin had turned as dark as ebony. His eyes were as brown as the great mahogany trees. They could be as fiery as blazing coal.

**

They called Micheal, Miguel. His size gave him away. Natives were neater. More compact. In Galway his mother used to tease him that he was like a haystack in a cyclone. Straw coming out everywhere. But you're a grand big boy Micheal so you are, she'd smile. Big enough to run the money lenders out of the temple. His hair was thick, black, curling on to his massive shoulders. A beard as wild and prickly as a blackthorn bush. The women giggled when they had him on the orange box on the porch. Setting about him with their combs and scissors. You're huge and hairy Miguel, they'd laugh. Clucking round him. Running their fingers through his hair. You're like the big monkeys over the river. They loved him with all their hearts. He liked reading them stories. Eyes smouldering as he glanced over the small gold spectacles nipping at the end of his nose. He liked Brendan Behan.

"That Quare fella. Now there's a story," he'd say. "He knew about the world."

Sitting at the open bar with its grass roof at the edge of the track. Above him blue-fronted parrots screeched and tore at the soft bark of the Capirona tree, offering only meagre shade from the pitiless glare of the sun.

**

With his thick neck and muscled arms he'd tell them he was as strong as an ox. Ready to fight your damn land owners. Your soldiers in their fancy uniforms.

Your glib politicians who smile a lot. Your fat policemen on the take. All of them taking bribes and useless.

"They're all as corrupt as Hell. One day I'll tear them apart. So I will. Limb by bloody limb."

Then he'd throw back his great head and burst into laughter. And everybody would join in. They'd open bottles of Xingu black beer and the women would bake Torta Gelada de Moranges, strawberry shortcake. As it turned into a party they'd drink cachaca, made from sugar cane. And everybody would smile and sing. In the middle would be Flaherty, towering over everybody, dancing and singing. His wild black hair being flung from side to side, hiding his face and his bright, burning eyes. Telling anybody who'd listen that in the Amazon most of the people had nothing. But they were still the kindest and most generous in the world.

**

In thirty years in Brazil Flaherty and his compatriots had strayed far from the pomp and purple of Rome. He was a gentle giant. His great hands delicate if stroking the brow of an old woman close to death. The same hands which had pinned a policeman to a wall, pressing his throat so hard he'd begun to choke. He'd demanded to know why the police were prosecuting a family for stealing food from a stall in the market.

69

"What are they supposed to do?" he'd shouted. "Starve? And while they go hungry you'll go home with your fat belly and your big pension."

He'd been jailed for a week. And was lucky not to have been kicked out of Brazil. He'd been lectured by the magistrate. His Order castigated. The Vatican said he was more Marxist than Catholic. His long-suffering Bishop told him that a touch more diplomacy might have been judicious. Flaherty had yelled at the magistrate:

"It's not stealing when you're so poor. People have to live. This time it was the food stall. Next time it'll be the tourists. Tourists are just bread on the water."

***

Worker priests and Liberation Theology were poison to the Vatican. The climate worsened when Oscar Romero, the Archbishop of El Salvador, was murdered by land owners. Shot as he took Mass in his church. A quarter of a million people attended his funeral. In South and Central America most of the land is owned by a tiny minority. It incensed Flaherty.

"There will never be justice until the land is distributed fairly. It's not right that so few control so many other peoples' lives and destinies. It's wicked, beyond defence. There's so little education, so few proper homes, no real infrastructure, so many people without sanitation or even fresh water. It makes me sick so it does. What sort of society is this? I'll tell you. It's one ripe for a revolution. And one day it'll come. It's a tinder-box that's waiting for a match."

***

Brazil was assailed by environmental and economic problems. The wanton destruction of the rainforest. Numerous assaults on indigenous peoples. Attempts to force them off the land had met with violence. Several murders included that of Chico Mendes, a Brazilian rubber-tapper and Amazon activist. Killed at his home in Xapuri by a rancher. Such events helped galvanise Flaherty and his confederates. Steeling them in their efforts to defend the dispossessed. They lived with the people, sharing their deprivations, the corruption, the oppression, catching their diseases.

"We try to be decent people in an indecent society," Flaherty told the magistrate, in his soft, lilting brogue. Then his temper flared again and he shouted at the Bench.

"There's fuck all else the people can turn to. If we don't try and look after them there's nobody else who will."

The magistrate had banged his gavel. But Flaherty had refused to be silenced.

"When was the last time any of you bastards spent time in a settlement? You daren't even go there. You're a bunch of arse-lickers."

They had had to wrestle him from the dock. Dragging him down to the cells, wrestling with the guards, yelling and protesting.

**

The Amazon was in full flood. Trees wrenched out by their roots. Swept along in its current. The vultures had gathered. Waiting for the afternoon deluge. Squatting in hunched rows on the limbs of a dead tree. The tree looked diseased. As if cloaked in black scabs. Like the scars of a biblical plague. Motionless, hooded, the vultures waited for new flesh. Hopping in a clumsy dance at the river's edge. Scouring the bones of fish gutted after the morning catch. Today Flaherty was more angry than usual. A trickle of stories about vanished children had become a torrent. They filtered in from Fransiscans, Jesuits, Oblates and Holy Ghost priests scattered across the Latin continent. From priests who toiled deep in the green silence of the forest. Or in the choking dust of stifling city slums. From priests now retired, too infirm to labour. Those who'd returned to their philosophy, their poetry and their doubts.

From young firebrand priests inflamed by the corruption and deprivation. From wherever the stories came, from forest or city, from young or old, from the strong or the stricken, they ignited in Flaherty a rage which could never be quelled.

***

The Antonino
Favela Rio de Janeiro
Brazil

Long before the London killings, Roberto Ligueira had been happy on the day he ran barefoot to the cemetery to play football with his friends. He was five years old and still too small to be much of a player. It was his task to retrieve the ball when the older boys kicked it off the pitch and it became lost in the tangle of brush and weeds and collapsed graves. Once, he had jumped onto a grave, and it sank inches into the ground, cracking and groaning and tilting at a crazy skew into the mud left by the torrential rains from the day before. A bone had poked up from the mire. It so scared Roberto it caused him to run back to his friends. When he told Eduardo about it, who was a little older and bigger and who everybody said would one day be as good as Pele, Eduardo had gone back to the collapsed grave. He'd scrabbled in the slime and pulled out a skull. Laughing and shouting, throwing it to the others, telling them to use it in a game of kick'n catch.

***

The graveyard which doubled as the soccer pitch was on waste ground. Littered with broken glass it was close to the shack in which Roberto lived with Isabella and Pedro, his mother and father. Isabella bore her first child when she was fourteen, and her second at sixteen. Both were now under the ground. The first was still born. The second died of tuberculosis. Maria, the nurse, who for thirty years day and night had tended the diseased in the Antonino Favela, warned Isabella that she was to have no more children. Roberto must be her last. Pedro was just skin and bones, dying of AIDS. Lying still and silent, as if he already departed, in the gloomy fly-blown heat at the back of the shack, curtained off from the rest of the hovel by torn sacking which had once held the cassava. Isabella, too, was HIV positive.

***

To those in the favela Maria was an angel. Stooped, old, she walked with a stick. She had shiny silver hair and fine skin and smelled of soap. Her eyes were as blue as the ocean in the bay. She offered belief and kindness when all around was despair. In the privacy of her own shack she'd break down, clutching her crucifix. Whispering of her sadness, pleading for forgiveness. For fifteen years she'd been a nun with the Little Sisters of Pity. In the Order she'd trained as a nurse. She grew up in County Clare. In a white-washed cottage in Liscannor Bay. Where Atlantic gales howled and icy winds clutched at the shutters. In the molten gloom of the shacks, catching the hot, putrid breath of the dying, pressing her ear to their lips, to catch their final murmurings, she'd remember the clean cool air of County Clare.

***

Maria knew that Roberto's father, Pedro, would soon be dead. His skin yellow, flaky as parchment. In his shrunken face his eyes were like dark saucers. She'd heat water on the fire to bathe him, gently turning him from side to side. But he was still wracked with bed sores. She'd turn up the kerosene lantern. An oily vapour filling the shack, shadows dancing in a hissing, puthering, orange glow. Cupping the back of his head she'd hold a beaker of water to his lips. Thousands were dying of AIDS. She could only stay for a few minutes. Others, elsewhere in the favela, were always pleading for her mercies.

***

Maria's days began before dawn, negotiating the scrambled confusion of mud alleys and slimy duck-boards which ran between the jumble of makeshift homes. She'd still be out and about dispensing her compassion hours later, working into the early dawn. Offering forlorn hope. Stroking the bony arms and the trembling hands of those passing from a hovel's half-light into the blackness of an unknown universe. And as the dying took their leave she'd try and comfort those left behind. Calming the children, cradling the wives and husbands, the mothers and fathers, who had watched and waited in the furnace gloom.

***

Little Roberto would not see his father die as so many children saw theirs. Nor would he see his mother die, a year later, ravaged by AIDS. Her spirit crushed by his disappearance. He had left a game of football. Running back for the black bean stew his mother had cooked for him on the open fire. Threading his way through the sunken graves. Skipping along the track near the mortuary. The door of a parked Jeep with smoked windows had suddenly swung wide in front of him. Blocking his way. Before he knew what was happening. Before he could scream out. He was bundled into its back and driven away. A man and a woman gagged and hooded him. Trussing his hands. Pushing him to the floor. Pressing him down with their feet to stop him squirming. Four adults, three men and the woman. They drove sixty kilometres to Petropolis in the mountains. Where the air is cooler, where the emperors once lived. Where tourists gawp at the palaces of old Brazil.

74

***

They took him to a mansion near an ornamental canal where back-packers rested, close to the elegant Avenida 7 de Setembro. Ornate electric gates swung wide. The house was cream coloured. A large colonial villa with white shutters and many windows. In a high-walled park. Lawns, trees, a fountain playing on a lily pond. The Jeep parked in a basement garage. The abductors took the lift to the ground floor. Carrying Roberto, trembling and tied. The four were in good spirits when the owner of the house appeared. Congratulating them. Roberto was stripped of his clothes. The owner was an industrialist. Called Lascelle. While the others held him Lascelle minutely examined the child. Instructing them that he be bathed and given a sedative to induce drowsiness and to relax his muscles.

***

They removed his hood and bonds and filled a bath. Pushing him into it, laughing. The boiling water made his skin red. He was taken into a bedroom and caned and sodomised by Lascelle. While Lascelle forced himself into him the others masturbated on his face and hair. Like the men the woman was nude and helped pin him down. When Lascelle had finished the others took it in turn to sodomise him. He bled so profusely it caused them alarm. Lascelle telephoned a friend, a doctor, one driven by the same lusts as themselves. The physician pronounced the injuries superficial. Telling the abductors they could continue with their pleasures. The doctor was so excited he too sodomised the boy.

***

To stop him screaming the woman slapped him hard several times on his face. Leaving red and angry wealds on his cheeks.

75

Lascelle left the room to return with a hooded Falcon. Strapped to his wrist by a chain. While the others held him down Lascelle brought the bird close to Roberto's face and slowly unlaced its hood. The falcon tossed its head. Eyes gleaming and blinking in the sudden light. Kicking out with its clawed foot. Its talon gouging Roberto's forehead. Lascelle took the bird to a corner of the room, transferring the chain from his wrist to a stand.

"He'll claw your eyes out boy."

The others laughed.

"You'll have no eyes. Just little black holes."

***

Lascelle whipped the boy. With a riding crop. His small frame flinched and arched. While he was being held he saw another face. That of Gleeson. Naked and smiling. While Lascelle sodomised him, Gleeson stood close. Recording on a video camera each scream and the tears which ran down his cheeks. He was taken to a basement snooker room, winched up by his wrists and suspended on a rope from a hook in the ceiling. Gleeson continued to video him. Crying and naked, twisting and turning on the rope. As he dangled they took it in turns to beat him with snooker cues.

***

Gleeson talked of Roberto's mother and the agony of her loss. And of Roberto's terror. It added to their excitement and they beat him more frenziedly. When they'd finished they left him hanging by his wrists. Bleeding, virtually unconscious. They drank and played snooker. The woman keeping the score. Clicking the sliding brass counters on the scoreboard. Occasionally she forsook the game and walked over to him. Inspecting him as he hung on the rope. Checking he was still alive. When they let him down he couldn't stand. They screamed at him to stand up. To do as he was told.

Pulling him up by his hair, wrenching a clump of it from his scalp. Then the four of them beat and raped him again.

***

One of them brandished a machete. They told him that when they'd finished with him they were going to chop his little head off, parcel it up and send it back to his mother. Every hour or two for a month, day and night, he was tortured. Gang-raped and sodomised. Then they tired of him. Like a toy his novelty wore off. They craved new meat. They sold him to another group in Gloria. An expensive suburb of Rio where the streets are cobbled. Quaint shops sell antiques. Ancient houses tumble down a hillside giving views of Guanabara Bay. In a friendly-looking house, pink-painted, window boxes, marigolds and scarlet geraniums, he met the same fate.

***

That is how it was for three years. With Roberto being passed from one group to the next. There had, at the start, been some semblance of police activity. An initial flourish when he first disappeared. His absence even made a paragraph in the local free sheet. The police chief promised he'd do his utmost. But children went missing all the time. Most, he said, left of their own volition to join the street gangs. A wealthy industrialist from Sao Paolo, not Lascelle but one who shared his tastes, was paying for the police chief's daughter to attend an expensive school in Switzerland, overlooking Lake Geneva. It was an opportunity for the policeman's daughter. All he had to do was turn a blind-eye to the industrialist's habit of having his agents scoop up street children who would never be seen again. Roberto's mother had been too weak and too poor to make her own protests. His father had lain still and frightened in the blackness of the shack.

77

PART 3

LONDON

The early hours. Raven and Miriam in bed. He woke with a start. The wail of an ambulance. A police siren. Bathed in sweat. Pillow soaked. She tried to comfort him. But he was beyond solace. Later, as he stepped from the shower, she told him what she had learned at work. Looking into his tired, pale eyes. Stroking his hand. Fingers settling on his wedding ring. She'd heard a whisper at Blue Star. The porno publishers in Soho. Where she worked. The advertising manager had been talking to a sidekick while she was getting water at the dispenser. His door was slightly ajar. The manager was well-built. A bully. She heard him mention the name Gleeson. Saying he'd read about the killings in the papers.

"He said something about meeting a man in prison who knew Gleeson. Then he said something I couldn't hear and they both laughed."

"What's his name?" Raven was suddenly alert.

"Michael Wall. He's not particular. If a girl's got a pulse it's good enough."

Raven slipped away into London's morning mayhem. The Alfa gently burbling, asking to be unleashed. Heading for Blue Star he rang Leach. Telling him to run a check on Wall. The office was in St. Mary's Court off Wardour Street. He ignored the girl on the desk. But in an instant he'd memorised her. Red blouse, cleavage, butterfly tattoo. A dyed blonde. A habit he'd cultivated over the years. Olivia said he had become a walking camera. He ran up the stairs. Past a gallery of salacious covers. Crotches and nipples. Barging into Wall's office. Raven was tetchy. He had a hangover. His back hurt. He'd slept with Miriam. Guilt gnawed at him.

"Wall?" He closed the door. "I'm a copper and you're going to tell me everything you know about a man called Gleeson."

Wall rose from his desk. Miriam was right. He was tall. Heavily-built. Bull-necked. Black greased hair combed back.

"What the ..?"

Raven cut him off.

"Tell me about Gleeson?"

"What you on about?"

Raven moved to the window. In the street below a cleaner swept dead fruit from the previous day's market. He pounced, pinning Wall to the desk. Flicking his arm up his back. Sweat spouted from Wall's forehead. Raven forced the arm higher. "Shoplifter, mugger, protection rackets. The old biddy at Sidcup. Couldn't find her son so you beat her up. Turned her into a cabbage. Brain damage. Knifed up one of your girls when she wouldn't perform. Used acid when she made a run for it. Messed her up, didn't you Wall? Her own mother wouldn't recognise her. Vice'll crawl all over this dump and the bed-sits you think we don't know about. Where you've got your little Lithuanian hookers doing their tricks."

He released his grip. Wall staggered to the door. Raven hadn't finished with him. He hit him, hard. Splitting his lower lip. Knocking him to the floor.

"Bastard .." Blood trickled from his mouth.

Raven stared down at him. Foot on his chest. Eyes glacial.

"I haven't time to mess about with scum like you. I'm in a rush."

Soon enough Wall told him what he wanted. While doing three years for keeping brothels, and carving up one of his girls, Wall met somebody called Kimble who'd mentioned Gleeson. Kimble was an untouchable. He spent most of his time in solitary. It was for his own safety. He'd been given it after being razored by an inmate. Kimble was a nonce. A child abuser.

***

Raven took Rosie. All prisons smelled the same. Stale, disinfectant, yesterday's left-overs. They sounded the same. A jangle of keys, footsteps, the slam of doors, shouts, unexplained cries, screams. A warder led the way. Locking and unlocking floor-to-ceiling gates. Long straight corridors. White strip lights. Inmates with buckets. Mopping floors for the thousandth time. Eyes raking over Rosie. Another gate, another corridor, quieter, no wolf whistles. Two prisoners shuffling towards them. She looked rigidly ahead. As they passed she could sense them turn and stare after her. It was her first time in a prison. They wanted her, hungry for her.

***

Kimble was stooped. Slight, thin-faced. A livid scar ran from his left eye to a speck of foam at the corner of his mouth. Hair mousy, soft dead eyes, round steel glasses. Skin pallid, dry, yellowy. Bereft of wind and sun. He squatted on the edge of his narrow bed. Staring at the floor. Clammy handshake, a snail's trail. Rosie wanted to wipe her hand. Near the sink, a black and white photograph. A woman with two children. Kimble glanced at it.

"They used to come." His voice a whisper. "Not anymore. Went off with somebody. Bitch."

He had met Gleeson at a party in London years before.

"Through a friend of a friend. You know how it is."

His eyes roved across Rosie.

"Nice and discreet."

A house in Haverstock Hill. The star turn had been a small girl. Brought to the party by Gleeson.

"We had some fun. Lovely little thing."

He smiled at the memory. "Fair hair. Very pretty."

Yellow teeth, mouth pink and gummy. Spittle on his lip.

"She led us on. Proper little monkey. You'd never believe the things she did."

He paused, looking at Rosie.

"Bit like you with your big eyes. White though. Only a kid, of course. About seven or eight she was .."

He smiled.

"Gleeson's sort don't do time. Too well connected."

His gaze turned to Raven.

"Ain't that right, Mr. Plod sir? Too many friends in high places."

"Like who?"

Kimble had been close to divulging a name. But Raven had been too quick. His eagerness had scared him off.

"Are you kidding?"

He ran a finger down the scar.

"Get another of these?"

He rose stiffly from the bed, back bent. Filling a yellow plastic beaker at the sink.

"Saw him here once."

Raven stared at him.

"Not like that .. here, on the telly. Some afternoon thing. Going on about insurance. Older, fatter. But it was him alright. Colonel bloody Gleeson. Or whatever he calls himself."

"You're certain?"

"You don't forget things like that."

"Like what?"

Gleeson's eyes were boring into him.

"What he did to that little girl."

A slight smile. A flicker of life in moribund eyes.

"It was a turn on. He was very strict with her. You know what those army types are like. Very imaginative."

He stared at Rosie's breasts. "I can remember it now. Clear as a bell. Everybody egging him on."

"Were you?"

"Now why would I be telling you things like that? I've got memories. Filed away up here."

He touched his head.

"They're what keeps me warm at night. Specially since they don't come no more." He looked at the photograph by the sink, curling at its edges.

BRAZIL

The Vatican had called a conference to forge co-operation between missionaries and charities. Truculent priests thought it an attempt to nurture their obeisance to Rome. Delegates gathered in Manaus. The capital of the Amazon. The most compelling question was not togetherness. But vanished children. Newly-weds Bill and Alice Lamb worked for the charity *Our Land*. It fought for indigenous peoples in Rondonia. Thousands of city slum dwellers had been lured from the shanty towns in southern Brazil, the barrios, and dumped in the northern wilderness of Rondonia. The authorities thought the shacks scarred the landscape and frightened the tourists. After the people left, their hovels were razed. The space used to build new hotels and offices.

***

Politicians said it would be a fresh start for the slum-dwellers. Rondonia, they promised, would be transformed. There would be new homes, schools and factories. It would be like the rubber boom. When there had been a bonanza of jobs and money. When the Teatros Amazonas was built in Manaus. The great opera house of the jungle. Where Hollywood stars performed and all the people loved it. Politicians said those who moved to Rondonia would be in paradise. Free of the stinking favelas of Rio and the choking dust of the chabolas of Sao Paolo. The chabolas were ruled by drug lords. With diamond ear-rings, mirrored-shades and Uzi machine-guns.

***

So the poor from the shacks in the teeming south were decanted into the barren lands of Rondonia. But no development would follow. Governments came and went. Politicians smiled and spun their lies and moved on. Mismanagement and corruption emasculated the economy. AIDS and narcotics and killings plagued the barrios. In Rondonia the urban throng who'd moved north were forgotten. Bereft of rural skills. Abandoned without money or resource. They had to cobble together ramshackle homes made of tin and straw and plastic sheeting. Like those that they had tried to escape in the festering cities of the south.

***

They had to beg at the roadside to feed their families. Sons and daughters sold themselves to the lumber merchants, land agents, soldiers and police. Peddling knick-knacks. Running stalls selling fruit juice and hamburgers that nobody wanted. They stood in rags at street corners selling matches. Or tried to grow coffee on patches of rock and red unyielding clay. Their search for halcyon horizons had vaporised in a litter of broken promises. Criminals roamed the land. Narcotics flooded in from Colombia. Children began to disappear.

***

Bill and Alice Lamb blamed the drug lords. Two weeping mothers came to them. A little boy and a small girl had disappeared. They had dark curls and chocolate brown eyes and mischievous grins. Somehow, they'd been spirited away. They'd been playing in the woods where the tall trees formed a parasol. Casting shadows on the forest floor. A friend said he'd seen them in the back of a black car with white-wall tyres. Somewhere close to the Mamore river. Heading for Guajara-Mirim. Near the border with Bolivia. The Lamb's travelled great distances badgering the police. Becoming a nuisance with the army commander and the land agents. The agents ran the haciendas for absentee owners who lived in stucco mansions in London. Or in fine brownstone houses in Manhattan.

Or sprawling villas set amid golf courses on the Portuguese Algarve. Each had promised to do their utmost.

***

Nobody trusted the police, the army or the land agents. The mothers heard nothing more. The children were never seen again. With the influx of dispossessed the problems in Rondonia became overwhelming. Two people with the slender resources of *Our Land* could make little impression. The head office of the charity, based in London, thought it wise to move the Lamb's to Candela, on the Amazon. Where Flaherty was based. Where their endeavours could be utilised more effectively. In Candela they fell in with the boisterous coterie of worker priests.

***

Proselytising, spreading the Word, was not top of the priests' priorities.

"You won't find any of our lot down on their knees foaming at the mouth," Flaherty told Bill Lamb. "It's called Liberation Theology. That's what we're supposed to be about. But there's still a Hell of a way to go before anything round here is liberated. We're too busy sorting out the medicine and schools and fighting the police and the soldiers. There's not a lot of time for praying and singing hymns. We're too caught up for a lot of yawping. We're organising the birth control and to Hell with what the Vatican says. The Vatican's so far removed from the reality on the ground it hasn't a clue. When we give the girls the pill they aren't swallowing them. Oh no! Mother of God they're putting them somewhere else entirely. And I for one won't be boring you with the detail. You really wouldn't want to know the minutiae. That's the level we're at, Bill, so it is. There's no health education. There's no proper schooling. There are lots of politicians who say all the right things

85

but don't do much. And when they actually do something they usually do it badly. There are plenty of two-bit officials with clip boards. And they're all as bent as the devil himself and a damn sight more heartless."

***

Flaherty looked up at the merciless sun. Running his hands through his wild black hair. Wiping at the sweat.

"It's the loveliest place on earth. But you can't even get decent coffee. All the good stuff's been exported. All we've got left is the rubbish. We're Beggar's in bloody paradise."

***

When Flaherty made one of his speeches his compatriots laughed and jeered. They told him he was a good man with a big heart. But for everybody's sanity would he please get the Hell off his soap-box. His friend Bernard was an Oblate missionary from Tipperary. He'd spent thirty years in the favelas of Rio de Janeiro.

"Mother of God you're worse than the politicians," he'd tell him.

And Flaherty would burst into laughter. Clutching little Bernard to him. Wrapping his huge muscled arms round him. Pressing him to his massive chest.

"Come on boys we'll have a toast with the Jameson," Flaherty would laugh.

"It's because there were seven of us at home and I wasn't brought up to know any better. I'm an ill-mannered bugger for sure and that's all there is to it."

And they'd all laugh, passing the whisky. Knowing how clever Flaherty was. The quickest mind in the Order. A rambunctious man mountain. His abilities hidden behind a shield of blarney.

"You get more from folk if they think you're not too smart," he'd tell the Lamb's .

"It's a fine theory so it is. It would definitely work if only I was smart."

And then he'd mop at his brow and his face would light up with a beguiling smile.

***

The Lamb's were fresh out of university when they arrived in Brazil. Bill had studied anthropology at Liverpool University. He came from the monied enclave of Hampstead in north London. His parents were both doctors. Athletic, broad-backed, he was good at sport. Especially sailing, like his father. Alice studied medieval history at Bath University. Her father was a school master. He taught English. Her mother worked for the library service. Home was a pebble-dashed semi-detached in Ealing in west London. It had a monkey tree in the small front garden. And rusting wrought iron gates in need of paint and oil. On its front door a galleon sailed gaily across a stained glass ocean. They had met at a university sailing regatta. The in-laws were happy. It was a union made in heaven. Perhaps their motives in journeying to Latin America had been altruistic. Maybe it was a chance to go somewhere exotic. Perhaps their post-degree options had seemed mundane. Whatever alchemy had brought them together and wafted them off to Brazil Providence would be the better for it. They had taken their leave so quickly after the champagne and the handshakes that they were still almost shaking the confetti off their shoulders. They left behind loved ones on both sides who wished them health and happiness, safety and success. All remained stoic. Moist-eyed but stiff upper-lipped. It had once been the British way. There was not a handkerchief in sight. At the outset of a great adventure it was not a time for histrionics. Nor London's Heathrow airport the place.

***

Flaherty's confederate Bernard was small and wiry. A worker priest he'd been bitten by a rabid dog on the steps of that which passed as a hospital near the shack in the favela in which he lived. He should have died. But he'd been pulled inside and given injections in his belly. On the mend, lying on his torn and sagging mattress in the gloom of his hut, he told well-wishers:

"The dog biting me was a miracle."

A miracle they chorused. Pulling aside the casava sacking which served as a curtain. Peering at him round the door of his hovel.

"It had rabies. The soldiers shot it. It bit you. How could it be a miracle Father?"

"It was a miracle because it bit me on the steps of the hospital."

***

Bernard knew of children who'd disappeared from Rio's favelas. Tourists on Copocabana's beaches thought the favelas looked pretty. Especially at night. A necklace of twinkling lights tumbling down the hills overlooking Sugar Loaf mountain. But they were told not to go there. The favelas were the fiefdom of gangs. Awash with narcotics. At night there were shootings and stabbings. In the morning fly-covered corpses littered mud alleys which wound through the jumble of shacks. The rains turned the alleys into streams of water and blood. Later the sun would burst through making everything steam. Stretcher-bearers took the dead to the morgue to lie in untidy rows. Black with bluebottles and mosquitoes. Bodies with knife wounds or bullet holes had to be identified by loved ones. They'd scream and become hysterical and be taken for a sedative at the clinic. But the clinic was usually out of sedatives. The cemetery was full. Corpses had to be buried one on top of the other. When the rains came every day the water washed away the earth. Creating bone yards. Broken skeletons and muddied skulls poked through the mire. Eye sockets plugged with slime. The urchins of the favela with dark eyes and laughing smiles played football with the skulls.

Only Bernard knew how many families lived in his favela. Who among the thousands had died or disappeared. Bernard in his bare feet and hand-me-down sandals. Ragged jeans. Shirt torn and frayed. The colour bleached out of it by the sun. Washed a thousand times by the old women who did for him. Brazil's bureaucracy trailed behind reality. Hard-eyed clerks brandished paper-work and death certificates. But they couldn't keep up with the killings and disappearances. They never stayed in the favelas very long. Their forms went unfilled. They were frightened of being maimed or murdered by the drug lords.

***

Outside the favelas lived those vested with protecting them, in the fancy villas and apartments of Ipanema and Copocabana at the bottom of the hill. The police, the army chiefs, the financiers and the lawyers. The businessmen and the bossy council officials. The dandy politicians smelling of lavender. With their quiffs and smiles and shiny suits. Each was feared and distrusted. Tainted by corruption.

***

Some children fled the hillside of their own volition. Joining the gangs who preyed on the tourists on the beaches and sidewalks. Vanishing down to the sea where the pickings were plentiful. Big hotels and fine apartments begged to be robbed. Tourists gazed and stared. Taking holiday snaps. Seeing nothing. Leicas and Chanel bags swung like bait from bronzed shoulders. Children lived in the sewers. Only coming out at night. Stinking of sweat and faeces. Scavenging like rats. Fleeting, sharp-eyed. Lost in the blur of tourists, coconut-sellers and the scarlet-lipped hookers on

Copocabana's marble sidewalks. Some families gave their children to strangers. Volunteered them. They were always fed the same story. This was a wonderful opportunity for their children. They would grow strong on good food. Be educated. Even attend university. Become rich. Send money home. Live in Brasilia with the important people. Weeping parents would hand them over. Kissing and hugging them. Imploring them to be careful. Believing this was a rare chance for them. That they were doing their best for them. To reject such an opportunity would be selfish and unloving. They would never see their children again.

**

The priests had taken vows of poverty. Giving away what little money they came across to the dispossessed. To the rascal children who trailed after them. Begging and laughing and clasping at their clothes. To the wizened and to the diseased. To those dying in the half light of the shacks. To the young girls aching for a fix. With their old faces and sad eyes.

"What would you do?" Flaherty was talking to Alice Lamb. Her fair hair caught in an Amazon breeze.

"The little girls are drugged up so they are. If I give them the money they'll buy drugs. If I don't they'll sell themselves anyway and buy a fix like that. What in Hell's name am I s'posed to do? The drugs and corruption .. it's not just here. It's all over south America."

**

Two of Bernard and Flaherty's friends were Dominic and Declan. Worker priests in Peru and Bolivia. They too knew of vanished children. Dominic had laboured thirty years in Yauri. A remote settlement on arid plains in the province of Sicuani, in Peru. A universe away from the familiar tourist trails of Macho Picchu and

90

Cuzco. Fluent in Spanish he'd mastered Quechua. The original Inca tongue. So difficult that even those with an ear for language would abandon its learning. He covered hundreds of miles by horseback in the Andes. In the summer with his sombrero pulled low against the glare of the sun. In the winter his poncho offered scant shelter from driving rain and biting wind. On his horse he'd forge swollen rivers. The water so high he could hardly see the horse's head. Swirling currents threatening to wrench him from the saddle. He'd ride high into the mountains. Where the air was damp and thin. Bringing what comfort he could to impoverished hamlets lost in the cold and mist. Riding in the shadow of Sendero Luminoso. Shining Path. The cruellest terror group in south America.

***

Sendero tortured those they thought educated. Teachers, nurses, shop-keepers and engineers. A posse of Sendero would arrive on horseback in a remote settlement. They'd round up the people. Making them watch as they tortured a victim. They murdered a nun. Stripping her naked. Tying her star-like to the ground. Inserting sticks of gelignite into her. Blowing her to bits. The villagers and their children forced to stand and watch. It was how Sendero imposed its will. Terrifying the people. When the posse galloped away the villagers cleaned themselves. Picking at the fragments of the nun's flesh which clung to them.

***

In Yauri Dominic was told of a brother and sister, Aurelio and Maria, seven and nine. Taken away in a big jeep. Maria screaming. The parents knew nothing until they returned that night from the fields where Los viejos, the elders, had been looking after them. As the elders had done with the children for generations. Their mother, Maria Alejandrina, had sobbed. She had five children. Three were dead. Under the ground, she said. She wanted Dominic to take her confession. But the ruined church of San Isidro was too far away, on the other side of the valley where the llama grazed. She was too weak to walk so he held her to him, cloaking her head beneath his poncho. Taking her confession. As he stroked her head she whispered of her guilt and begged forgiveness. Child, he told her, we're the guilty ones. You have nothing to confess. She died two weeks later of tuberculosis. Her husband said she lost the will to live. Her heart was broken. She was thirty one. In Peru mothers died young.

***

Father Declan worked in Siglo Veinte, in Bolivia. It means Twentieth Century. A name so ironic it eclipsed all humour. Siglo Veinte lay in a morose valley. In the shadow of a mountain of grey rock. Its people scratched for tin in black and airless tunnels deep inside the mountain. The best of the mine was long gone. Its innards scooped out decades before when it had been a jewel in the Patino mining empire. When the roofs of the chambers fell in, as they did all the time, the miners sealed the shafts. Sometimes the dead and dying were still inside. Their screams turning to faint cries. Their comrades would strive to save them, sweating and cursing and straining their sinews to get at them, to shift with bare hands the rocks and boulders. But they would be beyond rescue. A mile underground miners built a twelve-foot high effigy of an Inca god. In a lofted cavern hacked out of the mountain. Painting it in garish colours. Giving it burning eyes and monstrous teeth. Teeth big and sharp enough to bite the heads off the snakes. To thank him for sparing them they'd share their liquor with the god. Holding their beakers to its terrible, gaping mouth. Then they'd pour their home-made liquor on the floor of the mine to thank Mother Earth for letting them live. For allowing them to scrape remnants of tin from her breast. They had blackened faces and horrified eyes. Backs bent double in the damp and heat. They'd squat on their haunches and look up at the god with its piercing eyes, drinking themselves into oblivion.

**

Declan knew of children who'd disappeared. He'd journeyed for two days by jeep from the railway sidings at Oruro where sooty trains pregnant with tin had once helped to swell the Patino coffers. Higher and higher he'd climbed. The air so thin his chest felt it would implode. The height making his veins stand out. Blue and swollen. Eyes red with burst blood vessels. The clouds hung low. Bulbous with rain. He'd driven up vertical tracks used only by goats. The wheels scrabbling for grip. Shale spinning into the ravine.

**

It was a hamlet on a ledge. Chilled and unforgiving. Its people made slow by the cold. Swathed in blankets. Two sisters had been taken away by strangers. A white man and a woman. The villagers said the strangers were friendly. They'd brought cheese and Xingu and chocolate. Nobody had ever tasted chocolate. The girl's mother was tiny. Her teeth black and rotten from chewing the coca. The staple of cocaine. Her skin was pocked, burned by the sun, creased like leather. The diet was poor. Medicine scarce. The mountain streams ran yellow with sulphur. She sat cross-legged on the floor in the door of her hut and told him how sad she was. A red and yellow poncho wrapped tight around her. Black hair in plaits beneath a small brown bowler hat. Declan asked her age. Twenty three she said. But she wasn't sure. She looked fifty. Declan knew she'd be dead by thirty. The Campasino had their children early and died young. How many children did she have? Five she said. But three were under the ground. Her two little girls which she'd given away were the only survivors. Her eyes filled with tears and she asked him to forgive her. He told her there was nothing to forgive. She thought she'd been doing the right thing. It was a chance for the children. He said he understood.

***

She'd sobbed when the children went. Hand in hand with the strangers. Down the mountain in the big black Nissan jeep with all the chrome. One of them clutching her old doll. Its broken arm hanging by a thread. She thought they were going to Brasilia to a rich family. To live in a big house where water arrived hot from a pipe. They'd be well fed, clothed, educated. Life would be better than in the mountains. Where the wind blew wet and cold. And lungs felt they'd burst with the soroche. The crops were poor. There was more rock than grass. Nobody wanted to buy the goats. They were as thin and wasted as those who herded them. Declan held her small dark hand. Bony and veined. Her long soiled nails pressed into his skin. He had to leave her to her tears and drive to La Paz, Bolivia's capital. He managed to see Juan Panosa in the Town Hall . The Campesino said those with gold braid had the fattest bellies. Panosa was squat with podgy fingers and four gold rings. Two on each hand. A wet handshake. He was with Fransisco Sanchez. His right hand man, the chief of police. Slicked-down hair and Zapato moustache. Paunch squeezed into an olive green uniform. Braid and medals on his chest; epaulettes, tiny silver-stars running along his shoulders. Sanchez liked village women. But he preferred their daughters. Declan knew about him. And his special tastes. Priests heard things. The councillor and the policeman said they knew nothing. The disappearances were a mystery. They said they were shocked. They'd look into the matter. Panosa's gold fillings glinted. The fan on the ceiling hummed. Sanchez lowered the blind. He'd keep a look out. If he heard anything, rest assured Father, he'd be the first to know.

Outside in the baking sun Declan walked head bowed along the Plaza Murillo. Gazing up at the cathedral spire. The church was newly-built. Starkly modern, richly opulent. If the Vatican had money for new temples dripping in gold why did it not build hospitals, schools and homes? Give the millions of dispossessed clean water, sanitation, *hope*? The gangrene of corruption added to his sense of impotence. To whom could he talk? Sometimes, even the priest needs support. His people were the meek, the downtrodden, the voiceless. If the Kingdom of Heaven existed it would one day, *surely*, be theirs. He tried to quell his doubts. But all he saw was despair. Only misery. He was becoming like those who turned to him, who trusted and believed in him. He had grown ravenous for a miracle.

In Candela on the Amazon Bill and Alice Lamb had settled in. They had fallen in love with Brazil. The charm of its people. How those with nothing danced to the rhythms of the samba. The Lambs had little or no money. Like those they helped, they too lived in a shack made of tin and tarpaulin. They feasted on black bean stew cooked on an open fire. Bill had caught the anger of the priests. He was fired by the deprivation of the people.

"You're flesh and blood," Flaherty told him. "To get angry is to be human. This is not Europe with its grey, insoluble problems and indeterminate solutions. Here it's black and white. Good and bad. Everybody knows what's right and what's wrong. It's abundantly clear."

The higher the mountain, the more impossible the task, the more the Lamb's ran at it. They worked from dawn until late into the night, when the cicadas sang and the sun started to melt back into the forest.

***

A welter of stories about disappearing children had begun to circulate. Some had gone missing in Manaus. The capital of the Amazon lay down river from Candela. A hard journey on the paddle steamer, pressed low into the tide by the weight of its burden. Pink river dolphins and clouds of mosquitoes in its wake. Flaherty had caught it many times. Struggling to find hooks on which to hang his hammock. Teeming with Campasino taking their livestock and produce to market. Pigs, goats, rubber, bananas, nuts, figs, sacks of cassava for the flour. Reports of disappeared children came from the slums of the sprawling industrial city of Sao Paolo, where AIDS killed more people than Weill's disease carried by the rats. The rats scurried when the rains came and the sewers exploded, inundating the shacks. And the rains came every day. Flaherty had heard whispers in Candela. On his own doorstep. In the straggle of huts along the river. Roofs held down by tyres. Walls of flapping polythene. Corrugated iron stained orange by rust. Creaking and groaning in the wind. The other day he'd canoed deep into the woods. Slowly navigating poisoned streams. Shaded by the Mogno and Coqueira trees. He slept on the jungle floor. At the foot a giant Kapok tree. A bone-handled knife at his belt. The Miranha were once a proud nation. But their numbers had been decimated by European scourges. Tuberculosis, measles, influenza and pneumonia.

***

The dark-eyed elders of the Miranha told of white strangers who'd appeared in the clearing. Offering wads of Real, bottles of pinga and Schincariol beer. They'd wanted to take the children to Brasilia. But the elders had refused to let them go. Hiding them away. The strangers had become abusive. Eventually they left, melting back into the darkness of the forest.

96

In Brasilia a ring of abusers had been exposed. The Vatican was outraged. How could it happen in a Catholic nation? Around the world Catholic priests were being exposed as paedophiles. The Vatican made flimsy excuses. No one believed its apologies. Instead of confessing it had tried to cover up. The integrity of the Church had been sullied. Rome had been wrong-footed, unable to cope. On the ground some turned their ire on the worker priests. Those like Flaherty and Bernard striving amid the diseased and disaffected. It had made their efforts that much harder.

***

Curls of grey blue smoke drifted over the shacks of Candela, deep in the Amazon. The hot breeze carried the spicy tang of Portuguese sausages. Every day to the minute the rains lashed down. The afternoon deluge had just ceased. Banging like a drum on tin roofs. Flooding the track. The big leaves of the Brazil nut tree hung forlorn and dripping. Then came the sun, garnering its strength, becoming furnace-like. The grass steaming. Casting a silver vapour along the shore. In minutes all would be dry, as clean and washed as the white bones of the fish at the river's edge. The downpour would begin and end at exactly the same time the next day. Flaherty could set his watch by it. Not that he had one. Amazon time, he'd say. There is not a watch in the universe which could match its regularity.

***

From the dead bough of a fig tree the vultures looked down, watchful and sombre. Bavarian chemists from a drugs company had been in the village, testing species of trees which locals used for medicinal purposes. The fig tree, which the chemists knew

97

by its proper name of *Ficus insipida*, had been there as long as anybody could remember. The locals would soak its bark and drink the concoction to cure intestinal worm. The chemists had injected the tree with a special hormone to see if it could be made to grow more rapidly. If they were successful the elixir could be utilised for commercial purposes. When they left the village the smooth trunk of the tree, mottled and spotted by lichens which grew on the outer bark, began to shrivel, and the whole tree died. It looked as if it had been caught in a fire, or been hit by lightning, Once a source of medicine for the people, it was now disfigured, a gaunt perch for vultures, its skeleton limbs as black as their plumage.

***

In the distance a small child clutched a ragged doll. Her feet bare, dark hair plaited. She danced outside her shack in the warm mud of the track. Singing softly to herself. The rhythm in her head. Flaherty thought those in Candela were like the Irish, full of poetry and dance. Music running through them like the streams of Galway. The vultures were beginning to dry out. Sharp-eyed, hook-beaked, hungry for flesh. Wings sodden, black as an undertaker's frock-coat. He watched the swirl of the tide. The Amazon was running high. The vultures squatted in a mournful row on the blackened bough, then flapped to earth, making an ungainly, clumsy hop along the river's edge. Picking and scouring at the parched bones of the fish.

***

Flaherty was consumed by wrath. Two children had disappeared from Candela. *His* Candela. Taken from *his* people. He saw them as *his* family. Guarding them as a father would his progeny. He had been away for three nights in the forest. On his return the people had gathered at his shack beseeching him to do something.

Anything. He'd called on the police, the army, the land agents. They all insisted they knew nothing. There had once been a time in Candela when people had cared.

***

Candela had grown with a sudden, mad invasion. The world and its vices had discovered the Amazon and its rain-forest. It had become the latest must-see location. The place to go. Environmentalists. Mineral hunters. Bankers from Chicago. Lawyers in cream suits from New York. Tourism was one of the main propellants. It drove Flaherty into a rage.

"Tourism .. it's the most insidious, pervasive vice which has ever diseased this ill-begotten continent," was how he described it to his Bishop. "Cheap ideas. Bogus values. The promise of false horizons and the offer of crap, itinerant jobs, for rock-bottom wages. Tourism brings nothing but heartache. The people here need proper, long-term jobs. They need education, sanitation, hospitals. They need to feel secure. Free of threats from businessmen and bankers who simply want to kick them off the land or make money out of them. They need to get back the dignity that's been stolen by the colonisers. They shouldn't be waiting on tables or cleaning lavatories for tourists. Then having to go back to their hovels after sweating in hotel kitchens and making beds for tourists. It's disgusting. I can't abide any of the bastards connected with it. They're all on the make. They're all exploiters."

***

When Flaherty went into a rage his Bishop would smile benignly and advise him to moderate his language. The Bishop had fought many battles on Flaherty's behalf with the more authoritarian wings of the church. And he always forgave him, knowing that he meant well, that what he said was true, that his heart was pure. The

Bishop couldn't abide careerists in the church, and after difficult years at his post he had learned it was stuffed with them.

"Micheal's the one you'd always want at your side," said the Bishop. "You couldn't find a more faithful friend than Flaherty. He's not a politician. He doesn't want high office. He doesn't mince his words. He's not a crawler. The thing about Micheal is that he'd never let you down. Bernard's less fiery, but just as angry, just as determined. They've both got what we need out here. It's a little thing that's in rather short supply. It's called courage."

**

In Candela hamburger bars had sprung up on every corner. Entrepreneurs wanted to pile-drive the forest to build hotels on stilts. With champagne bars, silk sheets and infinity pools. There were plans to build viewing platforms in the tops of the trees. Twitchers would be able to climb rope ladders and peer into birds' nests. Candela was bursting at the seams. Botanists, lepidopterists, zoologists. Wastrels, drifters, hucksters. Thin-hipped, red-lipped girls, promoted eco-tourism for fat Californians squashed into slim canoes. All certain they were doing their bit to save the planet. Flaherty was unmoved. "Eco-tourism! Have you ever heard such oxy-moronic balls? There's no such thing as eco-bloody-tourism. All tourism contaminates. It spreads false values like the plague. It's just rich, over-fed bastards, trying to salve their consciences. I wish they'd all sod off back to San Francisco and Beijing and Berlin and stop screwing up others peoples' cultures. And take their money with them. Never have I met such a bunch of self-righteous plonkers."

**

Flaherty stood in the dust of the Rua dos Negro. Builders were at work on a new casino. There had at one time been a softness about

100

Candela. Now it felt as transient as the flaky settlements which had surged to life in the rubber boom. When thousands of seringueiros poured in to the Amazon lured by latex. The gummy white sap of the rubber-tree, the seringueira. He sensed the menace. Innocence corrupted. There was no *love* anymore. Hard-faced strangers, self-seeking and glint eyed. Everybody on the make.

***

He remembered the seminary where he'd studied. Keen minds and eyes burning bright. After each tutorial a wave of eager assertions. They'd all wanted to spread hope. To conquer injustice. The radicals thought they had the answers. One man's profit was another's misery. How ingenuous it seemed now. Marxism. Just another *ism*. A lie. The sort the poor of Brazil had been fed for decades. He walked on. A little girl ran after him.

"Pick me up Miguel Flaherty, pick me up," she begged. She clutched at his tee-shirt. "Give me some money."

He pulled out the pockets of his faded shorts. A theatrical gesture. Laughing and teasing. Showing her they were bare but for a tattered rag, his handkerchief.

"It's all I've got Juanita. Old but clean. The ladies wash it every night."

He pretended to make a giant sneeze. To blow his nose with huge harrumphing. The girl screamed with delight.

"Get you home child and stay away from these places."

He nodded at one of the new bars that had sprung up. Rows of men. Dark-haired companions in tight skirts. Tottering on red high heels. Certain to be glued in the ooze when the rains turned the track to mud. Juanita ran home. Throwing a ball high into the air. The sky a cloudless brilliant blue. Catching it as she ran.

***

He watched the bar. So many strangers. Anybody could have taken the children. He walked past Ribeiro's hardware store. Selling its shovels and nails and kerosene for the lamps. Past the construction site where mountains of red earth had been heaved from the ground. At the Lamb's shack he mopped with the rag at the sweat on his temple. Kicking off his sandals. Rubbing the sand and clay from his feet. They sat on the back porch in the shade of the famous makeshift shower. Bill had concocted a platform eight feet high. It supported an old oil drum. From it ran a hose with a stopper and a spray head. Inside the drum he'd fixed a muslin filter bought from Ribeiro the ironmonger. He'd fashioned it into a trap for the mosquitoes. The Amazon's daily deluge filled the drum to overflowing. The sun made the water so hot that when the Lamb's pulled the stopper they sometimes couldn't stand its heat. To everybody around it was the finest shower in the universe. Hot rain as soft as milk. Around it Bill had built a screen offering a modicum of privacy. To help deter the giggling children trying to peep at the lady with the white skin and the fair hair. Flaherty said it was a magnificent feat of civil engineering.

"It's up there so it is with that fella Brunel. It's like a Hollywood shower if ever a poor boy like me should see one."

Bill laughed. One day he'd build a similar shower for Flaherty, to stop him being scratched by the rusty oil drum which he used as his bath. On that sweltering night thunder and lightning rumbled through the heavens. A tropical night. Parrots preened and screeched, toucans cried in the treetops, flights of parakeets swooped to and fro. All trying to outdo the massed choirs of the cicadas. They drank too much Xingu and shared their fears. Flaherty became subdued, his energy draining away, staring into his beer. For once, his rage had become so incandescent it had rendered him inarticulate.

PART 4

Children who vanished were used and abused. Discarded or sometimes murdered. Roberto Liguiera was more fortunate. He managed to escape. In a careless moment on the first floor of a house near the sea, where the crash of the waves drowned the screams of the children, his tormentor had fallen asleep. Spent with lust and the boiling heat of a summer afternoon in Rio. A fan rattled in another room in which three men were engrossed with a little girl. Recording her cries. Videoing her plight. Roberto seized his chance. He was gagged. But his blindfold had been removed and his hands and legs untied. He had crawled naked to a half open window. Summoning reserves of strength known only to the desperate. He climbed out and dropped on to a ledge. Jumping onto a flat roof and slithering down a pipe. Flakes of rust and slivers of decayed paint cutting into his hands. He'd run and run and never looked back. Tearing off the black duct tape with which he'd been gagged. He ran so far and so fast his heart pounded and he had violent pains in his chest. People stared and laughed at his nakedness. Shouting after him. But he kept on running. Nothing could slow his flight.

***

Finally he collapsed. Legs wobbling like jelly. Head and chest pounding. He hid crouched behind garbage bins over-flowing with waste. In an alley at the back of a cafe. He stayed there for hours. Quaking with fear. Until the evening shadows when he was befriended by Alberto. A teenage pick-pocket. The leader of an urchin gang living in the stench of Rio's sewers. The gang only broke cover when darkness fell. When the tourist pickings were rich. When holidaymakers thronged the sidewalks of Ipanema

103

and Copocabana. Alberto calmed Roberto and tried to help him, finding him an old tee-shirt, shorts and plimsolls. He would later visit the favela where Roberto had lived. He discovered that Roberto's parents were dead. A neighbour said she'd known the family. She could remember Roberto. She told Alberto to bring him to her. But he didn't trust her. He didn't trust anybody. She'd sell him on or tell the police. They'd send him to an orphanage. Or to a magistrate. He could be sent to a hospital for the insane.

***

When Alberto first found Roberto he wouldn't speak. As the weeks passed he started to get a little better. Though he would never mention what had happened to him. At night he had bouts of terror. Waking suddenly. Cold and screaming in the sewer's stinking damp. The smell made the urchins sick. Vermin scurried in the gloom. Water gurgled. Yellowing tiles, oily with slime, dripped with condensation. Alberto tried to train Roberto as a pickpocket. Gang members would sidle up to tourists pretending to be blind or dumb or both. With silken fingers they stole wallets and credit cards. Then bolted along Copacabana's glittering pavements to empty accounts at cash machines. But Roberto lacked finesse. Whenever he was close to strangers his hands began to tremble. Fear made him inept and clumsy.

***

In desperation, Alberto turned to the one person he trusted. Bernard. The wiry little priest bitten by a rabid dog and who'd lived to tell the tale. Alberto's hovel where he grew up had been in Bernard's favela. When Alberto's parents died of AIDS Bernard had tried to look after him. But as soon as he was strong enough he fled the favela and ran down the hill to the beach. Joining a gang. When the gang's leader was shot by the police he took his place.

Like Alberto, Bernard had no faith in the authorities. They agreed that Roberto should temporarily stay with Bernard. Sharing his shack until a better solution could be found. There was nowhere else for him to live. At first Roberto was terrified. Cowering like an animal in a dark corner of Bernard's hut, flinching when he came near.

***

Bernard called in a friend, Sergio Flamenga. A psychiatrist. Bernard had used Flamenga before with other damaged children. Dr. Flamenga tried to get through to the boy. He never charged the priest for his services. He said his reward would be in heaven.

"I wouldn't bank on it," Bernard told him. "I don't."

Flamenga laughed. "I always knew I was a failure. The boy confirms it."

"No luck?"

"No. God knows what he's been through."

Flamenga sat on Bernard's collapsing bed. Face running with sweat. Outside children played. The shack was shadowy, humid, its air fetid and stale. On a tea-chest a small fan whirred in listless defiance.

"How in Hell's name do you live like this?"

The stench of sewers in open troughs inches beneath the shacks made visitors retch. Bernard said compared with some of the others it was a little palace. Flamenga should see the other hovels.

"I've seen them," he said. "But you're an educated man. You're cultured. You've known better. These people haven't. You weren't born to this."

Bernard smiled. "And thank God for that."

"You'll be ill."

"We've all got to go sometime. If you look at the others, I live like a king."

"Of what? Squalor? You'll crack up. Then you'll be no use to anybody."

"It's irrelevant. What are we going to do about the boy? He's the problem."

"Let me buy you a little air conditioning unit. It'd work if we blocked up the holes." Slivers of light seeped through cracks in the walls, the wood warped by the sun.

"And what would I tell my neighbours? I'm sitting in my bathing trunks in my little air-conditioned fridge and they'd all be baking in the heat."

Flamenga knew if he gave him an air conditioning unit he'd only take it to the mortuary to keep the mosquitos and bluebottles off the corpses.

"You're hopeless Bernard."

"We all are."

He fiddled with the fan.

"It's a useless bloody thing. You're right. We're all hopeless. Especially shrinks. All this psycho stuff. It's as useful as Murphy's rag and bone cart, with one wheel and Murphy drunk as an English lord."

Flamenga nodded. Mopping his forehead.

"We shrinks are all crackers. I haven't met one who's sane. They're madder than any of the patients."

"So what's to be done?"

"Perhaps he needs some prayers. A few hymns. Get you dolled up in a dog-collar." Bernard stood at the door.

"That'd finish him off for good."

"He's very traumatised. But what's happened to him .. and for how long .. I can't get two words out of him. The only time he reacted was when he saw the vultures at the tip."

Bernard nodded. Pouring him water.

"I'm afraid it's a bit warm. I've fished the frogs out. What tip?"

"Where the trains run near the shacks. Where that kiddie was killed."

He sipped from the beaker.

"Kids scrabbling around on the tip for junk. Suddenly the vultures arrived, picking at stuff. He went mad. Hysterical.

Shouting and screaming. But he wouldn't tell me what it was about."

"That scar on his face looks like a claw mark," Bernard said.

Flamenga nodded. "Could be. I don't know. Anyway, he went berserk, crazy."

***

After some months Flaherty and the Lambs journeyed from the Amazon to see Bernard in his favela in Rio de Janeiro.

"I hate cities," Flaherty said. "The only reason we're here is because we're on the scrounge."

"What's new?" Bernard smiled.

Our Land was in the running for a modest grant. Flaherty had been called on to vouch for the Lamb's and their work.

"I'll lie my head off if it means rich bastards are going to part with their cash. The bureaucrats said they wanted to meet me in person. It's all baloney. Naturally, they couldn't come to the Amazon .. said they were too busy. They're worried about catching a disease. So they paid our fares. Can you believe it? If they sacked all the apparatchik and saved the money on the fares they could have just sent the cash."

"Apparatchik?" Bernard smiled. "Haven't heard that since the seminary." Flaherty looked at him.

"Aye .. that's it. Uncle Karl. I used to think he knew the lot. You get out here and you realise it's all bollocks like the rest of the clap-trap."

"Ah, please. No politics," Bernard said. "Politicians get up my nose, so they do." Flaherty's eyes blazed. He ran his hands through his shaggy hair.

"You're hairier than ever," Bernard said. "Where are all your women barbers?"

Flaherty said he was thinking of giving up the priesthood and taking a wife.

"There's nobody who'd have you. There's no woman daft

enough. There's no wife who'd put up with that tin drum of a bath of yours so there isn't."

Flaherty reminded Bill that he'd promised to build him a shower. Alice's green eyes sparkled. A shaft of sunlight pierced the gloom of the shack.

"Take no notice Micheal," she said. "You're a handsome fellow .. there are plenty of girls who'd like a nice big man .. all that lovely hair."

"Now there's a lady with taste," Flaherty said.

"Why give up the Order?" she said. "Take a lover."

The fan had begun to squeak.

"Needs oil, like me," Bernard said. "The heat's got to it. It's on its last legs. Like the rest of us. You know things are bad when it's too hot for the bloody fan."

Alice smiled. She looked round the hovel. The makeshift table. A row of hooks for jeans, shirts, Bernard's fraying straw hat. The sagging mattress. A water-colour of the River Liffe, glass cracked, frame broken, its colour drained by the sun.

"Would having an unofficial wife be such a sin?" she asked.

Flaherty laughed.

"There's some doing it already. They're doing all sorts of things that Rome wouldn't like. But it gets complicated if you start taking wives in secret."

***

Bernard had a coterie of women who fussed over him. Tidying the shack. Washing his clothes. Baking him sweet Rossylongan cake like his mother used to make.

"It's a fine cake so it is," Bernard said, cutting it into slices.

"You're s'posed to use Guinness. But you can't get it round here so they use Xingu. If you haven't got any money that's what you have to do. Improvise. That's why it tastes a bit different to the Irish. I prefer the real thing but it's still very nice."

"My women feed me so well," Flaherty said. "Soon I won't be

able to get into the drum. It'll scratch me to bits. So I'll have to stay a dirty bugger."

***

To Bernard's pleasure in the hours his visitors were with him Roberto appeared to warm to Alice more than he'd seen him respond to anybody. He'd even offered a few shy words of conversation, whispering into her ear. When he was out of earshot Flaherty said quietly to Bernard:

"Why doesn't he come back to Candela with us? There are too many memories here. His poor wee mother and father are dead. He'd have a grand life in the Amazon so he would. It's a good place for a little chap to grow up. Away from all this damn mess."

They were at the door. Looking at a sea of dilapidation. Shanties strung together with plastic sheeting and corrugated iron. Black smoke rose into the sky. A pile of tyres had been set alight. The acrid stench of burning rubber.

Bernard said: "It's easy to despair. It's nothing but drugs and killings and AIDS. The boy doesn't stand a chance. Even if I get him to where he'll go out on his own he'll probably fall in with a bad lot. But for him to move to Candela – well, it's an idea alright, so it is, and I'd be foolish indeed not to have a good think on it. The problem is this. It's taken me all this time to build up a little trust with him. If he gets carted off to some strange place in the middle of nowhere he'd be petrified. Whatever's happened to him is still locked away inside."

He told Flaherty that soon after Alberto had brought Roberto to him he'd given him a sleeping pill to try and calm him down.

"The boy was exhausted. When he finally fell asleep I got to see his wee back and the backs of his little legs. Mother of God it looked as if he'd been flayed, whipped. He'll have the scars all his life. And those are the marks you can see. God alone knows what's going on in his head. And what the Hell sort of internal injuries he might have. Sometimes he yells out. I hear him in the latrines."

109

A row of lavatories stood yards from the shack.

"Anybody'd scream if they had to use those," Flaherty said.

"No, I'm serious .. he cries out Micheal. He's in such pain. I tried to get the doctor to have a look at him. But he became as mad as a Dublin whore house. He's a proper little soldier. One of the fallen. If we can't help an innocent like him .. well .. we might as well call it a day."

He slumped on a rickety chair in a dark corner. Head low, shoulders down.

"Bernard .. this is not like you. So it isn't. Not to get so low. We'll have a drop of the Jameson's. It's the best medicine when you're in your condition."

But his torment and frustrations couldn't be deadened by whisky.

"I'll have a dram. But I don't know how to help the little mite. He's been brought to me to be looked after. Everybody's let him down and nobody gives a two penny fuck.. if I tell the police .. well, you know what they're like .."

Flaherty put his massive arm round Bernie's shoulders.

"Don't worry. We'll get it sorted. We always do. It's what we're here for."

In the months since he'd seen him Bernard had become even thinner. Eyes tired, face pale, clothes like limp rags on his puny frame.

"Don't let yourself go Bernie. They need you here. There's nobody else. You were always skin and bone. But you're wasting away. You're in a mess."

Bernard in his frayed jeans, bare feet, the sandals with the flapping soles that he'd glued back in place. Sitting on the wonky chair he kicked at the dirt floor.

"I'm not a penguin. Best bib and tucker. They're only clothes. They don't mean a thing. They're clean. What more do you want?"

"You mustn't get too down at heel. And I don't like to see you so dispirited."

He took the Jameson's from his tattered holdall. Rummaging

round the shack for beakers. The Lamb's were outside laughing with Roberto on the muddy track.

"They're getting on well with the boy," Flaherty smiled, showing Bernard the bottle. "Given me by a rich supporter who thought God didn't mind him having a drink or four. I said I couldn't speak for the Lord but I knew the man's poor wife and family were worried about his boozing. So I took it off him for safe keeping. He had a bad liver as well so I was doing him a favour." He laughed. "I was certainly doing the Lord's work that day. What was it they used to say Bernie? Whisky wrecked Scotland and Guinness did for Ireland. There's lot of truth in it."

Bernard stared at the floor, head in his hands.

"Try praying," Flaherty said. "Doesn't do much for me. But some speak highly of it. Got to be worth a go. Doesn't cost anything."

Bernard looked at him.

"D'you think prayers aren't answered because we haven't fulfilled our side of the bargain? You can't keep asking for things unless you've earned them."

Flaherty gulped his whisky.

"Everybody prays when they're afraid Bernie."

"It doesn't matter how hard I work I can only do so little. I'm just me. One man can't make any real difference. It's hard to see any good coming from it, so it is." Flaherty said: "What did Teresa say? Something about the sea? She could only help that bit which was in front of her."

"We need a miracle Micheal. You look at children like Roberto and you begin to wonder. He's done nothing wrong. Why was he put here? Just to suffer? Was he put here to be in torment all his life?"

Flaherty pulled him to him. Hugging him.

"Stop feeling sorry for yourself. We all know how inadequate we are. We've all grown up with Catholic guilt. There's nothing you can do about it. Look around, it could be worse. You think what a Hell of a day you've had and then you see others and what they're going through and you think to yourself 'it's bad but it's not as bad as what they're having to put up with.' There's always somebody worse off. Life's one bloody great compromise. What you need is some proper sleep. You're spending half the night playing Florence Nightingale. I've told you .. if you go down ill you'll be no use to man nor dog. We'll get you some proper food. You can't go on living on bananas and Rossylongan. You're not a bloody monkey. Think about it. You could have had rabies. That dog could have done for you. That was your miracle. How many more do you want? This is not like you, so it isn't. Pull yourself together man. You're not a bloody child. It's the child out there who *needs* you."

He refilled Bernard's beaker. "Get it down you. You're a wee little bugger. But you always had more stamina than a cart horse like me."

Bernard smiled. "I never read these days. Used to love *Animal Farm*. So you're Boxer?"

Flaherty laughed.

"He was a bit more equable than me. But you're right .. round here some animals are a damn sight more equal than others. Orwell's Boxer was a patient old dobbin. I haven't his temperament. I've got a bit of a temper."

"I hadn't noticed," Bernard said, draining the beaker. "If you didn't get angry.." he waved his arm, a gesture of futility, words trailing away.

Flaherty completed the sentence:

"There'd be something wrong with you .. yeah, I know. I told Bill the other day. It's the price of being fully developed. That's my excuse anyway."

***

Bernard had to rush away. A family of five in the favela were infected with AIDS. Three children, the mother and father. His rusting Volkswagen Beetle had broken down.

"It conked out. Rubbishy old thing. Bit like me."

He told the others he'd walk. The mother was dying and he'd promised to be with her.

"I tell you what we're going to do," said Flaherty. "We'll tell the Bishop you need a break. We're going back to Candela. All of us. You as well Bernie. We'll take Roberto. He'll have a new life. You'll be with him. You're the one he trusts."

Bernard protested.

"There's no way .. there's too much to do here."

Flaherty interrupted.

"No buts. It's decided. You're too worn out to make any decisions. Your head's gone. You're sweating like a pig so you are. Your heating system's gone wrong. Your thermostat's gone haywire."

Alice came into the shack, holding Roberto's hand. She laughed. "It's his thermostat is it? Is that a medical diagnosis?"

"It's the nearest I get to being a medic."

He turned back to Bernie.

"A change of scene is what you and the little lad need. Instead of this slum you can come and stay at our slum. We've got the river and the greenery and some big monkeys and the tall trees. You and the boy will love it."

Bernard still protested, half way out of the door.

"Be off with you," Flaherty told him. "Go and see your poorly family. They're the ones who need you. And it's decided. We'll have no more arguing."

The sun blazed down. Bernard turned his back and made off down the track. Tripping on the flapping sole of his sandal. Tightening his backpack round his bony shoulders. Shouting that he wouldn't be ordered about by Flaherty or anybody else. He was his own man. Flaherty could get stuffed. He'd decide if and when his thermometer was buggered up. Nobody else.

Flaherty grinned, pouring another Jameson.

"Take no heed of him," he turned to the others. "No matter what he says we'll all be going back to Candela. Bernie as well. It's just the sun that's getting to him. He's gone a bit barmy. He'll be fine."

***

Eventually Bernard was persuaded to make the trip, temporarily leaving his Rio favela. In Candela Roberto would begin to find a new confidence. Though for many weeks he remained suspicious and listless. Hiding away for hours at a stretch. At Bernard's insistence he had reluctantly allowed a doctor to examine him. Dr. Manoel da Vicente Silva was one of Flaherty's supporters. Like Bernard's friend, Flamenga the shrink, Silva never charged for his visits.

"I try and be a good Catholic." His face was lined and sad.

"If the big man up there lets me through the gates it'll be because I haven't been a Shylock down here. Anyway, you've got no money."

Bernard smiled. "Where did you learn Shakespeare?"

"Guy's Hospital in London. I trained there. I could have stayed. I'd probably have been treating rich widows in Harley Street with a clinic in Switzerland by now. But the wonders of Brazil lured me back. I'm getting like you and Flaherty. Addicted to deprivation. It's the squalor. It grows on you."

"Like leprosy," Bernard said, looking down at his shirt, wringing with sweat.

"I'll choose somewhere cooler next time. Live in a cave."

He explained to the doctor that Roberto wet himself at night. In the day he sometimes soiled his clothes.

"It's classic stuff," Silva said. "It's what happens with abuse. We'll never know what he's gone through."

He cajoled Roberto into letting him take a sample of blood and, after much persuasion, to conduct a cursory examination.

"I suspect he's HIV. We'll have to wait for the results."

***

Days later Dr. Silva returned to Bernard's shack. Trudging back along the track. Mopping his head. The hut was shady but like

114

an oven.. He took a clutch of papers from a scratched leather briefcase. Carefully laying them out on the tea-chest.

"It's not good news."

"Mother of God." Bernard's eyes filled with tears.

"We mustn't give up on him. He's HIV. We can start treating him. But the scars in his mind .. well, I can't do much about those."

He was his usual morose self. Baggy face, eyes old and tired. Bernard sat on the edge of his bed.

"What about the other problems?"

"Nocturnal enuresis. Common in these cases. I found anal fissures. Tears in his skin. They cause excruciating pain."

He sat next to Bernard on the dilapidated bed, his voice soft.

"After the fissures begin to heal they can split again. The discomfort is intense. The sufferer tries to stop using the lavatory because of the pain. This creates hard stools which tear at the skin even more when they eventually exit the body. It's a vicious circle. Laxatives can help to soften the stools and we can give him those. But there's no quick magic cure. Let's hope that time will help him. As for soiling himself .. it's a form of faecal incontinence."

Bernard nodded: "And the AIDS? How long's he got?"

"Who knows? You've seen as much of it as me. It's not AIDS. Not yet. He's HIV. He'll have to be on anti-retroviral drugs for the rest of his life."

Bernard had seen enough families destroyed by AIDS to understand its path. He was familiar with the effects of the drugs. He'd seen the violent nausea. The radical re-distribution of fat. The sufferer's appearance changing beyond recognition. The shack in which he and Roberto were now living had been home to a family of six. All had been wiped out by AIDS. Dr. Silva described the parotitis. The changes in the parotic gland. The tell-tale rash if HIV is converting to full-blown AIDS. Bernard felt helpless. At the door the cassava sacking shifted in the humid breeze. Later, on his own, he knelt in the dark of his hut. Elbows on the bed, head in his hands, his eyes clenched, praying that Roberto be spared the anguish he'd seen in so many others. He's done nothing, he

115

muttered. He's suffered enough. He doesn't deserve this. Take me instead. Give me the disease. Not the boy, please not the boy.

***

Flaherty and the Lamb's had suspected the diagnosis. They had no money to buy the drugs. Bernard and Flaherty said they'd plead the case with their Orders. The Lamb's said they'd try and get money from *Our Land*. But the promised grant hadn't materialised and the charity was almost bankrupt. They pledged that one or other would stay with him. Filling his days as best they could with interest and diversity. He'd accompany them on their rounds. Visiting the mayor, the police, army commanders, the landowners. Learning from them as they castigated, charmed and harried.

"He'll see more things than most people do in a lifetime," Bernard said. "It's the university of life."

"Strife," Flaherty laughed.

***

Roberto would join Flaherty on expeditions deep into the forest. Sitting in the front of the canoe. Navigating streams. Sleeping in a hammock in Indian settlements. Stars peeping through the canopy of tall trees. He learnt to handle a boat and tie special knots which held the shacks together. Keeping them safe from tropical storms which bent the trees double and turned the sky as black as jet. He would learn to cook, lay bricks, master the intricacies of plumbing and electricity. He'd sometimes ride Flaherty's old trail-bike on lonely tracks, the roar of its engine echoing through the forest. Visiting the frail, the elderly, those dying of AIDS.

***

Alice said she'd never met anybody more patient and forgiving

116

than Roberto.

Bernard was delighted.

"He's stronger than I thought he'd ever be. It's the drugs. If we hadn't been able to pull strings in raising the cash I don't know what would have happened. If we don't know anything else at least we know how to beg and scrounge."

Bernard had badgered his Order, teetering on the edge of bankruptcy due to a fall in recruitment. It had somehow managed to scrape the money together, helped by contributions from Flaherty's Order and the Lamb's charity, both of them on a financial knife-edge.

"You can see why the Orders can't recruit people," Flaherty said. "Who the Hell would want to put up with all this? We're living in the ruddy Stone Age."

"It's amazing how the drugs are helping the boy," Bernard said. "The thing that's really noticeable is that he's just so gentle. I think it's because he's been very hurt himself. He knows more about pain than we'll ever know."

***

Roberto attended Candela's tin-hut school which Flaherty had set up. He had a facility for English. Though still defensive and withdrawn he'd started to confide, especially in Alice, about that which had happened to him. She, in turn, had quietly shared what she'd learned with Flaherty. Flaherty was convulsed with rage.

"But what can we do?" Bernard said: "There's not a lot. The people who did these things are long gone."

"I'd wring their bloody necks," Flaherty said.

Bill reminded him about the policeman he'd threatened. If he was in more trouble he'd be thrown out of Brazil. Flaherty wouldn't have it.

"If we're always frightened it won't do anybody any good. Maybe I could do more if I packed it in? Take a wife. Have some kiddies. Join a charity like you."

He reached for the Jameson.

"What about all the other children out there? Those who are still being hurt. Suffer little children? What a bloody joke that is."

He stalked off. Turning back, shouting: "It's everywhere .. unfairness, corruption, cruelty. Any of us could have been like him. You only have to be dropped out of the wrong womb in the wrong country and that's it. You're screwed. He was snatched away. Abused. It's not right. We're just bloody useless priests. We don't have any real power. Behind our backs they're laughing at us."

Bernard ran after him. "You married into the Church Micheal. You made that decision. It was your choice. You know life isn't fair. It never has been. What did you tell me about Mother Teresa? We can only do something about the bit that's in front of us. And if we go making accusations about Roberto it'll only make it a damn sight worse for us all. Particularly him. It's better to keep as low a profile as we can about the boy."

***

As the months passed the time came when Bernard had to return to Rio de Janeiro. In his absence a young priest had stood in for him in the favela. But he'd come to the end of his term and was to be moved on to a rundown area in Sao Paolo. Bernard's farewell was emotional. He'd been a whirlwind of energy and steadfastness. News of his impending departure spread like a fire. Gifts of cakes, sweets, fruits and flowers filled his shack from villagers distraught at his leaving. Each morning fishermen brought some of their catch.

"It's s'posed to give you brains," he said. "But I can't see any improvement."

He arranged that Roberto pass the gifts to the poorest.

"Make sure you don't give them back to those who gave them to me. That would be terrible. Try and be diplomatic."

"What do you know about diplomacy?" Alice smiled.

"As much as I do about repairing my car. Nothing."

Bernard, Flaherty and the Lamb's had grown to love Roberto. To him they'd become the family he had hardly known. Flaherty set to work on one of his supporters, a clerk in a government ministry. He wanted to see if the Lamb's could adopt the boy. It was a laborious process. There was a welter of red tape.

***

"The Bishop's good at politics." Flaherty said. "He's patient and cunning. And unlike me he's very diplomatic. That's what we need."

Whether the breakthrough came because of the Bishop's politicking or through Flaherty's mithering was unclear. But there was great joy when the official papers finally arrived. Roberto's adoption gave him a new sense of belonging and security. His adoption and Bernard's departure was cause for a party. The Xingu flowed, the craic was good. Bernard sang in bad Gaelic. Flaherty misquoted Behan. The people brought more cakes and beer. Pigs were roasted on spits. Everybody danced. The rhythms of the samba echoed deep into the night. The cicadas were in full voice. Gaudy parrots preened and screeched in the trees. The sun melted back into the forest and thunder boomed and rolled round the heavens. Sheets of lightening lit up indigo scudding clouds. The Lamb's hugged Roberto. Tears stung at Bernard and Flaherty's eyes. At night Alice lay awake listening to the cicadas. To the warm wind clutching at the straw on the roof. She worried that she was mothering Roberto too much. Bill whispered she was silly to be concerned. That it was better to give him too much love than too little.

***

After three years the time came for the Lamb's to return to England. Roberto was downcast at the thought of leaving. But dismay turned slowly to expectation at the prospect of a new country and the excitement of the unknown. *Our Land* had staggered from one funding crisis to the next. It had had to reduce its commitments. The long recession had seen a fall in donations. Bill was to succeed its chief executive in London. Neither he nor Alice were happy about the move. In England the previous two years had been fretful for Bill's family. His father had died. His mother rattled around in the large family home in Hampstead. *Our Land* could pay only small wages. On his move to England Bill's stipend would marginally increase. Alice too would have a new role with the charity. But even a combined income would be hopelessly inadequate for life in the capital. Bill's mother suggested they lived with her. She had met Roberto previously when she and her husband had made the long haul to Brazil, tolerating the primitive circumstances in which their son and daughter-in-law lived. Her pleasure at their return to England was shared by Alice's parents, who consequently put into abeyance vague retirement plans to flee London for the country. The idea of being able to spend time with their family and their new grandson was a happy prospect not to be hindered by distance. Any move to pastoral England would have to wait.

***

The Lamb's departure heralded another big leaving-party in the favela. Some days later, loaded with luggage, they took the ferry to Manaus. Roberto knew the Amazon and Manaus and Brazil's major cities such as Rio. On the farewell journey he had leaned over the rusting stern rail of the ferry. In its wake came skimming dolphins and darting blue fish. He knew the ways of the rainforest. Its birds and creatures and peoples. He had acquired skills and knowledge and wisdoms of which others had barely heard. At the airport Flaherty said farewell. As the plane left he was enveloped in a loss so intense it bordered on despair. As if he had suffered a bereavement. He would grieve over their absence for many months. Roberto, now making such a fine young man, and the

Lamb's, Bill and Alice, had become the family for which he had always yearned.

*****

Though Roberto had learned much, nothing could have prepared him for the shock of London. With his parents, his two grandmothers and grandfather, he gorged on its wonders, goggle-eyed, soaking it in. *Our Land* gave the Lamb's a short break before starting their new jobs. Roberto and his family joined the throngs of tourists exploring the capital. All the sights: The Tower of London to Buckingham Palace. From Trafalgar Square to Piccadilly Circus. Over time he would come to know its every part. Its brassy boulevards to its quiet backwaters. From its scuffed tourist traps to its hidden corners.

*****

Alice's mother took him to see *Buddy* playing in the West End. He danced in the aisle with her. *Les Miserables* seemed less agreeable. He fell silent. His grandmother concerned her choice had been careless. That she had awoken ghosts. With his grandfather he tapped his foot to Ray Gelato at *Ronnie Scotts*. Tate Modern had him spellbound. From the top of the London Eye he tried to see Hampstead in the far distance. Bill's mother was an avid cinemagoer. In Roberto she found a new and wide-eyed companion.

*****

For Roberto, that taken for granted in the West held curiosity and excitement. Even a house on two-storeys was something of a novelty. In the shower he revelled in controlling force and heat by turning a tap. Alice had heard him in the bathroom. He was sobbing. He told her his hot bath had reminded him of something in his past. But that today his tears were of happiness. He was an able cook. Filling the house with the spicy waft of black bean stew. Bill said it was like perfume and that it reminded him of the old days. In the rain Roberto would sit and watch puddles forming on the drive. Remembering as a child how he had had to run round with a bucket catching leaks in his mother's shack. He was fascinated by his late grandfather's collection of motorbikes. And cases of wine stored in the garage.

***

Too soon Bill and Alice's holiday came to an end. It was time to start their new jobs and for Roberto to begin school. His trepidation slowly vaporised and in some subjects he would excel. He had an aptitude for natural sciences and spoke excellent English. The teachers said he might one day be a scientist. Or perhaps utilise his Portuguese and English as an international lawyer. His grandmother still had her late husband's small racing yacht on the Solent. Roberto would sometimes take her sailing. As she sat in the craft, watching him, she couldn't bear the thought of him being ravaged by AIDS. She tried to block from her mind the depravities in his past. "I feel free when I sail," he told her. "The boat's alive. She's talking to me."

He'd drive the yacht hard. Making it heel. Reading the wind and current and the swell of the tide. Feeling the craft's compliance as it surged through the water. When sailors more timid and less instinctive spilled the wind from their sails he'd do the opposite, pulling them taut for greater swiftness.

"She feels like me .. she feels free," he'd tell his grandmother.

"Listen to how she creaks and sings."

His grandmother told him about her youth.

"When I was young there was a shop in the King's Road with the tail of a flashy American car sticking out of its window. As if it had flown through the air and crashed, hurtling into the front of the shop. I loved the King's Road. All the fashions, the music

– Jimmy Hendrix, the Beatles, the Rolling Stones. Because of the car the shop was called *Granny takes a Trip.*"

Roberto laughed.

"You'd have loved it," she told him.

"One day, when I've got enough money, we'll take a real trip Granny. We'll go back to Brazil and I'll take you sailing."

The wind whipped at his dark hair. Spray streaming down his face.

PART 5

Fred Burns and Raven had never got on. Burns ran Operation Wildflower. Its remit being to track down child abusers. His number two was Alan Lomas. Lomas had a put-upon air. Raven guessed Lomas did the work and Burns took the glory.

"Abusers are cunning bastards," Burns said. "All walks of life. Chameleons. They know how to hide themselves."

Burns and most of his team had been seconded from Vice. They led Raven and the squad through a maze of web sites. Penetrating supposedly secret portals using code words and pass numbers. Each site filled with violent images of abusers and victims. Raven's squad had spread its net to Europe, America, South America. Checking locations in Gleeson's past. Enlisting Interpol and the FBI. A welter of information which threatened to swamp the investigation. Wragg had stretched the budget and sanctioned more officers.

He told Raven. "I've got no choice .. if I pull back now it'll look as if I backed the wrong horse."

"Thanks. That's a ringing endorsement."

***

Raven and Rosie went back to Brazewood prison to grill Kimble the nonce. Kimble stared at the floor of his cell. In a reedy whisper he said he couldn't add anything. "Who's been getting at you?"

"You've no idea."

"Meaning?"

He gave them a note pushed under his door after their previous visit.

'Talk to the Scum again and your kid won't recognise you. We'll take his eyes out.' Kimble turned to the yellowing photograph near the sink.

"Our lad. I won't risk anything happening to him by talking to you."

"Who sent it?"

"How the fuck do I know? Probably the governor and some screws? Perhaps they like little boys?"

He gave Rosie a gummy, half-smile.

"Men in uniforms and little boys. Never fails."

**

They returned to the army to scrutinize once again Gleeson's career. Back to Cathedral Insurance. To Stocking Easter, Gleeson's village. They'd garnered fingerprints, blood samples, DNA. Blurred images from cameras. Files bulged with statements. From members and servants at *The Imperial* to known paedophiles. Witnesses who knew about motorbikes, knots, special dyes. Each lead drew a blank.

"We've found no evidence Capes was a paedophile," Raven told the squad.

"But she *had* to be. Her sort are duplicitous. They don't hide their tracks. They don't leave any. Capes and Clarkson were abusers. All we've got to do is prove it."

**

Sylvia Capes had been fresh out of university in Austin, Texas, when she visited Europe for the first time. She'd travelled with a boy friend. In Cannes, on the French Riviera, they'd visited a tiny restaurant called Les Joie. It stood on a narrow cobbled street, Rue Meynardier, running parallel with the Mediterranean. She'd been taken to an upstairs room above the restaurant. From a window she could see the rooftops and Notre Dame de l'Esperance, the church of Le Sucre, the old town. From another, beyond the Palais de Festival, lay Cannes harbour, white yachts gleaming. She'd had too much to drink and her boyfriend had been smoking pot. She'd been carefree, light-headed, in love with her companion and with France. In the room was a black iron bed with a grubby mattress. On a wall, a washed out print of Matisse's 'Le Peintre dans son atelier.' A girl was brought in, no more than six or seven. She told them her name was Aimee. She said she couldn't remember her parents and began to cry, asking them not to hurt her. It made no difference. Capes' boyfriend and the patron raped her. Capes helped, sating a lust which had burned in her since she could remember. She had no idea what befell the child. As she lay in the bath, the glowing tip of the cigarette inches from her skin, she told her tormentor that she didn't much care what had happened to the girl. "She'd just be sold on," she told him. She'd been in child trafficking ever since, moving around the world, using false names. Taking different jobs which brought her into contact with children. She'd been a teacher and a charity worker. She'd tracked children to order. She'd be given a specification and told to find a child who matched the requirements as closely as possible. When she'd fulfilled her role other members of the ring snatched the child that she'd targeted. She'd been paid large amounts of money in cash. The few people she got to know in child trafficking included Gleeson and Clarkson. She and Clarkson had worked together, playing a husband and wife. "If kids see a woman they think it's alright. They see them as they see their mother. They thought I could be trusted. I was the bait." She had been in Berlin hunting for a child. The specification demanded that it be a boy, aged three to five, with blue eyes and blonde hair. Ideally, he'd have a sister, of similar age and characteristics. If she could find both she'd be paid double. They had to be from a good home with professional parents. Capes had tracked down a brother and sister. Their parents were busy architects. They had their own practice and a house close to the Kurfurstendam. During the day the children were left in the care of a nanny. Capes found that the nanny was more attentive to the demands of her boyfriend than those of the children. She'd contrived a plan in which the children would be taken while the nanny canoodled with her boyfriend in the architect's house. The children were playing in the small orchard at the far end of the garden when they'd been snatched. Neither had been seen or heard of again. She learned subsequently that the architect and his wife had broken up. The wife later committed suicide. As she sobbed in the bath he asked her if she had felt pity for the parents. Tell me the truth, he told her. Not what you want me to hear. "Not really," she told him. "That sort of thing occurred. It was collateral damage." What happened to the children? "I haven't a clue. I'd done my job. What happened after that and where they were taken to was none of my business. I had to ring a number and give the code meaning that the children were ready for collection. Snatched? "Yes, stolen." What was the number? "I don't know. I was told to destroy it after I'd used it." Did she? "Yes." Could she remember it? "No. If the ring told you to forget a number that's what you did. You were scared of doing otherwise." Why? "There was a rumour. They'd found another girl in the ring. They'd told her to write the number on a bit of a paper and destroy it immediately after she'd used it. But she hadn't done so. She'd broken a cardinal rule. It was imperative you never left a clue. They were paranoid about security." What happened to her? "She was gang-raped and they cut her tongue out.." What else did she know about the number? "It was complicated. Too long to remember. With pauses that you had to make in between. It must have been to a mobile. Probably somewhere overseas." What was the code? She hesitated. He held the cigarette close to her eye. She could feel its heat. "Knock down ginger." What did that mean? "It's a game children play. Banging on peoples' doors and running away. It meant whoever I was talking to could make the arrangements." For snatching the children? "Yes." Was she well paid? "Fifty thousand in sterling. There were two of them. First rate specimens." Her fee was paid into a Geneva account. In Berlin she had met a young army officer. They had a brief fling. He had taken her to a cocktail party at his headquarters in Paderborn. There she met Gleeson. Soon afterwards they'd begun their relationship. Gleeson was married. His vivacious wife Vicky was the toast of the mess. Famously flirtatious. Soon after her wedding Vicky was sleeping with one of Gleeson's fellow officers. Capes and Gleeson had similar tastes. But they knew little about their paymasters. The world they'd entered was so shadowy that on occasion neither knew if they were even working for the same ring. As an expert on irrigation Gleeson had been seconded by *the army to help engineers in Peru. He'd concentrated on street children in Lima. "Nobody cared about them. If one went missing .. so what?" Sometimes, before passing them on to his paymasters, Gleeson took them back to his villa in Miraflores where he held 'special parties' in which she'd sometimes participate. Gleeson spent a long period in Brazil. His work as an irrigation expert was the perfect cover. It took him to the poorest parts where the pickings were plentiful. Where there were always vulnerable children. "It wasn't difficult," Capes told her persecutor. Her skin red from the boiling water. Sweat mixed with her tears. "The places were so chaotic you could do anything. The police and the army were a joke. Everybody was bribed. People do anything for money. Kids are a valuable commodity. There's a big demand. It's not just people like me and Gleeson. People who can't have kids will do anything to have a family. They pay a fortune." She said several gangs were stealing children. "South America's a big place. With terrorism and drugs occupying everybody it wasn't difficult to line up a few kids. Many of their parents were dead. The kids were on their own. Nobody gave a damn about them. There was always a good market for Brazilian kids. They're so beautiful. Lovely skin and eyes. And they're so innocent. They're not like Western kids. You can tell them anything. They're so ingenuous, so naïve. They believe everything you tell them. We were sometimes permitted to avail ourselves of the children. It was a perk. Sometimes it wasn't possible. There'd be no time or they wanted them untouched. Virgin pure and all that. Other people came in and helped with transportation. They were just cargo. We didn't know who anybody was." How were the children shifted around the world? "It's not hard getting false papers. You can easily change their looks. Dye their hair. Bit of plastic surgery." The ring had ordered that she be moved to London. It had fixed a big job for her with Global. Her confederate would be Mrs. Melody Lockhart, ostensibly her boss. As her principal it was Melody Lockhart, steely hair swept back into a flawless chignon, with her specialist tastes and insatiable hunger, who ensured that Capes was never hindered by irksome banking duties. It was she who encouraged Capes to roam continents. In a ravenous, ceaseless quest for new young flesh. All costs and expenses reimbursed out of one of Global's many contingency funds. Her real job would have nothing to do with banking. The ring looked after her references. The ring bought the flat in Docklands in her name. The paperwork was arranged by Lockhart who disguised its purchase through the immense and complex Global accounts. The ring preferred cash. But sometimes the amounts of money were so large they were paid into foreign bank accounts. Hers was in Geneva, How was it arranged? He held the glowing tip of the cigarette inches from her flesh. She didn't know. She imagined there was a sympathiser in the Geneva bank. A paedophile. Who was he? Or she? She didn't know. One didn't ask questions. That's how the ring maintained security. Capes had never married let alone divorced as the HR department in Global thought. To colleagues she was just another smartly-dressed banker. She claimed she'd tried to quit the ring. But it had threatened her with blackmail. It might kill her and her family. Consequently she'd agreed to toe the line. Trying to get out was not worth the risk. There were compensations. She had large amounts of money. The freedom to travel when and where she liked. She could indulge herself with an endless supply of children. Of parents and families whose lives she'd destroyed, of the vanished children enslaved, tortured, murdered she said: "You must think me heartless. I'm not. It was usually the kids who led us on." She'd begged him to untie her, to let her go. She told him what he had wanted to know, everything she knew, each detail. She'd give him anything. Whatever he wanted. Herself, money, anything. She was rich. There was cash all over the flat. She would never tell anybody about him. But he didn't care. He wasn't interested in money. She was a liar. People like her always are. The children she and her confederates snatched and tortured would have screamed and begged like her. He watched and listened and felt nothing. Just deadness. He cut a lock of her hair and clubbed her. She slithered under the water, eyes fixed and staring. He caught a fleeting glimpse of himself in the mirror. Hammer raised, face demonic. He hated himself as much as he hated her.*

***

Roberto did well at school. Distinguishing himself as both scholar and sportsman. He achieved a good degree at Leeds University. Bill and Alice doted on him, offering boundless love and stability, at times almost over-compensating, knowing that he was carrying the AIDS virus and terrified of what the future might hold. He was the child that they were never able to have, an endless source of happiness and joy.

**

The fog had suddenly thickened. The black Range Rover was travelling too fast in the outside lane of the M25 heading south. The driver was using his telephone. He'd ploughed into the back of the Lamb's car. The motorway was closed for hours. The jam stretched ten miles. The police said they'd never seen such carnage. The coroner said it was a tragic waste of life. The Lamb's were killed instantly. Roberto's grandmother was cut from the back seat. She died minutes later in the ambulance. The judge sentenced Paul Wilkinson, thirty-four, a hedge fund manager from Haslemere, Surrey, married with two children and a wife called Christine, to six years in prison. He'd been made redundant a few weeks before and had been hurrying to a job interview. Some thought his sentence too lenient, banging on the side of the van as it sped from the court house.

**

After university Roberto had found work at a rundown former leather factory in Oswald Terrace, Kiburn, in north London. Its roof patched, walls daubed with graffiti, clumps of grass thriving in its gutters. A shabby refuge for derelicts run by the tiny Order of the Blessed Sinners. He laboured from dawn to dusk amid a stream of shuffling vagrants who sought sanctuary in its dank and ruined gloom. He had not become a lawyer as his teachers had predicted and while at college, instead of law or languages, had decided to study electrical sciences. The mission in which he worked was dubbed the Beggars Palace by its immediate neighbours, and others living in the vicinity who were worried that its looming presence and unsavoury tenants were having a detrimental effect on property values. Roberto told his parents that he'd work there until he found something which more properly utilised his degree. In his heart he knew he'd found his calling. As did his parents.

***

The Beggar's Palace was a draughty hodge-podge. Held together by mercy and meagre funding. It was in dire need of an overhaul. The plumbing, brick-laying and rewiring skills which Roberto had learned in Candela would be invaluable. The Order had shrunk to a wizened core. At sixty-six Brother Wilfred was the youngest. When the police came he assumed they wanted a word with a client, as he called his ever-growing family of beggars and down-and-outs. A policewoman called Pamela told him what had happened. Wilf said it would better if he broke the news to Roberto. She'd not been in the police long and had at first demurred. Wilf's suggestion ran counter to the rules. But Wilf said Roberto was asleep and given the circumstances it was surely more merciful to let him remain so for as long as was possible. She had been dreading the task and was secretly grateful for his intervention.

***

Roberto was not asleep as Wilf had maintained. Amid the ramshackle sprawl of rooms and corridors on different levels, he finally found him in the laundry room, in the basement. He had been coping with an alcoholic called Bishop. The unkind moniker given to him by other clients was Stinking Bishop, a reference to his fondness for cheese, his reluctance to wash, and his refusal

132

to let anybody launder his putrid rags. Roberto's patience and persuasiveness had succeeded. Bishop's clothes were in the washing machine, while he luxuriated in a steaming bath, grasping a bottle of Newcastle Brown and ranting about its medicinal qualities. Wilf told Roberto as gently as he could.

***

Roberto went silently to his tiny eyrie at the top of the building, Slowly climbing a dusty wooden staircase. The loft had a small electric fire. Bare boards, a camp bed, a grubby roof-light wedged shut for years. Its glass obscured by pigeon dirt. His bright yellow and blue duvet printed with sail boats had been a present from his mother. He'd laughed when she'd given it to him, protesting that he was no longer a child, as young men do with their doting mothers. To use it, he told her, would embarrass him. When clients in the refuge became too boisterous or aggressive his tiny space in the roof offered an inadequate respite. He sometimes spent the night there, wrapped in the duvet, trying to keep the draughts at bay, rain tapping at the tiles, shouts and screams drifting up from below. Sometimes he'd have nightmares, seeing the houses and rooms in which he had been hurt. His abusers' faces, cackling at his plight. He'd wake with a start, trembling with fear, soaked in sweat. Or he'd find an uncertain peace. Dreaming of the rain forest. Warm Amazon nights. A velvety universe far above the trees, star-spangled, twinkling. After Wilf told him what had happened he had clutched the duvet around him, as if they were his mother' arms, and drenched his pillow in tears.

***

Born in poverty, reared in cruelty, Roberto was now of considerable means. The sole beneficiary of an estate passed down from his grandmother. In circumstances less dreadful her house, its contents and savings would have gone to Bill and Alice, Roberto's parents. But they had been wiped out and the estate had now passed in its entirety to him. Alice's mother and father, stricken and despairing, had implored him to come and live with them. In the rubble of his mind he had decided to stay in Hampstead, at least for the time being, until his head had begun to clear a little. His grandparents had become suddenly weary, devoid of spirit, their grief quickening the usual maladies of old age. For weeks he shuffled between the mission and the cold, ghostly silence of his home. His mind as unkempt as his appearance. Lost in uncertainty and confusion. He took to spending hours at home. Curtains drawn, the incessant flicker of the television, the sound turned low, Alexander the fish his only company. He and his grandmother had won it at the Easter fair on Hampstead Heath. He remembered how they had laughed as they brought it home in its small polythene bag.

***

The Beggar's Palace once rang with Roberto's laughter. No repair had been too daunting. No derelict unworthy of his care. But the clients now rarely saw him smile. Stephen Mwenepembe, another helper, had taken him aside, worried by his decline. Roberto assured him that he would be fine, once he had come to terms with his overwhelming sense of loneliness, the new circumstances with which he was now faced. Mwenepembe was unconvinced. He remembered his old aunt on the homestead. When her children died in the big fire. She had said then that time would heal. Time would salve the wound. Her husband had found her. Hanging from a beam in the barn. At her farewell the Masai sang their lament and wept. Mwenepembe spoke about his concerns to Wilf. When young Wilf had been the most fiery Brother in the Order, strong and determined, intellect matched by physique.

"He needs all our support," Wilf told the young Kenyan. "But we mustn't smother him. Pain is never one-dimensional. Think what the driver of the car is going through. His wife and children.

Hurt always spreads. Suffering is never contained. It always consumes others."

"It's unfair."

"So's life."

"Roberto's the innocent one."

"That's true. And the driver's family were innocent. The driver made a mistake. He didn't set out to kill. I make mistakes every day. We all do."

***

Wilf's room was tiny, chilled. A monk's cell. Its plaster grey and cracked. He lay on his bed staring at the ceiling. A dead spider hung by its thread. The room had been the foreman's office. Where post-war factory girls with dangling cigarettes and headscarves came to be reprimanded for clocking-in late. Or idling on their shift. A small window let on to a high walled yard. The blackness of night yielded to the foggy drizzle of a grey dawn. He listened to the swearing. The clatter of cutlery. Mwenepembe ladling out breakfast porridge from black vats bubbling on the old range. As fretful as the boiler which fired it. He closed his eyes. Blocking out the ragged curtains. The window with rusting bars and smeared glass. The lurid blue print of Lake Como. The small crucifix on the cracked plaster. Its tiny brass Christ in need of polish. A present from his mother fifty years before. When the priest in the Killarney village mentioned her four strapping sons. And how she might think of giving one of them to the church.

***

Roberto was slumped in front of the television. Curtains closed. Alexander circling the bowl. At his lowest ebb he had suddenly seen Gleeson's face flash onto the screen. Talking about insurance for flood damage. He had been transfixed. Hurled back across the years. The scabs on his wounds violently ripped away. Madness ousted sorrow. Remorse, lethargy, despair, all swept away by a demonic vitality. The unhinged energy of the crazed. In seconds on the internet he had traced Gleeson's company. Gripped by a furious insanity he took the immaculate old Velocette motorbike from the garage, a powerful bike, one much loved by his grandfather, and rode to Norfolk. Tears poured down his cheeks. He was HIV. Gleeson and his cohorts had given him a life sentence. He'd lost everything. Those he'd loved. Those who had loved him.

***

In Norwich he waited for Gleeson outside the offices of Cathedral Insurance. Tracking him to his cottage. His frenzy slowly turning to a quiet, determined menace. Later, in London, he would follow him to *The Imperial*. Lingering in its shadows. Watching, listening, immersing himself in Gleeson's habits. Where he went, who he met, the intricate patterns of his life. Thinking about how he'd kill him, Torture him. Watch his anguish as Gleeson had relished his. He'd make him betray his confederates. Meting out punishments to mirror the myriad hurts and abuses which had been inflicted on him.

***

Rosie was at home in Hither Green. In the shower, exhausted. She'd slept badly. Her mind filled with the minutiae of the case. Another murky dawn. Where did Gleeson go on leaving the train? Why practise snooker and never play? In Holland Park Raven pored over the timeline. Shifting paper on the floor. He'd been up all night. What had Charlotte Clarkson said ? Her husband's snooker partner died. That was it. 6.05 a.m. He rang Rosie.

"Find who services snooker tables in London."

"Are they serviced?"

"They have slate beds. They can be temperamental."

"Like me."

"They run hot and cold."

"Yeah .. just like me."

"Slate sweats. They have to be set up correctly. Cushions lose their bounce."

"Don't we all?"

"There can't be that many snooker tables in London."

"What am I looking for?"

"I'm not sure. It's just an idea."

**

Clarkson the optician didn't know who ran the rings. Where their headquarters were. Or how they were financed. Their tentacles crossed borders. He'd been told that many politicians were paedophiles. They were in powerful positions, able to cover things up. He knew they were in governments in Britain, in France, Germany and Switzerland. All over the place. In Austria and Belgium, too, so he'd been told. But he didn't know who they were and he never caught the names of those who told him. There were others, in every profession and walk of life. Sometimes they ran care homes. Institutions. Places where children were supposed to be looked after. There were paedophiles in local councils, in the civil service, everywhere. Making sure that nothing ever came to light. The great and the good. The leaders and the civic worthies. The ones who everybody thought could be trusted. For Clarkson it had all started a lifetime ago in Thailand. At a bar called Johnston's Place. Where a neon sign flashed all night and girls danced nude in cages. Customers picked whoever they wanted. Taking them to a cubicle. Buying and using them by the hour for a handful of Baht. Johnston's Place was in Bangkok. Near a slum called Klong Toey. The Slaughterhouse. Off-limits to tourists. A vast huddle of shacks built over an open sewer. Only inhabited by Catholics. Outnumbered by Buddhists in surrounding districts.

The Catholics had to live among pigs which they slaughtered for a living. They slept in the straw of the pig stalls. When a child was born a pig was the first thing it saw. Clarkson was young, travelling. Spoiled by his parents who financed his trip. After he had outlined his special preferences to a red-bellied European in shorts and a floral shirt in Johnston's Place, he was taken to a hut just outside the Slaughterhouse, stepping on duck-boards which ran between the hovels. He was met by an old Buddhist Thai woman, with black teeth and sharp eyes. She took his Baht and put him in a tuk-tuk. Instructing the driver where to take him. Leaving a trail of blue smoke as it snaked through Bangkok's traffic. To a flat at the back of the Wat Traimit temple. Close to the chaos of Hualamphong Station. Teeming with back-packers, addicts and hookers. At the flat he met a Belgian man and a Thai woman. They brought him a little girl, assuring him that she was a virgin. She was seven. He paid them two hundred pounds in Baht. When they left they told him he could have the child until the following morning. The next day the little girl was taken away and Clarkson was recruited into a ring. He thought it the perfect job. He was paid large amounts of money deposited in accounts in Jersey, the Caymans and Geneva. The ring had sent him round the world. Asia, Europe, the Americas. Bonus time arrived with natural catastrophes: earthquakes, tsunamis, famine and despair. When the rings' operatives, sometimes posing as aid or relief workers, would move into grief-torn neighbourhoods. Amid the chaos children made homeless and often parentless were vulnerable and alone: an easy, tempting target The ring would detail the type of child required. Boy or girl, fair or dark. Age, characteristics, details of the family background. Clarkson found them, spied on them, forwarded photographs and details to a series of ever-changing box numbers. He couldn't remember any of the addresses. He had to identify the safest time for others to move in and steal the child or children which he'd targeted. He'd trained as an optician and started his own business. The ring had helped finance it. Paying the wages of the staff so he could spend long periods abroad supposedly on ophthalmic business. It was a front. The ring was well-resourced and cared little if the business was profitable or not. He'd heard rumours that there were many such businesses. Seemingly respectable companies used as cover-operations to launder sizeable chunks of money. In their ledgers, the administrative procedures and costs in stealing and transporting children around the world could be neatly disguised. After his marriage, Clarkson bought a flat in Switzerland's St. Moritz. Charlotte enjoyed skiing. She thought the money for the flat came from his business. According to him she knew nothing of his past. Clarkson's killer took a bird book as a souvenir. And forced him to his knees. Yanking his head back by his hair. What had he meant by 'the perfect job?' Clarkson stuttered about the bonuses. It wasn't just money. It was the little girls. As many as he wanted. His killer stared down at him. Letting him feel the weight of the axe on his neck. Did he still indulge? Oh no, never. He'd grown out of it long ago. But his killer didn't believe him. People like Clarkson didn't change. They can never stop. It was beyond them. It was a disease. There was no cure. He re-taped Clarkson's mouth and decapitated him. Fixing his head on the bird table. He felt nothing for his victim. There was only one thing on his mind. How to deal with the new name that he'd extracted from him He'd think about it. Later, at home, he fiddled with the video machine. Pulling Papa's raggedy old armchair closer to the screen. He lit a Player's. Filled his glass with a good Burgundy. And settled down to watch.

***

Miriam's flat in Greenwich. She and Raven were in bed. The throb of a motorbike. The wail of an ambulance. Echoing through the night. He had had another row with Wragg.

"He went crazy .. you'd think I'd done the killings."

Miriam pressed herself to him, letting him talk. Hoping her warmth would help. Midnight. The street lamp which cast a forlorn yellow glow flicked off. The recession had forced local authorities to make cuts. The blanket of dark over the capital accelerated its menace. A rise in stabbings and burglaries. Across the Thames Wragg was hunched over his desk. His budget drained by terrorism. By the increase in knifings and assaults. By the everlasting Raven case. As His Nibs had taken to calling it. In the imperious way that Wragg had grown to hate. Lockhart's murder had triggered another outburst from the Chief Constable. Wragg in turn had leathered into Raven. In his heart he knew he was being unfair. How Raven and the squad were at breaking point.

***

He'd dropped the hammer in the furnace in the basement in the Beggar's Palace. Stepping back from its roar and heat. Throwing in his clothes. Those he'd worn in the old days. Made for him by those he had left behind in a faraway land. When he had been happy. He took a shower. Cracked tiles, mildew, black grout. Reminders of the sewers in Rio. He remembered his escape. Running naked through the streets. Chest heaving. Legs shaking. Crouched, terrified, behind dustbins. His new life, with Alberto and the pickpockets. With Bernard, Flaherty and the Lambs. The water mixed with his tears.

***

Greenwich Park was in blackness. Rain teemed from a moonless sky. Splashing in white dashes on the boating lake. Puddles grew at the feet of a man in a crash helmet and a long dark riding coat. Rain streamed down his goggles as he watched Miriam's window.

***

In the bedroom Raven drew her close. Outside in the pouring

rain a motorbike exploded to life. Its violence splitting the damp stillness. For weeks sleep had eluded Raven. Killings and corpses skidding in and out of his brain. Miriam had been asleep. Her breath steady. A languid arm across his chest. He sprang to the window, jolting her awake. Catching only a receding tail light. Its vivid red becoming faint. Blurred in the rain. A wisp of memory swayed in his mind. Fuzzy, half-forgotten. He'd parked at the arts cinema. Walked to the flat. His usual route. Head down. Lost in thought. A motorbike had turned into the car park. Raven, the human camera. He cursed. He should have inquired. It might have been over. At the window soft-edged suspicion hardened into certainty. Later, in the darkness, Miriam pulled him to her. Delicate fingers traced beads of sweat trickling down his face.

***

Wilf had found the hammer head in the boiler's ash. It meant nothing. With his clients the unusual was customary. They lived on the margins of conventional behaviour. Crazy-eyed. Minds addled by booze or drugs. That deemed strange in the outside world was unexceptional in the confines of the refuge. The Beggar's Palace was an ocean of bodging and patching. Tools were always scattered about. The hammer had broken. Somebody had thrown what was left of it in the boiler. It meant nothing. For Wilf the world and its agonies were mirrored in the stubbled rage of the clients. His immersion in their despair excluded all else. The wider society which lay beyond the parameters of the hostel rarely intruded. Ordinary forms of communication had broken down. Newspapers arrived spasmodically. There were more vital things on which to spend the slim resources of the mission. The television had been rendered unwatchable. The picture scored by static. It had been thumped too often. Tampered with by calloused fingers more used to clutching at needles or bottles.

***

Had Wilf even been aware of shocking headlines they would have failed to whet his interest. Or trigger any undue curiosity. Each day at the Beggars Palace brought its own quota of calamities. It quenched any thirst for tabloid excess. But in his damp cell he had talked with Roberto. Wanting to share his burden, to lessen his pain. Roberto had hung his head and sobbed. Dark eyes fixed on the brown lino floor. He had confessed all. The bursting of a dam. An insanity that had become too immense to contain. Wilf had learned the full horror of his crimes. The depths of his torment.

***

In a quiet corner of the Beggar's Palace, the former drying room where hides once hung in morbid rows, now served as a makeshift chapel. Here Wilf sought sanctuary. When young he'd worked among the dispossessed of Nicaragua and El Salvador. When revolution had swept central America. Inappropriate diets and exotic diseases had told on his once athletic frame. Over the decades his faith, too, had started to fray. He had seen too much suffering. Doubt had come to him slow and dissembling. Like a catch in his charity-shop jumper. First a run, turning into a small hole like the trace mark of a moth. Untended it would spread and the garment would unravel. After years overseas his Order had summoned him to England. To missions in Liverpool, Glasgow, Hackney in London's east end. And then to here. To Kilburn and the old tannery. In each he had lived with the downtrodden. Those who had slipped through the net. Giving a voice to the voiceless. In the chapel a roughly carved, primitive cross, had been fashioned by a client in a sober spell. Here Wilf came to pray. Trying to quell his doubts. Pleading for strength. All his life he'd listened to the confessions of others. Some avowals so harrowing they'd provoked a despair which had threatened to overwhelm him. His sense of entrapment sometimes so urgent he had wanted to seal his ears and eyes. To block out the miseries of others. In all that he had witnessed he never heard anything as terrible as Roberto's

142

admissions. Nor had he learned of anything which would help him solve the dilemma with which he was now confronted.

***

Raven assembled the squad. He began with a frank admission. He thought he'd missed his opportunity. Rosie had tried to console him. Saying it was tiredness. His imagination getting the better of him. But he was beyond sympathy. She knew her words sounded hollow. Raven's instincts were strong. He *knew*. He ordered a check on riders, motorbikes, manufacturers, clubs. Each stockist and garage. Wragg whinged about the money. More CCTV footage. People quizzed in Greenwich. The car park at the arts cinema. Miriam's street.

Leach said: "It's not much to go on. Early hours. Raining. Nobody about."

Leach re-read the porter's statement. The porter had heard a motorbike after Capes's murder. Leach pored over Cook's interview. His garage rewired before Clarkson's killing.

"Cook said he had always been a car man. Never took much interest in bikes. He seemed to think it was big and black. Probably Japanese but he couldn't be sure. It was all he could remember."

"He saw more than me," Raven said. "I was too slow and it was too bloody dark."

***

In the small hours at his flat Raven was on his second gin. Resentful of the way his quarry had impinged on his life. It was past midnight by the time he had left the nick. He'd combed more files and a fresh stack of statements. London was in darkness. He'd taken a circuitous route. At one point pulling in to the kerb. Turning off the lights. Peering into the dark. Waiting to see a motorcyclist in the shadows. He'd parked the Alfa some distance from his flat.

143

Walking side streets. Crossing and re-crossing roads. Using basic surveillance techniques learned years before. Sleep was impossible. I'm paranoid, he thought. He telephoned Miriam. He wanted her to move into his flat.

"Right now?"

"Yes."

"Jack .."

"He thinks I'm there. I want you out. Now."

He'd already booked a taxi to bring her to Holland Park.

"It's two in the morning .."

"Just do it."

***

It was the first time she'd been to his flat.

"Jack .. you're frightening me."

"I'm sorry. He's a maniac."

She went immediately to bed. He poured another gin. Padding around. Blaming himself. Angry at his missed opportunity in Greenwich. Reproachful of the way his prey had encroached on his life. But it was his guilt at inviting Miriam into the sanctity of his and Olivia's home. To join him in their bed. It was that which gnawed at him the most.

***

Old Brother Wilf knew how to make things happen. In the past he'd been the salvation of a remote community in the mountains of El Salvador. The Switzerland of Central America. A naive name for a nation disfigured by tumult. The village was tiny and barren. He'd galvanised share-croppers into a co-operative to safeguard its supply of food. He'd ensured that the children went to school each day. Irrespective of the violence that wrought havoc all around them. Rupturing daily life. He'd begged medicines from soldiers and freedom fighters and all the other crazy-eyed vagabonds of conflict tearing Salvador to shreds. He'd pleaded compassion for the innocents. For the old, for the frail and the infants. He'd dragooned the strong into felling trees for fuel. And concocted a makeshift pump at a spring which burst from the mountain. Installing a plastic pipe two miles long. Pumping water to the hamlet on the high plateau to which it clung with a fragile tenacity. He looted pipe and pump from a burnt-out builders' yard in San Salvador. Its proprietor had been killed in the war, the premises torched. He'd led a party of raiders to get what was needed. The men from the village had been afraid of taking action. Weren't they committing theft? The owner's dead he told them. So nobody owned the pipe. How could you steal something which nobody owned?

***

The Thames ran black as an oiled snake beneath a starless sky. The shoreline cast into gloom by the curfew of recession. Sean Heaney of Deptford Towage edged his tug *Lily* away from the green slime wall of Gibbet Wharf, hung with a necklace of tyres. A forgotten dyke of glutinous silt when the tide ran low. Seamus, his grandfather, began the business in Liverpool. When his prosperity grew he moved to London and built a fleet of four muscular steam tugs with red funnels and gold hoops. Small ships with stout hearts. They trailed black smoke and plied for business day and night. Harnessing hawsers to the bows and sterns of the cargo carriers which loomed above them. Laden with spice and ore from distant lands. Nudging them into their home berths. Seeing them off on perilous journeys to the furthest corners of empire. Sean's father Liam had taken over. Running the company through the war. Towing warships. When the docks were blitzed. Alight from end to end. Fire on the water. Liam and his wife sheltered little Sean, his two brothers and two sisters, under the stairs in their back-to-back terrace in Limehouse. Where the flats of millionaires now

145

stand. After the long years of tumult came peace. And in London's dockland, four decades of decline. Blight crept over wharves and warehouses. Rotted hulks sank in the ooze. Cranes stood gaunt and forbidding. Morbid sentinels to a robust past. As a child he had watched with his father as the contamination on the shore had spread, standing at his knee in the wheel-house. Feeling the deep, steady throb of the engine beneath the plating of the warm cabin floor. He loved the tug boat business. The heady mix of oil and grease, sweat and tar. The slow pitch and roll as the river coiled and uncoiled. As he grew older, when his father retired, he watched from the river the transformation of the shore. Through the cracked glass of the wheel-house he saw empty warehouses being converted into apartments or flattened for new offices. The bankers had begun their colonisation. Tall shrines to finance now lined the river's bank. Shimmering with light. The servants of usury knew how to generate money but produced nothing to profit Sean and *Lily*. Bewildered by change, knowing only the Thames and its caprice, Sean's skills which had been passed down from his father and his grandfather were now almost redundant. The little tug-boat fleet built up by his forebears had shrunk from four vessels to just *Lily*, the rivets on her powerful, squat hull, beginning to corrode.

***

In a lifetime of sharing the burdens of others Wilf had learned that any solution to a difficult problem always entailed compromise. It guaranteed that his conscience could never be stain-free, without blemish. He had agonised over what to do about Roberto. A terrible conundrum he had turned this way and that. If he betrayed him to the authorities his incarceration was inevitable. He would die in prison, a husk. In the Beggar's Palace Wilf had seen in him a depth of tenderness and compassion which could only have been borne out of unimaginable suffering. Born an innocent, scarred by abomination. The love he had always craved, and had at last found, wrenched away by insidious fate. The lusts of others had left him with the AIDS virus; he was already under a life sentence. His murderous rampage could never be forgiven, though Wilf knew that vengeance was a potent element in the human condition. In a lifetime of confessions he had heard penitents mutter of its joy, eyes downcast, their voice a whisper. Without Roberto's deranged intervention it was a reasonable assumption that his abusers, or those acting in a parallel way, would never have faced justice. They'd have been left to roam. At liberty to inflict further indecencies. To destroy more innocents. Their families bereft, left with shadows and sorrow.

***

What if he, Wilf, had been subject to years of cruelty? If abusers had infected him? How would he have reacted if the kaleidoscope had been shaken with such violence? Would not the instant obliteration of one's' entire family destroy the sanity of most people? Especially if one had been as scarred and brutalised in the past as had he?

***

Professor David Elsworth. Sports jacket, leather patches at the elbow, check shirt, the tang of black shag. Round-shouldered, bushy-browed, lost in contemplation, wreathed in a permanent curl of blue smoke. He'd sit for minutes at a time on a bench beneath his laboratory window in a small walled garden, deep in concentration. Catty younger colleagues, at the Institute for Indigenous Studies at Twickenham, in London, said he was a scientist of the old school. A scholastic research centre it was old-established, respected and averagely impoverished.

***

When Rosie took Elsworth's call he said he'd checked his findings. Elsworth was the antithesis of his peers: rushing out their slender conclusions in time for the six o'clock evening news, relishing the dubious fame of being on breakfast TV the next day. To Elsworth the limelight was anathema. A Hell to be endured only because Fielding the director said that in some curious way public exposure of the Institute and its research helped secure it grants. Elsworth's wit was as dry and cutting as the flint in Norfolk where the thread had been found. His examination had been characteristically impeccable. To Fielding's consternation, and growing impatience, it had also been costly in the extreme. Elsworth had bent over his microscope, scoured the laboratory for long-forgotten chemicals, mixed bizarre concoctions which released odours so foully pungent his fellows had had to seek escape in the garden. He engaged with his colleague, the short-tempered Robinson. Together they plundered the botanical research library in Kew Gardens. Fretted over antique tracts in the Hospital for Tropical Diseases; spidery script on faded pages. At noon each day they shared a damp bench on the green at Kew. Two tetchy coves watching the traffic snarled up on Kew Bridge. Elsworth spluttering on his shag, Robinson rolling incendiary cigarettes. Eating sandwiches. Arguing about potassium and sulphates and other things comprising birds' droppings.

***

Elsworth spoke softly. Rosie pressed her ear to the telephone.

"Brazil, Amazon-ish. Made by some clever chaps. Crushed berries, coconut hair, sap from tree roots. Parrot droppings, animal hair. Inca-ish. We got rather excited about something in the dye. It's from a Hoatzin."

"Sorry. What was that?"

Rosie scribbled on her pad.

Elsworth was seized by a coughing fit.

"Bloody pipe .. locals call it a Shansho. It's a 'stink' bird. Dreadful ruddy smell. Orange and green feathers. They crush the feathers for the dye."

Rosie tried to keep up. Scribbles filling her notebook.

"It's vegetarian so you get good droppings. Never learned to fly much. Young stinkers have claws on their wings to do a bit of climbing. Clever eh?"

She was still trying to spell Shansho.

"So there you have it. Dried by the sun – calcium and nitrates – banks of a river. Probably the Amazon or a tributary. Very polluted round there."

He paused, wheezing and spluttering.

"Can't thank you enough. Wonderful journey, really was. Good of you to call us in. Tricky little so and so but we got there in the end."

Fielding urged Elsworth to tell the world. How the Institute helped in a manhunt. Donations would roll in. Elsworth politely declined. As did the short-fused Robinson, more bluntly.

***

The Herald's Bert Moffat had assigned his finest. Moffat was having a fling with a columnist. An opinionated harridan and by some stretch the worst writer on the title. She compensated for an inability to express herself with an acrobatic ingenuity in Bert's bed in Bromley. Moffat was the news editor. A legendary drinker and foul-mouthed expert on greyhounds and horses. He'd scaled the journalistic heights after a rum start in a tenement in Glasgow. After several weeks a maniac was still terrorising London. Raven didn't seem to have come up with much. *The Herald* wanted to know why. At the morning editorial conference its editor, Lewis Daley, demanded something be done. Famed in Fleet Street as both workaholic and tyrant he slept and dreamed the *Herald*, keeping a bed in an ante-room off his office. If excited by a story he had been known to run into the sprawling newsroom and leap on a desk shouting:

"Go reporters go!"

With that they'd scatter. Usually repairing to the *White Swan*. Better known to its habitués as the *Mucky Duck*. There to mutter about Daley's growing madness. Daley and Moffat had grown thirsty for blood. They wanted a scalp and cared little if it was that of a policeman or a politician. To have both on a platter would be a bonus.

***

Raven and Rosie were snapped outside Lockhart's mews house. He had been caught whispering to her about the case. The photograph was plastered across the front page.

'Proof in black and white: Raven shows Rosie the ropes,' ran the headline.

It continued: 'Killer roams free but has top cop other things on his mind?'

Details of Rosie's university background included quotes from a former boy friend who said they had once crashed on his motorbike and were sent flying across a verge locked in each others' arms. Her dead father was described as a hard-drinking West Indian bus driver. *Herald* reporters found illegal immigrants living on benefits in Lewisham where she grew up.

Neighbours remembered her as a 'quiet girl who kept herself to herself,' which Rosie interpreted as 'blue-stocking intellectual snob who thought she was above everybody.'

An unnamed police source said Raven 'almost went off his head when his wife died,' which Raven read as: 'Loony-toons copper not up to the job.'

Albert Moffatt's semi-literate lover penned a diatribe which a world-weary sub-editor made half-intelligible. It suggested that a young black girl might be personable and clever. But was she sufficiently experienced for an axial role in the Snooker Room Slaughters? Had the Met been seduced by brains and beauty? Or was it being politically correct while London quaked with fear at a serial killer in its midst?

***

The *Herald's* splash induced meltdown in Toe Rag. He thumped his desk and said the innuendo brought the Force, and in particular the squad for which he was responsible, into disrepute. Raven had walked out after threatening to punch his lights out.

***

While Fleet Street worked itself into a lather, and squad morale took another dive, Roberto's demeanour remained relatively calm. He had returned from blackness to a state of some ordinariness. The inferno which had consumed him appeared to have been quelled. As if he'd been purged by the killings and his confession to Wilf. Wilf had taken over Roberto's affairs and assumed responsibility for his estate. He had called in Professor Tom Balchin, a psychiatrist at Guy's Hospital in London. He had known him during the years of tumult in Salvador. They'd been young firebrands together. Wilf had been fresh out of the seminary. Balchin was newly-arrived from university. Both were ingenuous and idealistic and were quickly caught up with the rebels' cause. Balchin had been picked up by the police, not noted for their gentleness. Wilfred's exertions, backed by his Order, and the tardy intervention of the Vatican, had eventually secured his freedom. Balchin had returned to London where he had forsaken his revolutionary ways to forge a stellar career in the research and the care of the disturbed, most of whom languished in prison or some other type of secure institution.

***

Wilf told Balchin that he wanted to share with him an awful secret. Its knowledge would incriminate Balchin. If his involvement became known it might devastate his illustrious career. Wilf wanted to give him the option of saying no before revealing his dilemma, before compromising him. Without hesitation, Balchin pledged his help. He trusted Wilf more than any other, and over the years he had become immune to shock from the terrible things he'd heard while closeted with the tormented. He'd spent four days with Roberto, subjecting him to a psychiatric evaluation.

***

Balchin said: "It's not an unknown condition. Extreme psychosis. Total withdrawal from reality. In simple terms a person is consumed by another personality. The new, assumed personality, acts in a way which can be entirely alien to the person that it's effectively devoured. Such a state can be triggered by shocking events which have lain buried and then healed and which then have suddenly sprung back to life. We know the boy was abused. That he's HIV. We know the horror that he's endured. His family being wiped out. They were his protectors. He'd felt with them a security that he'd never known. Their sudden destruction would have been enough to tip him over the edge. By focusing on those who persecuted him, or who in his mind represented those people, he has managed to save his own sanity. By their death he's cleansed himself. They abused him – he'll die through the AIDS virus which they gave him. This other personality took over and acted on his behalf. He was in no way responsible for these events. Nor could he in any way control this second person by whom he had been, in effect, utterly consumed."

***

Wilf stared at Balchin.
"So you're saying he's purged himself?"
"Yes."
"Could he revert back?"
"No .."

"Sam .. I need the truth .. if you tell me he could kill again, I must turn him in."

"He won't. This was bottled up all his life. It's sated now, finished."

"He'd always been so kind .."

"He still is. Because he went through so much as a child he has a far deeper level of compassion than you or I. He feels his emotions much more intensely than others. He knows what it's like to suffer. We can only imagine .. and that's easier to bear."

Wilf looked at the little battered crucifix on his wall.

"He knows what he's done," Balchin continued. "Or, rather .. that which this other personality has committed in his name .. and he's genuinely horrified. To think that he tortured them .. well, that's unrecognisable to the person he really is. But you have to remember that Jung said it wasn't the healthy man who tortured other people .. it was usually the tortured who turned into torturers."

"The psychiatrist?"

"Yes .. Carl Jung. And we know Roberto's been tortured .."

"He won't revert ..?"

"This is the end of it. From now on he'll be rational. Give him time, it's been a Hell of a shock – for the real him, not the one who did these things."

"If I turn him in – which I should – he'll be incarcerated. What would you do?"

"It won't just be imprisonment for the rest of his life. He'll be gang-raped on a regular basis. The authorities are powerless to stop it. He's a good looking young man. He'll be subject to every torture he suffered as a child. And worse. I can guarantee it."

"What should I do?"

"God only knows. But I can tell you this .. he'd certainly die in prison. And he'd die a terrible death, as bad as the AIDS which is one day going to claim him anyway. That's the one thing which could protect him .. if news got out that he's HIV .. the other prisoners might just give him a wide berth. But I really wouldn't bank on it."

"I'm not sure .."

"Revenge can be very calming. We might not like it ..but it's in most of us. He hasn't taken revenge. It's the other personality which has extracted it for him, on his behalf."

"Would you send him to jail ..?"

"He deserves it. There's no argument about that. But if you want my opinion .. well, frankly, no. It would be a terrible waste. He has such talents .. he's a total charmer .. and I can see the kindness and the compassion that you have recognised in him. To condemn him to an agonizing death would be what you might call a sin. What he really needs, of course, is absolution."

***

Four members of the squad had been assigned to checking on the numbers and identities of Brazilians in Britain. They worked with hard-pressed immigration officers and Customs & Excise. A laborious task made worse by inadequate documentation. Nobody knew who was in Britain or not. *The Herald* campaigned for tighter immigration laws. Its stories lambasted the Home Secretary, speculating that she'd be chopped in the next Cabinet shuffle. The squad's eager Sam Lake was sent to Brazil to galvanise the authorities into assisting with its inquiries. Wragg had questioned the efficacy of the mission saying there was no money for jaunts. Envious colleagues told Lake to remember his sun tan lotion. Lake had e-mailed Rosie saying anybody who thought UK immigration files were lacking should take a squint at those in Brazil.

***

Raven's request that snooker table repairers be checked out had led Rosie to London's Bell Maker Lane, in the heart of the Asian rag trade in the capital's East End. A bustling market had long

154

since disappeared. It had once rung with the cries of stall-holders hawking baskets of fruit and vegetables freshly arrived at the nearby docks. Bell Maker Lane was cobbled and narrow. Hemmed in by satanic warehouses now abandoned to well-fed pigeons. Some had been brought back to life as Asian textile emporiums. Roof tiles askew, grass in gutters, grubby windows with mesh screens. Inside rows of girls with long dark hair. Bent over Singer sewing machines from the 1950s. Saris and gold slippers glittering in the gloom and dust. A grey sky, more rain on the way. A chill wind funnelled between the warehouses. She checked the address in her notebook. The lane was a shabby hotch-potch of family enterprise. A peeling sign for the Calcutta Import Agency. The art deco architecture of the old Adelphi cinema, where Ava Gardener and Errol Flynn once cast their spell on Cockneys wearied by the Blitz. It was now a decrepit bingo hall with lairy signs and special rates for pensioners. Moustaffa's Kebab, a crescent on its door, meat sizzling and spitting on a slow revolve. The Maharashtra Balti, a forlorn palm in a lace-fringed window. Jamshedpur dry cleaning, Mr. Joshi leaning at its entrance, waiting for the rush which never comes. A pub, wreathed in infamy, where the ritual execution of a man in a hat signalled the end of East End gangster rule. Close to it, a drab doorway in flaking brown. A brass plate dulled by time. The headquarters of the once renowned Union Jack Cloth company.

***

At Roberto's home, Wilfred dealt with the wine and the vintage motorbikes. He garnered the gruesome keepsakes. Transferred Alexander into a small plastic bag to take him back to the Beggar's Palace. He filled a suitcase with clothes and sent several curt and enigmatic emails.

***

The last thing on George Masefield's mind at the Centre for Distressed Seafarers at Nail Wharf in Tilbury was a message from Wilf telling him he was coming to share a bottle of Bushmills with him. George's refuge, carved out of an abandoned warehouse, fronted the Thames and its mud flats. At its rear lay the vandalised *Admiral Hood*, long closed, corrugated iron at its windows. In its heyday the *Hood* was known across the oceans from sailor town to sailor town. For a week George had been coping with nine stranded Indonesian sailors, their ship impounded in lieu of monies owed to its import agency. The captain had disappeared. The crew spoke only rudimentary English. They had no money, nowhere to stay, no way of returning to Cilicap, on Java's southern coast, from which their rust-bucket had embarked many weeks before. Masefield had limited accommodation at the Seafarers' Centre. Each well-used bunk was spoken for. Under the rules he was not supposed to do that which he was now doing, fixing hammocks in a ruined outhouse next to the *Hood*. Where beasts had been killed a century before when its purpose had been that of a slaughter house and holding bay for foreign foodstuffs, prior to the invention and arrival of freezer ships from the Antipodes, laden with frozen carcasses of lamb and beef.

***

The illicit sheltering of a few foreign deckhands was far from the gravest offence among the many which Masefield had committed in a colourful life. Wilf had found him his job after they'd met at the Liverpool refuge which Wilf ran on his return from Central America. Masefield was a seaman like his forebears. He'd girdled the globe, his ticket stamped a thousand times. His last run had been on an ominous hulk plying its trade from the West Indies to Liverpool. Heavy with molasses, alive with rats. He'd lost his footing in a sudden torrent of white spume which crashed and raced across the deck, knocking him over. He'd slid sideways across the plating, smashing his face against a bulk head. It cost him an eye. He'd just turned fifty. A one-eyed sailor with a piratical scar, muscled limbs heavily tattooed, in an industry caught in a slow, inexorable decline. His prospects were not rosy. The rolling gait of a sailor marked him out as a punch-bag for every yob in town. He sought sanctuary in whatever bottle was at hand.

***

It was then that Wilf encountered him. He had shouted, bullied and now and again thumped him into straightening himself out. Refusing to give up on him. In Ugly George, as he was known in every bar in Liverpool, Wilf had seen something worth saving. Twice Wilf had punched him to the ground, pinioning him in the mud, screaming at him to sober up. When younger Wilf had been a useful boxer. But he was now frail compared to the lion of his youth when he'd been revered by the cowering villagers of Salvador. Once, Wilf had wrestled a bottle of bourbon from George's grasp and hurled it into the River Mersey. The bottle had been quickly followed by George, desperate to retrieve it. Wilf then had to jump in himself on the sudden realisation that George's capacity as a swimmer did not match his astonishing ability as a drinker.

***

From such entanglements sprang a friendship as deep as the Mersey, which on that dark night had very nearly claimed the two of them. Under Wilf's brutal tutelage George had finally begun to curb his drinking. Though the odd bender was never totally eradicated. Wilf utilised George's brawn. Using him at the Liverpool mission in a diversity of roles, from bodger to bouncer. When a vacancy for a warden arose at Nail Wharf, in London, George got the job, sponsored by Wilf. George never fathomed Wilf's faith, and he remained happily unaware that doubts had started to impinge on Wilf's once unshakeable convictions. During a session at The Boscowen in Wapping they'd agreed that faith, like politics, could be divisive. So they had agreed never to discuss it. To George, Wilf was simply a smashing geezer, steadfast when he had been at his lowest ebb, and when all others had forsaken him. Wilf's constancy was a debt George had long wanted to repay. At his different missions Wilf's resourcefulness had been tested in many ways. From coping with brigands in central America to officialdom in England.

"We spend so much time on the peripherals, the bureaucracy, lighting all the damn candles," he told George, "that more often than not we lose sight of the cake."

George told him: "Writing's never been my strong point. So I throw any paper work that's sent to me in the incinerator. I haven't got time to mess around with all that stuff."

Wilf wondered what George would do if council officials came to check on his refuge?

"I'd throw 'em in the incinerator as well."

He looked at George's barrel-chest. The black socket where his eye had been, the livid scar on his cheek. His arms buried in tattoos. It would be a rash bureaucrat who'd take him on.

***

Toe Wragg had called in Dr. Gideon Henshaw. An American profiler who had featured in previous high-profile investigations. A Berkeley graduate. Early forties. His confidence rankled with Raven. A blond pony-tail. Jeans and sneakers. His initial deliberations were vacuous. A string of banalities. He had urged the detectives to think outside the box. To step up to the plate, Observations so clichéd Raven had been close to walking out. The latter part of his talk to the squad was less fascile.

"They're ritual murders. They reflect something in his background. It's some bizarre form of re-enactment."

Leach glanced at Raven. Henshaw's thesis chimed with what Raven had said earlier about symbolism.

The heyday of the Union Flag Cloth company had been at the turn of the 20th century. When gentlemen played billiards in country estates. Dressed for dinner. Passing the port. Leaving crinolined ladies to their gossip. Retiring with their cognac for a frame or two. The perfumed haze of Havana's lying in lazy curls between the green of the baize and the glare of low-slung lights. A halcyon interval obliterated by the carnage of the Great War. When teams of retainers who knew their place polished plump mahogany legs and shone the top sides. Rubbing out chalk marks. Brushing and ironing the cloth. Horace Green looked as old and sad as his business: shoulders bent, head bowed, a soldierly row of felt-tip pens and pencils in the breast pocket of his brown overall.

"We've been going down the pan for a hundred years. All they want today is anything that's quick and cheap. Getting a table in trim is like tuning a grand piano for a concert. It ain't easy. But when you get it right snooker tables have got a sort of music all their own."

His forlorn features creased into a tired smile.

"Sorry .. you're too young," he said. "It was all a long time ago. Days of empire, eh? Like some tea?"

A tin kettle on a gas ring. Chipped mugs. On the wall a sepia-tinged photograph. A snooker player in bow-tie and waistcoat.

"Joe Davis. Now he was a real gent. Posh houses. Gentlemens' clubs. We did the lot. Who've we got now? Footballers .. pop stars. Most of 'em yobs. We were craftsmen. They treated us proper."

He pulled at a drawer in a scuffed pine chest.

"This what you're after? They go back years. Everybody we've dealt with. Who was it you're looking for?"

She clutched the mug, feeling its warmth.

"Not sure yet."

A buff folder. Its cover stained by tea rings. The first entry dated 1911.

"Ah," he said, as if knowing what she meant.

159

"Like that is it? Police stuff? Confidential."

"You're right."

She gave him one of her most engaging smiles.

"It's a bit like that .. very confidential."

***

Sean Healey at the wheel of *Lily* had known Nail Wharf all his life and the winding dyke which led to its rotting quay. At its conclusion lay a small basin, in skilled hands its width sufficient to turn a tug. A skewed jetty in its last pangs poked from the bank; splintered, wormy, tilting into a fetid pool hazy with the blues and golds of spilled oil. All around, a morbid clutter waiting quietly for the wrecker's ball. The sad detritus of a nautical age long ceased. Sean remembered being in the wheel-house at his father's side. The twisting dyke had been wider then, busy with traffic. At its end, a bustling repair yard; black-tarred barges up on stocks, ready for new planking, like patients on stretchers awaiting their transplants, hulls prised open to wood-ribbed skeletons.

***

His voyage tonight had been slow. He'd kept *Lily's* power curbed, her engines muffled. The tide and wind building up, pushing against him. To starboard, the white and silent colonnades of the Old Royal Naval College at Greenwich, now the University of Greenwich, Christopher Wren's masterpiece, its Painted Hall a glorious tribute to Nelson and Britain's maritime past. To port, the Isle of Dogs, where his Gran once lived. Its shore now lined with blocks of showy flats, favoured by bankers and lawyers, and counterfeit-types in public relations and advertising *Lily's* heart beat steadily. The rich waft of diesel on the wind. How he hated the newcomers. The financiers and the fund managers and the pension chiefs. Past the Trafalgar pub. Where his father, and his grandfather, the tug-boat and the lighter-men, the sea captains back from their epic voyages, drank whisky and bitter, swapped tall-stories and sang bawdy shanties. Now the river pubs burst with smart arses sipping Chardonnay and Spanish lager.

***

We're the only ones left, he thought. *Lily* and me. Past the idiot Dome he went, now called O2, catching the scent of oil on the wind again. Still dubbed the Big Top by the few who could recall the circus pitching up on high days and holidays on the bomb site where the Dome had risen. Rag-a-muffin children, the urchin off-springs of the dockers, stevedores and shipwrights, the tug-boat and the lighter-men. Cheeky faces gummed up on toffee apples and sticks of pink and billowing candy-floss. Wide-eyed at the elephants, the lions, laughing at the clowns with their sadly-painted eyes. Dads and grand-dads staring up into the Big Top. Craning their necks. Blinking into the spotlight. Lusting after the trapeze artist, with her cascade of dark hair, high above them, acrobatic, long-legged, shimmering in the spotlight in her white, star-spangled leotard.

***

In the darkness a launch took shape. The river police from their base in Wapping. His radio crackled to life. The launch cutting across the water for a closer look. Bows rising as it gathered momentum. Falling as it slowed, bobbing gently on the swell. They knew Sean and *Lily*, his pride and joy. Laughing and joshing together, river people, a special breed. Bit late to be out Sean? Everything alright? Fine .. thanks .. got a run coming up tomorrow. New filters, wanted to be sure the pressure was holding. They'd waved farewell and opened the throttle, a cultured purr starting to rasp. Leaving a white-topped wake. Their spotlight dancing across dark waves.

Its beam flicking to the shore. Racing fleet and white across flats and houses and deserted office blocks. Waking a hobo wrapped in newspapers. His bed a seagull-stained bench on Millennium Walk.

***

In the oily heat of the engine room the pipe-work gleamed. It was down here that Sean would eke out his days when he had no commissions. Of late there had been too many. He'd polish and tinker and knew each screw and rivet. When the police launch slowed *Lily's* progress Wilf and Roberto had looked at one another. Anxious for the voices to die away. Nervous that the police would come aboard, take a look around. Keen for *Lily's* heart to thump back to life, for their journey to continue.

***

Earlier, in a derelict corner of the Beggar's Palace, tiles missing from its roof, grass in the gutters, a pool of leaked engine oil on the garage floor, Wilf had coaxed to life the elderly van which he used for collecting ancient beds and collapsing wardrobes, donated by well-wishers. It had even been pressed into service as an unlikely ambulance, when more than once he'd had to rush some client in a pitiful state to hospital. He'd hidden Roberto under old bedding. A ragged pile of thin sheets and mothy blankets, setting off to meet Sean and *Lily* at Gibbet Wharf in Deptford. Telling his fugitive: "Nobody knows who you are. But we can't be too careful."

***

The *Jose Antonio Paez* had seen better days. Voyaging for fifteen days from Lake Maracaibo in northern Venezuela to the Isle of Grain on the Kent coast. Having discharged her cargo of crude oil her owners had decreed that her return passage would be her last. On her journey to Britain she'd averaged nine knots and covered four thousand miles. She was a former Royal Navy tanker. Nearly fifty years old. At some point the navy had sold her off. Surplus to requirements. In her time she'd been owned by a Greek company and an Italian line. Finally she'd been sold to Black Funnel, its owners registered in Athens with a base in Panama City. The blue, white and red squares of the Panamanian flag of convenience fluttered at her stern. Using the for'ard and aft pumps it had taken a day to unload her twelve thousand tonnes of crude. Oil prices had plummeted in the recession. Tankers were laid up across the globe. To help stability on the return leg Captain Ernesto Borges had pumped thousands of gallons of water ballast into her holds. Making her ride lower and heavier and safer.

***

Borges had been a seaman forty years. Always a prudent mariner, he'd also been careful with his money. Salting it away for his retirement. He wanted to make up for the time he'd been absent from his wife and two girls. He'd missed their growing-up. One was now close to marriage. His passage to the Isle of Grain had been uneventful. One he'd made many times before. But the age of his ship had begun to concern him. The fresh water system was playing up, as it sometimes did even on newer ships. He worried about old pipes lagged in asbestos. The hazard of scavenge fires. Where fumes could build up in the boiler room, causing the diesel to take flame. At nineteen thousand tons and six hundred feet she wasn't the biggest carrier on the seas. Nor was she a plaything. She was his command, and as her Master he was affectionate towards her. They'd been through a lot together. He always made sure that his crew kept her up to the mark. The owner's intention of having her return home empty of any cargo had offended him. In his eyes it was an unseemly gesture, unprofessional. He would usually be under orders to utilise his vessel as a tramp steamer. That was her role. To voyage anywhere in the world to find the cheapest cargo to sell at the highest price, with the ship's operating company playing the spot market. To return devoid of cargo seemed an inauspicious way for his ship to end her years, and for him to conclude his long – and in the main – distinguished career. There was talk of her going to a breaker's yard south of Rio. Or to the breakers' beach at Mumbai, shipping's most ignominious graveyard.

**

The recession had come too early for Borges. Another year or two and his nest egg would have been ready to hatch. An envelope fat with sterling would help counter the deficit. He always liked sterling. It was less volatile than South American currencies. The money would be deposited in his account in the Caymans. He and Marika had holidayed on Lake Como in Lombardy years before. When his seafaring days ended they planned to return. Buying a small flat and a sail boat on which to wile away the hours. He had wearied of the sea. It was a more capricious mistress than even the hot-breathed harlots who had serviced him down the years in sailor towns. He hankered for placid waters. For air free of oil.

**

It was Borge's old, dear friend, Ugly George, who had sealed the deal with him. They had downed a bottle of Southern Comfort and remembered the old days. The brawls and the hookers and the ships that were rust buckets. They'd talked of drunken navigators and raging engineers. And border-line incidents which should have done for them and never did because they could always high-tail it back to their ship and take off into the blue. Bolting for their lives. Helpless with laughter or rigid with fear. They'd been free men. Unfettered by suburban shackles or domestic restraint, leaving in their wake a trail of smashed bordellos. Unpaid tarts and broken hearts. They were young, fit, bursting with life. Now they were older and everything had changed. Even the owners. Once they had been as bold as their skippers. Running risks, taking gambles. Hell bent on building giant fleets and doing down competing lines. But now shipping was run by pettish accountants, fretting over their ledgers.

***

George and Borges had braved waves as high as tower blocks. Ships climbing walls of water, crashing down, groaning and shrieking. They'd clamped their eyes in terror. Immutable bonds had been forged. Strong enough to withstand the decay of time and distance. The notion of offering a passage to a renegade held no terrors for Borges. He'd been a renegade in his time, most seamen had. The oceans were always a sanctuary for the hunted. Most of his crew were on forged papers. Their certificates dog-eared and dubious. He'd never cared for bits of paper. They were of no use in an Atlantic tempest. It was sufficient that his men knew their task. Coping with boredom or fear. Or the loneliness of keeping watch on a starless, freezing night. George and Borges had cursed and laughed and drained the bottle. Ugly gave him the money. They shook hands, embraced. Borges remembered when Ugly was young,with two good eyes, and every whore from Manilla to New York, had given him the nearest they had to love.

***

The early hours. In good time to catch the tide. Borges had insisted on an early start. Sean waited on *Lily* in Nail Wharf. Wilf and Roberto had picked their way towards Ugly George's mission. Side-stepping oily puddles, shards of glass and broken concrete. George handed Roberto two false passports and seafaring-papers.
    "For a couple of thousand quid you can get somebody killed in

London," he laughed.

Roberto looked at them. "So I'm an electrical engineer, first class."

"Only the best," George said. "Doesn't mean a thing. Everybody's on forged papers. I'll come out with you .. do the necessary."

Wilf and Roberto looked at one another.

"Not all the way."

He threw a tattooed arm round Roberto's shoulders.

"Wouldn't have minded a few years back."

Wilf looked at him, "You've done enough George."

"It's nothing. I could have got twenty passports."

"Two are fine," Roberto smiled.

Wilf said: "You shouldn't need a passport at all. But if you do, two are better than one."

George poured coffee from a battered aluminium pot.

"Real stuff."

Wilf looked at his watch "You're sure we've time?"

"Plenty."

Roberto looked at him. "Why are you helping me?"

George stared at the coffee.

"I've been an outcast. I know what it's like."

He raked at the black iron stove. Its glass bronzed and scorched. The air rich with coffee and simmering oak pillaged from some rotting hulk.

"Best Columbian. Say that today and they think you mean something different."

A fat black cat lay curled and purring by the stove. Roberto picked it up, cradling it.

"Old Hook." George said. "Outcasts are always good with animals. Always had cats on the ships. Kept the rats down."

He stabbed at the embers with a hefty poker. "I hate the fucking system. When nobody's got a brass farthing and you see some businessman whose kids spend his money on shoes and £50 million houses. Or some crap celebrity snorting cocaine – or caught with his pants down – or some politician on the make .."

166

He stared at Roberto, still cradling Hook.

"Helping you in a funny sort of way seems like giving the buggers one in the eye."

"Who rattled your cage?" Wilf smiled.

"I mean it Wilf. The council's been sniffing around again. Kids with clip boards."

"You didn't chuck 'em in the incinerator?"

"Should have done. These council bastards make me puke. They want to try being a bloody sailor washed up on a foreign shore. No money. Nowhere to live. Poor as church mice. Screwed by the owners. Bastards who run this country don't know they're born."

"How much were the documents?" Wilf asked.

"Five hundred. You gave me a grand. I bought a couple of bottles and shoved the rest in the poor box."

They stepped out into the darkness. Flames leaped in the stove. Hook curled in a warm black ball. Shadows dancing on the walls.

**

Sean had fired up *Lily's* engine. Anxious to be underway. He too had been recruited by George. They'd known each other years. George had told him that all he had to do was keep his mouth shut and his eyes to himself. Sean told him he wouldn't do drugs and George said neither would he. He accepted the fat bundle of notes. It was a God send. Business was slack. He had a family. *Lily's* bills were mounting.

"Who is he?" Sean had wanted know.

"No idea."

"What's he done?"

"Haven't a clue. My pal didn't tell me and because he didn't tell me I didn't ask. He's just another poor sod at the bottom of the heap."

Sean laughed: "He can join the club."

George had counted out the notes.

"Fair enough," Sean said. "We'll try and beat the sods."

Borges was waiting. They'd tied up at the jetty near the *Jose Antonio Paez*. Borges and his ship had been cleared to sail by the port authorities. They had twenty minutes to see Roberto to his cabin and say their farewells.

"I'm not interested in who you are or what you've done," Borges told him. "On my ship you're a free man." In the small windowless cabin Wilf and Roberto embraced. "I'll look after everything," Wilf said.

Roberto clutched at him. "I'm frightened."

"Who wouldn't be?" He faced Roberto. Hands on his shoulders. "Think what you've been through. How you escaped all those years ago. How you survived. You'll get through this. You've been through worse. You're a good man. I know you Roberto. The madness has gone. It's over, finished. You've done what you had to do." When Wilf and George left Roberto went on deck. Waving into the gloom. The lights of the tug disappearing into a grey dawn. In his cabin he slumped on his bunk, exhausted. From the suitcase he took photographs of his family. One was of Bill and Alice, arm in arm in the Amazon. Another was of Bill's mother, his late grandmother, at the helm of the sailboat. The third showed him with his surviving grandparents, Alice's mother and father, arms around him, in their pretty garden in London. He was a renegade. Tears stung his eyes.

***

Rosie had pored over the customers of Horace Green's Union Flag cloth company. She'd found nothing unusual. *The Imperial* had been a customer in the past but another company now maintained its table.

"It let the snooker room go to wrack and ruin," Green said. "They had it locked up while they were saving for a new roof. When they opened it again the work needed on the table went to the cheapest company. You give 'em good service for years then you're out on your ear. That's how it is. No loyalty no more. Committees change, members bring in who they know. It's all down to who's got a pal or somebody they know, and who's the cheapest. Most of these gentlemens' clubs are skint. Truth be told, so are a lot of the members, gents or no gents."

***

Immigration inquiries had become bogged down. Britain's Home Office was in mayhem, swamped by waves of immigrants. Some were in the country legitimately, others not. There was disarray in the steel and chrome headquarters of immigration in Brasilia. Roberto's change of name and circumstances had been lost in the files. A new Brazilian president and a pledge to cut red tape had paralysed the bureaucracy. Layers of clerks once familiar with the case had been sacked, leaving the files to gather dust.

***

Jolyon Wedd's company had purveyed fine wine to the gentry for decades. Its 18th century shop in the West End was all dusty boards and bulls-eye glass. In his dark blue blazer, pink cords and suspect regimental tie, Wedd had bought several cases for a snip from Dekker & Sons the auctioneers. The wine being described as the property of an anonymous collector. Dekker's Hubert Browne had given Wedd the wink. They'd done under-the-counter deals before. Browne told Wedd that the seller had scant appreciation of its worth.

"Just another mug," he said.

Browne had told Wilf that the market was flat and he could only expect a lowly price. Wilf thought Browne imperious, all accent and no brain. With two thirds of the world starving he felt it obscene to make a fetish of food and drink. Though Browne's

169

braying had grated Wilf simply wanted rid of it. Dekker's would normally have auctioned it. But Browne knew that Wedd was always partial to making a few pounds on the side, so he offered it to him privately. By way of thanks, Wedd gave Browne a useful backhander. Wedd would later get a handsome price from his patrons, unshakeable in their conviction that they were dealing with the most honest, and straightforward merchant in town. At the Savoy Grill Browne and Wedd had a laugh at Wilf's expense.

"Some prat of a priest out to save the world," Browne boomed. "Didn't have a clue."

***

Some miles from London's West End a small collection of vintage motorbikes attracted a good turnout at Taylor's auction rooms in an Acton side street, a long-time mecca for motor-cycling aficionado. They sold for what Wilf considered bizarrely high prices.

***

The next day Wilf instructed an estate agent to sell Roberto's house. The charming young man told him that it was not a good time to sell. His advice was especially honest in that he was desperate to hang on to his job in a falling market. It would, in reality, have been to his benefit to sell at any price. Though appreciative of his honesty, Wilf simply wanted it sold, and quickly. He accepted a low valuation and the buyer was delighted with the keen price. To Wilf it was an unimagined fortune. Roberto had been explicit with Wilf about what he wanted done with the monies. He had signed a book of blank cheques and written a carefully-phrased letter to his grandparents. While composing it he had been overcome with sadness that he had so betrayed their trust.

***

When the 'phone rang in the squad room Raven made a grab for it. Horace Green of the Union Flag cloth company wanted to tell Rosie that he'd taken another look at the names in the ledger. A number of entries were misleading. Would she please ring him? "Not moaning Horace again?" she said.

Green told her some names were misspelt.

"We keep getting young lads who fill the sheets in and don't have a clue. Most of 'em can't spell their own names let alone somebody else's. Anyway, for what it's worth, we've got an 'ardley who's an 'arding, that's with an 'h.' And we've got a Smith who's a Smythe and he's particular about his 'andle and 'is 'e.' Anyway, it's probably of no interest, but it's police business so I thought I'd best let you know."

"I'm very pleased you did."

As Green was about to put the 'phone down he said:

"Oh .. and there's another 'ere. It ain't Silk. It's Dilke."

"Dilke?"

"That's him. The judge bloke."

"Alistair Dilke?"

"That's the one. I think he's a Sir. Very nice old boy. Been to 'is place m'self. Up in Regent's Park. Lovely old Riley table."

She and Raven were on their way almost before she put the 'phone down.

***

Marlborough Place, Regent's Park. Dilke's home. An elegant curving terrace of Nash houses. White stone, sash windows, black railings topped by fleur-de-lys. Steps to a black-gloss front door. Portico, pillars, brass bell-push. To the right, a short flight of steps to a basement flat. The staff quarters. Dilke shook hands, guiding them down the hall with its black and white floor. Paintings on either side. Into the drawing-room. Silk curtained windows at each end. The gentle hiss of a fake coal fire. Flames dancing with an unnatural symmetry in a grey marble surround.

171

"I'd prefer a real fire," Dilke smiled. "These gas things always look so bogus."

Classical piano music filled the house. He chose a brown bucket chair to the right of the fire. Inviting them to take the antique brown leather chesterfield facing the hearth. He ran his hands through his thick silver hair, pushing it back from his forehead. Tall, slightly stooped. Face thin, finely featured, dark eyes set deep. He had the unassuming gravitas of a senior figure in the law, pulling at a bell set into the wall by the fireplace.

"Tea? Coffee?" A Filipino maid appeared.

"Grace," his voice gentle. "A few refreshments for our guests if you don't mind. Perhaps some biscuits? And you might turn the music down a little."

Raven wasted no time.

"I didn't know you played snooker."

Dilke watched him. As he might an accused. Getting his measure. He rose from his chair, moving to the window looking on to Regent's Park.

"Oh yes .. played for years." He turned to face them. His features shadowed by sun streaming through the window.

"Not lately .. used to be quite keen."

"You've got your own table."

Dilke smiled. "You've done your homework."

Rosie chipped in: "People talk."

"Yes, I suppose they do."

"You were in the *Imperial* when Gleeson was killed," Raven said.

"True enough. Downstairs .. one of your chaps spoke to me."

"They did sir," Rosie said. "Why didn't you tell Detective Sergeant Leach you played snooker?"

Dilke smiled, resuming his seat by the fire.

"Well, I'm afraid it doesn't sound very convincing .. but to be frank, I really don't know. We were all pretty shaken up. I suppose it didn't actually enter my mind. I can see what you're driving at .. and perhaps I should have done so. But when some poor fellow's been done to death not a stone's throw away .. well, the last thing you think about is playing snooker. Where he'd been killed didn't seem very relevant at the time – it was the fact that he'd been murdered – not the room where it occurred and not any connection that I might have had with snooker"

The maid brought a silver tray. Crown Derby china.

"Chocolate digestives. My wife used to say they'd make me so portly I'd not be able to get into the stockings and the fancy dress we judges are obliged to go in for."

His warm charm filled the room. "It's the most awful baloney.." he spread his arms .. "Judges dressing up like silly chumps. Choccie biscuits .. one of my vices."

"And the others?" Raven smiled.

"Too many to mention."

At their request he showed them the snooker room at the rear of the house. It was in darkness. A slight musty smell. He drew the long red velvet curtains. Folding back old pine shutters, light splashing in. A tall sash window overlooked a long walled garden, extensive by London standards. Well-shrubbed with specimen trees. A gate at its conclusion.

"Rather attractive, don't you think?"

Raven nodded. "The gate ..?"

"Goes to an alley. Runs the length of the crescent. Tradesmen used it in the past."

The antique Riley table was of a dark mahogany. A lustrous patina, the baize brushed and smoothed. Laid for a game, reds in a perfect triangle. Each colour expectant on its spot.

"How well did you know Gleeson?" Raven asked.

"I didn't really .. seen him around a few times. But that was about it."

He stood at the window. A wrought iron bench sat in the shadow of a Japanese Maple. As summer turned to autumn its crimson leaves had started to carpet the grass.

"You never played snooker with him?"

"Of course not. I'd have told you."

"You didn't tell us you played snooker. Let alone that you had your own table."

"Well, be that as it may. I can assure you I never played snooker with Gleeson. For what it's worth, I've rarely used the table at the club."

"Why's that?" Raven's eyes had turned to ice.

"There was gambling. Quite a heavy drinking culture had built up around snooker at *The Imperial*. Between games they'd play cards. All very unofficial and against the rules of course .. the committee has to turn a blind eye to that sort of thing."

"And your point?"

"Oh, it'll always go on, you'll never stop it. No matter what the rules might say. But in my position .."

He smiled, breaking off in mid-sentence, turning back to the garden, throwing wide his arms. "I can see the headlines: 'Former judge in gambling scandal.' Sounds a bit pompous but one can't be too careful. Some rag like the *Herald* would just love that. I don't think Gleeson had any part in it. The gambling and so on. He never seemed to play with anybody. Just a bit of practising they say. I never heard anything about him being involved with all that. He lived out of town, one of those country chappies .. as of course you know. I'm sorry to be unhelpful, but I didn't really know the fellow at all."

Raven joined him at the window, his voice barely a whisper.

"Still a bit odd you didn't mention your interest in snooker when Leach asked you?"

"I'm sorry .. as a matter of fact, he didn't."

"You know what I mean."

"Well, I really don't think it's odd at all .. for the life of me I can't see why I would have mentioned it. If somebody was mugged in front of you and the assailant ran off you wouldn't necessarily mention to the policeman that you did a bit of jogging yourself .. now would you?"

"Sophism. Isn't that what lawyers are good at?"

"Oh come .. please." He looked at Raven as if he was being

particularly silly.

"You've had plenty of time since you spoke to Leach," Raven said. "Why didn't you get back in touch with us and tell us about your involvement in snooker?"

"Frankly .. it never entered my mind. I can't really see why it would. I just can't see what my private snooker table, and the occasional game in my home, has anything whatsoever to do with some awful murder at *The Imperial*. It's hardly *involvement*."

"Still very peculiar isn't it? Your involvement .."

"Involvement? I have a table. I like to play sometimes. It doesn't make me *involved*."

"How would you put it?"

"Inspector, I'm a retired judge. I play a little snooker. Do you really think I'm the type to run around sticking scissors in peoples' eyes and mounting decapitated heads on bird tables. The servants at the club would vouch for my presence there when this ghastly business occurred. I'm sure you've spoken to them already? At least I certainly hope that you have. It would be pretty inept policing if you hadn't done so. All in all, if you don't mind me saying, it seems a pretty thin case you're trying to pin on me."

***

In the Alfa Raven said: "Crap. Even if Phil didn't ask him specifically he'd still have mentioned in passing that he played snooker. It's just semantics."

"But why?"

Rosie said she found him convincing. That his point about being shocked by the murder rather than in the room in which it occurred had validity.

"Balls. Why was the table laid if he didn't play much? *The Imperial* has a cloth to cover the table when it's not in use. The balls are kept in the pockets. But the baize on his table was brushed and ironed and the table shone with polish .."

"So?"

"It was all set up for a match. But he said he didn't play much."

"Just the way it is. Looks tidier, neater. The Filipino girl would do the polishing. It'd be all part of her household duties. Maybe he hasn't got a cover?"

"A table like that costs thousands. A cover costs a few quid."

"So?"

"It's like having an expensive outboard on a boat and not having a cover for it."

She frowned. "Don't let's get too hung up over the damn cover? He seemed pretty straight forward to me. What was that dry smell?"

"Precisely.. if the maid cleaned it every day why did it smell musty?"

"You're clutching at straws Jack."

"Probably. But it's bloody odd that three people – two of them victims – played snooker. And the first, who we know was sleeping with the second, was a member of *The Imperial* which Dilke just happens to belong to. The odds are too great for all that to be coincidence."

He started the engine, a puff of blue smoke.

"Anyway," he said, pulling out into the traffic, "What did you make of all that stuff about how shocked he was? He's a judge. He's tried as many murder cases as I've investigated. Murder's an everyday occurrence for him."

"Maybe," she said. "But it's always at a distance. To him murder is academic. Something to be played out in his court room. By then it's been anaesthetised, all the blood and gore sucked out of it and replaced by the lawyers' semantics and the sophism you mentioned. It becomes a game for the lawyers, like chess. And it doesn't happen under his nose, on his own turf. Anybody would be shocked by that."

Raven glanced at her.

"For somebody so clever.. you can be bloody ingenuous."

"Maybe I'm not as cynical."

"Give it time."

"Well, anyway, for what it's worth, I quite liked him. I can imagine him in his buckles and stockings at the Lord Mayor's do."

"Bollocks. If he was pig ugly and abrasive you'd hate him You're letting emotions cloud your judgement. What you liked was his charm. He's elegant and he's successful and he's a bright bugger."

She smiled.

"You might be right .. nice house too."

***

"Grace."

The maid was alarmed when Rosie stepped up to her in the street the next day, saying she only wanted a quick word and there was no need to be frightened. She'd taken her to a bustling Italian. Windows fogged with condensation. Office workers queuing for bacon butties to eat at their desks. A warm huddle in a back room, red-topped formica tables with white chipped legs. An elderly man in a fawn raincoat pouring HP sauce on a full-English. Reading the *Herald*: 'Still no breakthrough in *Imperial* killings.'

"Judge Dilke .. he doesn't like me talking to people," Grace wiped a stray hair from her forehead. Rosie hadn't realised how pretty she was. Dark hair, dark eyes, olive skin. A shy, fleeting smile. "Mr. Dilke's good to me. Treats me well."

A moment later Raven joined them. He'd stayed in the Alfa knowing she'd be less intimidated if it was just Rosie who made the initial approach.

"This won't get you into any trouble," he said. "Judge Dilke needn't know anything about it. We just wondered if he had many visitors at the house."

She looked away, avoiding his gaze. "Why don't you ask him?"

"Sometimes .." Rosie's smile was warm, encouraging. "It's nice to talk to other people, build up a picture, get a slightly different perspective."

"Mr. Dilke says he doesn't like me talking to strangers. He says London is dangerous."

177

Rosie mentioned how clean the snooker room looked.

"I polish, make it nice." She shrugged her shoulders.

"Does he play a lot?"

"Not much now .."

Rosie reached across the table, touching her hand.

"Why are you so nervous ..?"

"I shouldn't be here."

"Why do you polish the table if it's not used?" Raven stared at her.

"The judge .. he like it that way. It's how it is. No reason."

"Why don't you put the balls in the pockets and put a cover on the table? Have you got a cover?"

"Yes sir."

"Why don't you use it?"

"I don't know sir. Sometimes people come for game. Not much now."

"Do you know who they are?"

"No sir. I just take drinks through, whisky, coffee." She was agitated. "I mustn't be late back. I have to get the shopping for judge's lunch."

She had started to leave the table when Raven showed her a photograph of Gleeson.

"Do you know him?"

"No." She'd immediately pushed it back across the table, barely glancing at it.

"What about him?" Raven had a photo of Clarkson.

She shook her head, moving quickly away.

"I'm sorry. The judge will be looking for me."

***

Wilf watched the video tapes which Roberto had taken from Gleeson's locker in *The Imperial*. With the snooker ball, the bird book, the lock of Capes's hair, the small silver- framed photograph of Lockhart in an alpine setting, and four of the five tapes, he

178

wrapped them all into an ungainly parcel. Unhappy with its fragility he pressed the parcel into a cardboard box, padding it with wads of old newspaper.

****

Roberto shared his cabin with Alf. He'd grown up on an estate in Rotherham.

"We're all 'ard as steel and sharp as blades. Like the Sheffield boys."

He had an unruly mop of curly red hair. His large round face, red from the sun, was heavily freckled. He'd been at sea ten years. His mother was Irish. He had never known his father.

"Did a runner when I was a nipper. Me Mam and me Gran raised thee."

He exaggerated his Yorkshire accent to amuse his mates.

Roberto was tall, well-built. But Alf towered over him. He had taken the lower bunk.

"It's easier to get to the bog in the night if I've had a few."

In the evenings Alf played brag and drank whisky with the other donkey men and greasers in the cramped mess in the stern of the tanker. At night, lulled by the steady thump of the engines, they'd talk, Alf befuddled by booze.

"Half of 'em 'ere have been inside. I'm a bit of a reformatory boy .." his words drifting away. "What about you then? My little Brazil nut."

His inquiries reminded Roberto of his renegade status. He'd spin a fictitious tale.

Alf would say: "I don't believe a bloody word thee tells me .." and then he'd sleep, snores muffled by the beat of the diesels.

****

During the day Roberto fell in with the daily routines of the seafarer. The weather had been uneventful but for a day and a night in the south Atlantic. The wind had gathered and a grey sky turned inky black. The ocean, white and foamy, pitched and heaved. On the bridge, Borges lost sight of the bow as his tanker plunged into troughs, howling in its pain, throwing him off his feet, the wheel spinning. Bows rising up, scaling walls of water, plummeting down again. A sudden quiet had followed the tempest. A large grey sea-bird materialised as if from nowhere. Gliding calmly, leading the way, as though directing the ship and its company on the safest course. In those hours Roberto learned the might of the sea, the frailty of a ship and its complement.

***

To lessen the monotony faced by those making long passages, Borges kept a modest library. Its contents were a joy to his renegade passenger. He would read for hours, lying on his bunk, falling asleep over the words. At Borges' behest Roberto attended to the ship's electrical apparatus, paying careful heed to the alternator and its stand by unit, knowing its malfunction would disable the steering and render the craft helpless.

"Ah yes," Borges would say, standing at the wheel, sucking on a bottle of Jack Daniels.

"The alternator." As if he was discussing an old and quixotic friend, whose mild caprice over the years he had learned to tolerate.

***

Roberto would join in with the greasers and donkey men wielding their oily rags, pouncing on the tiniest chafing in the engine room. Sometimes he'd work with the maintenance crew, chipping away for hours on end at flaking paint and then repainting, a tedious, never-ending cycle made especially pointless by the knowledge that this was to be the vessel's final passage. Its owners had radioed

Borges, instructing him to take her to the breaker's yard sixty miles south of Rio. The sea, the sun and the wind had added to Roberto's tiredness. His nightmares were starting to lessen. The insanity which had devoured him had vaporised. England was beginning to seem far away.

***

In England, Alice's parents had also succumbed to an overwhelming fatigue. Their lives had become hollow, without purpose, the usual afflictions of age had been quickened by grief. They had abandoned the idea of escaping to the country. It all seemed too much bother. They had chosen, instead, the familiar over the unknown. Pottering around in God's waiting room, waiting patiently for death. Trying to fill their days.

***

The size of the cheque which dropped through their letter-box had been beyond their comprehension. Wilf had sent it on behalf of Roberto, and with it a letter.'

'My darling Nan and Pops,' it began, and Alice's mother's eyes had filled with tears.

'I want you to have this and to buy the house in the country which you used to talk about. I am sorry that all this must seem so secretive and strange. There is good reason and I will try at some point in the future to explain. There is no need for you to worry or to be frightened. I am very well and I am safe. If you should wish for anything at all please get in touch with Wilfred. He is the kindest and truest of men. He has been a wonderful and steadfast friend to me and I know that he would do anything to help you in any way that he could. As you will now know from Wilfred I have sold the house and its contents. The money is from the sale. When Mama and Papa and my other Nan were killed I simply had to get away. I pray that you will forgive me for leaving without saying goodbye; my head was in such a spin I didn't know which way to turn. Your loss is my loss and I am trying to come to terms with it as best I can, as are you. I love you both very much. I always will and I want you to fulfil your dream. I know you love me as much as I do you. You are all that I have left and I am so proud to be your Grandson. A move to a new home in the country will be a great adventure. It cannot end the grief, or lessen the loss, but it will give you new horizons and provide you with some small distraction which, hopefully, might help in some tiny way to lessen the pain. The money means nothing to me and I have little need of it. I know Mama and Papa and Nana would want you to have it. It can, at least, open up a new chapter for you. I can never repay you for all the love and the kindness, the affection and the support you have always shown me. As soon as I can I will be in touch again. You are in my thoughts, and will be forever.' Your loving grandson, Robbie.

***

The Church of St. Peter and St. Paul in Wapping, in London's East End, fronted a small green, its boundary marked by rusting black iron railings. A muddy path sliced it diagonally from corner to corner, an unofficial track used as a short-cut for hollering youths on mountain bikes. Clutching their bottles of Stella, faces hidden by hoods. The park had been built by the Victorians, a tranquil lung in a grimy corner of dockland. Its grass was now thin and yellowed, benches vandalised and graffitied. Once an oasis for harassed mothers pushing prams, now it was the haunt of addicts and drunks and the juvenile runners on bikes working for the drug gangs who had annexed it as their own.

***

Wilf knew the area. He had explored it when he first arrived in

London, getting to know its shadowy, cockroach-ridden corners. The concrete stairwell of a council block, sour with urine. Where youths had gang-raped a girl for showing too little respect. The railway arches where hobos fought over bottles of meths, lying curled in their rags round a glowing brazier. Sometimes he had joined them, sleeping among them, laughing at their raucous imprecations for him to share a bottle; the wild-eyed and crazy, the weak of limb and fragile of mind. It was what worker priests did. They had a soubriquet for him. They called him the walking man. In the past he had walked from dawn, when a damp mist wreathed the Thames, into the velvety blackness of the night. When the winos in their rags tottered and fell. And sad-eyed, lank-haired girls, with thin, needled arms, hitched up their skirts for the price of a fix from punters with whisky-stained breath.

***

In high-rise council blocks with broken lifts Wilf had pushed past huddles of stoned youths, sniggering and jostling him on the stairs. The air rank with reefers, climbing higher, flight after flight. Consoling the old and the wretched marooned in their tenements in the sky. They'd told him about another priest who visited them. Old Frank McCormack from St. Peter's over the Green. They loved old Mac. He'd never let them down. Even though the youths on the stairs beat him unconscious one night and put him in intensive care in the London Hospital on the Whitechapel Road. Even after that he'd still come to see them. When he was on the mend and off his sticks he'd come clumping up the stairs, breathless and wheezing. They worried Old Mac would have a heart-attack.

***

By the time Wilf had said his goodbyes they'd plied him with tea and shown him the views from their flats in the heavens. He'd headed for the Thames. In his shabby jeans and hand-me-down sweater, its wool coarse and matted. He stood outside The Cannon pub where locals once held knees-ups round a piano. Now it was a gastro-pub. Gastro-enteritis locals called it. He'd walked down cobbled lanes, between wrecked factories, through a children's playground. Broken swings lurched in the wind. A vandalised roundabout on a crazy-skew, never to spin again. He watched the nouveau riche in their costly lofts carved from warehouses which once held the spoils of empire. He sat sorrowful on a bench by the river. Thinking of those he'd met. With their distant views and limited horizons. The tide was out. The Thames a straggle of grey mud. A shopping trolley- and a bike lay entwined in the slime, half submerged. Like somebody drowning, hands imploring above the ooze.

***

From where he sat Wilf could see the cross of St. Peter and St. Paul peeping over the sagging roof of a ruined piano warehouse. Almost obscured by minarets on the mosque, where Bangladeshis answered the call to prayer. Frank Mack would be his man. He knew from what he'd been told that he'd be fine. He sounded like somebody he could trust. From what they had said he wasn't a holy bloody Joe. Or a mad careerist. He wasn't on his knees, every five minutes, foaming at the mouth. And thank God for that.

***

Raven had sneaked off to his boat on the Deben. Only Rosie knew where he'd gone. The squad had assumed that he was following a lead. They were familiar with his way of sometimes keeping things to himself. Playing it close to his chest. A lone wolf. It was the way he was, how he operated. The case had dragged on for weeks. Exhaustion had threatened to overwhelm him. He was near breaking point. As well as trying to unravel the case he'd had to cope with the constant fear that at any moment the killer might strike again. He'd had to contend with the politics, back-biting, irritatingly ambitious commanders fidgety about budgets. Editorials in the *Herald* had become increasingly shrill. He had put Dilke under surveillance, telling the squad to tread carefully. Dilke was a former judge. If he knew he was being watched all Hell would break loose. Knowing his move would lead to another bust-up he'd not told Toe Rag.

***

Raven's relationship with Miriam had become fraught. She was still living in his flat. But the arrangement had grown strained and claustrophobic. He'd failed to convince her that his tetchiness was not her fault but that of the case. She knew his affections lay with a phantom with which she could not compete. Olivia.

***

He rowed the tender out to his yacht. It bobbed seductively at its mooring. A cold dry day with a stiff breeze. He opened the hatch to the cabin and another at the bow. Letting a draught of air rush through. It smelled stale, unused. As he drew back the tiny curtains a shaft of sunlight splashed across Olivia's photo on a shelf above the starboard berth. Her berth, the one she had always preferred. Even as he parked the Alfa, the car she'd chosen, scanning the water for his boat, *their* boat, memories came pouring in. He had been determined to keep them at bay. But he'd failed.

***

With the yacht to wind he raised the main. Releasing the painter. Unfurling the jib. Easing the helm to port. The craft trembled to life, waking from its slumber, sensing the wind, the sails beginning to fill. He sailed for three hours. On the little gimbal stove he cooked soup from a packet. As night closed in, the distant lights of Woodbridge twinkled on the water. He mixed a hefty gin and tonic, and slept more soundly than he had in months. In Olivia's starboard berth. Her photograph smiling down at him. In his dreams he smelled *Joy*, her perfume. And felt once more the softness of her skin.

***

In London Dilke was at home. In his leather chair by the marble hearth. Fake flames dancing, the snake-hiss of gas.

"Tell me about it child," his voice soft, soothing.

Grace's flowing dark hair was swept back from her face.

"They showed me photographs of Gleeson and Clarkson. They wanted to know if I recognised them. If I knew them."

She knelt by his chair. Head buried in his lap. He stroked her hair, hand under her chin, tilting his face down to hers.

***

The launch scythed across the waves. Heading for the tanker. Three fifty-six a.m. Four minutes early. The ship had anchored off Macapa. The state capital of Amapa in Brazil's north eastern corner, on the north side of the mouth of the Amazon, at the point it joins the Atlantic ocean. Its name comes from a local palm. But it's familiar to navigators for a different reason, sitting exactly on the Equator at 0 degrees North.

***

Roberto had climbed quietly down his bunk ladder, being careful not to disturb Alf. He'd slept fitfully, continually looking at his watch. When sleep finally came to him he had a sad dream about Brazil's small green parrots. The male and female fly together. If one dies, the other starves to death because it will not fly anymore. When he woke he felt sick and clammy. On the lower berth Alf snored. Mouth agape, his head lolling to one side, breath sweet with rum from another night with the greasers.

**

On deck Borges wished Roberto good luck and farewell. He told him he was the best electrician he'd ever sailed with. At the helm of the launch was Luis, a tall young Brazilian. He had been given his instructions by a professor at the Universidade Federal do Amapa. Roberto told him to speak more slowly. It had been a while since he'd used his native Portuguese. Luis's face was stubbled, thick black hair curled over the collar of a black leather jerkin. He explained how he had discreetly nudged his craft with its pointed bow and rakish lines out of the port of Macapa. Past rust-stained freighters full of manganese, tin ore and timber. A mile out to sea he'd dared to open the throttle. Engines roaring, bows rising, leaping from wave to wave. The professor had told him that Felipe in Customs at Macapa would not try to detain him, and nor had he. Luis's orders were to take his passenger to berth thirty-eight in the port of Cidade das Mangueiras in Belem. The city of mango trees. Sited opposite Macapa on the southern shore of the Amazon's mouth.

**

Wilf's organisation had been impeccable. His reputation was such that it had taken only an enigmatic outline of his requirements on the Net to galvanise a network of friends around the world. They had asked for no details beyond those which he had volunteered. They had made no inquiries about Roberto's name

187

or status, though Wilf's guardedness offered a potent clue to his renegade presence. Their unquestioning compliance was a mark of the loyalty Wilf inspired. Some owed him favours for kindnesses shown by him. Or for battles against injustice which he had fought on their behalf. The greying, mild-mannered professor of philosophy at Amapa University, Carlos Ruiz, owed Wilf his life. Years before, as a young firebrand, he'd been cornered in a remote township by a posse of hacienda owners. They had accused him of fostering radical politics. He'd been tied and dragged behind a horse. Wilf had fallen to his knees in front of a posse of riders on charging steeds. He'd held aloft the small crucifix his mother gave him and which would later hang in his cell in the Beggars Palace. He told them those in the settlement loved their priest and that if they hurt him or the academic the police and soldiers would have to hunt them down. He lied that he knew politicians and that he had influence. And he told them that when the law had done with them they would still have to answer to a higher court. The hacienda owners had begrudgingly cut Ruiz free. Leaving him in the dust, coated in blood, his clothes shredded. They bound Wilf to a tree and lashed him with bull whips until there was no skin on his back and on the backs of his legs. Then they rode away, fuelled by liquor. Laughing into the night and asking where his God was in his hour of need. A share cropper and his wife had sheltered him in their hovel and nursed him back to life. He had lingered on the lip of death for weeks. Infection took root. It seemed as if his burns, and makeshift surgery by a well meaning medic whose skills had not previously extended to skin grafts, would spell his end. Ruiz had sat at Wilf's bedside in the gloomy sharecropper's shack saying that he thought their survival had been a miracle.

"I'm afraid not," Wilf told him. "I think you'll find that the big man has rather more important things to worry about than a couple of silly buggers like us who happened to have been in the wrong place at the wrong time and ought to have known better."

Wilf said he'd been bloody terrified and had a venomous snake reared up, spooking the horses and sinking its fangs into the riders, that would have constituted a real miracle. Especially as it was well known that there were no killer snakes in the area.

***

Wilf had anguished over recruiting his friends. Apart from the shrink in whom he had confided he alone knew the extent of Roberto's crimes. If his plan failed they would all be implicated. Without hesitation or inquiry they had put their lives in his hands. He had to get it right. It was conceivable that Roberto might have escaped in a legitimate way. But the risk was too high. Had he presented himself at dock or airport simply being a Brazilian would have been sufficient for his detention.

***

Wilf lay on his thin mattress worrying about the arrangements he had made. He watched Alexander swimming happily in his bowl, darting behind weed. Wilf thought about Roberto. The boy who could fix everything, from fitful boiler to intermittent stove. The boy who spent patient hours calming the clients. And what had he gained in Roberto's absence? A goldfish. He prayed for Roberto. For those he'd slain. For those endangered by helping him. For Raven the policeman he had never met but felt he knew. For Roberto's parents and grandparents. For the motorist incarcerated in jail. For the family of the motorist left behind, trying to cope. Outside his room drunks swore and shouted and thumped the television. That's the trouble he thought. We always overload Him.

***

From the box of keepsakes Wilf had taken the video tape which Gleeson had made of Roberto's despair, dropping it in the furnace in the basement. His discovery of the hammer-head which had

189

meant nothing to him initially had taken on, since Roberto's confession, a new and sinister importance. On his way back upstairs, returning from the furnace, he had met Stephen Mwenpembe who had anxiously inquired after Roberto. Wilf told him that he had gone away. That he had been traumatised and on the advice of a doctor had left for an extended break. Stephen nodded, but to Wilf he seemed unconvinced. The Kenyan had made no mention but Wilf was a keen judge of men. He'd been tempted to level with him. But it would have made him complicit. Stephen wanted to be a priest. His soft eyes hid a fire which reminded Wilf of his own early years. He liked his kindness and his mettle. One day he'd be a spirited defender of the downtrodden. He asked him to come to his room.

***

Wilf leant on the wall by the broken clocking-in machine, gently reminding him that his visa had nearly expired. That he was responsible for him and that he was very much looking forward to being his sponsor.

"Is this about Roberto?" Stephen interrupted, immediately seeing through him, making Wilfred feel cheap and crass.

"You don't need to do this. You don't need to make threats. You're the best man I know Wilf. I trust you. Can I go now?"

"Of course .. but Stephen, let me try and explain .."

"There's no need. Roberto's travelling. He's coming to terms with his grief. That's what you told me. That's what I believe. And if for any reason I was asked about him, that is what I would say."

Wilf stared at the floor.

"I must go," Stephen said, quietly closing the door.

Wilf slumped on his bed. Aching with regret. Asking that his lies and his clumsy attempt at coercion be added to his long list of heinous sins.

***

It was near midnight when Dilke left his house in Regent's Park. Young Lake who'd been detailed to keep an eye on him had fallen into a half-sleep in his car and had nearly missed him. Dilke sped off in his silver Volvo estate with Lake three vehicles behind, radioing for a second surveillance unit, exercised that Dilke might spot him. Dilke sped down Park Lane. Past Buckingham Palace. Left along Birdcage Walk. Into Parliament Square. As he crossed Westminster Bridge Lake turned left onto the Embankment. A second car driven by Leach took his place. Over the bridge, south of the Thames, Dilke swung right at the Elephant and Castle. Following a circuitous route through Brixton. Fifteen minutes later he turned into the tree-lined darkness of the Fitzgerald estate in Blackheath. Leach would have been seen had he followed him on to the estate. Instead, he drove past, parking near the heath. Sitting a couple of minutes in his car before walking quickly to Clarkson's house, anxious that Dilke might suddenly reappear. The house was in darkness. He crept into the drive, hugging the shadow of a hedge, convinced that at any moment the intruder lights would flick on. Dilke's Volvo was parked at the rear. He stole back across the gravel, each soft step seeming to him a thunderclap. The quiet of the Fitzgerald enclave did not lend itself to being spied on, offering nowhere to hide. Leach felt conspicuous. The estate was hushed, absent of traffic and people. A bossy notice warned that he was in a Neighbourhood Watch zone.

***

Rosie and Raven had been in Soho when the call came. Looking for a man called Hodgkin. He'd left prison after nine years for a string of assaults on children. As an untouchable his friends inside had been nonces. He'd have heard whispers. They'd run back to the Alfa. Hodgkin could wait. Blackheath and Dilke were now the targets. On their arrival Leach explained the difficulties of approaching Clarkson's house without being seen. Dilke was a knight. A former high court judge. It was late at night. They had

191

no appointment. No warrant. Raven had said that if things went belly up with Dilke's surveillance a ton of unmentionable would hit the fan.

"Bugger it." Raven said. "Judge or no bloody judge. Screw him."

They hurried along the road and into the drive. Feet crunching on gravel. The sudden white glare of intruder lights. A terrier next door began to yap. Raven leant on the bell. A light in an upstairs window. Moments later Mrs. Clarkson appeared at the door in a dressing gown. Raven wanted to talk to Dilke. She made an inept attempt at prevarication. Dilke appeared at the top of the stairs, suggesting it would be more sensible to talk inside.

***

Raven didn't waste time.

"Why didn't you tell us you knew Mrs. Clarkson?"

Dilke smiled. "Why would I do that Inspector?"

"You're hindering a murder inquiry."

Dilke had thrown on a dressing gown, fiddling with its belt. He said he'd had a long-term affair with Charlotte Clarkson. He'd known her husband for years.

"My eyes were always a bit weak and Charles was a first-class optician."

He smiled at Raven, his voice reassuring.

The two had shared a passion for snooker, he said. On one occasion Clarkson had invited Dilke to his home for a frame or two in his snooker room above the garage. It was then he had met Mrs. Clarkson. And subsequently they had become lovers. Dilke's slow, knowing gaze, moved from Raven to Rosie, settling on Leach.

"Just imagine that if I'd told you that I played snooker with Charles Clarkson and that I was in love with his wife .. what on earth construction would you have put on that? Let's not forget Inspector that I possess a pretty good insight into the way policemen tend to think. When the pressure's on two and two can so often be made to look like five. I'm not sure what case it is you are trying to build against me. But even you must admit it looks pretty flimsy. I'm also a lawyer. I know only too well how my own profession can sometimes construct a convincing case founded on nothing more than cruel coincidence."

Raven's eyes were glacial. "Coincidence?"

"I'm afraid it's true. It's the damndest luck that I also happen to belong to *The Imperial*. Believe me Inspector, if I was going to tell you and your colleagues a pack of lies I'd have dreamed up a far more plausible story than this. This is the truth and that's why it sounds as if it lacks credibility, as the truth, unfortunately, so often does."

Dilke turned to Mrs. Clarkson, squeezing her hand.

"There's something else. I didn't want Charlotte's name being dragged through the newspapers and splashed over the television. After all she's been through .. seeing Charles on that terrible morning .. I couldn't do that to her. If I'd spoken up, and my name had got into the 'papers, the reporters would have ferreted around until they'd found out about our relationship. They'd have been out here .. camping at the gate. It would have been misleading and it would have inflicted even more hurt on Charlotte."

***

Leach said: "You didn't even tell me you played snooker when we met. You didn't tell me you had your own table."

"Sergeant," Dilke smiled at him. "I've explained all this to your colleagues. You're tempting me to be facetious. I could say that I didn't tell you because you didn't ask." Raven's temper was rising.

"But that would be quite wrong of me. I know as well as you chaps that murder is never to be treated lightly. My error, and I confess to it, is that I've been .. how can one phrase this? .. I've been a little sparse with the detail. But to be meagre with the truth is hardly the greatest crime. It's not a hanging offence. And I have to say, in my own defence, if you like, that it was done with the best possible motives .. to spare Charlotte from any further misery."

"No sir. I don't see it that way," Raven said. "You've been playing games with us. You've lied and lied again by omission."

Raven had noted how Dilke's confidence had begun to reassert itself. He'd started his explanation with a semblance of contrition. As the minutes had passed he'd grown more cocky. Perhaps he imagined his performance to be persuasive? Raven had seen lawyers puff themselves up if they felt a case was going their way. Arrogant bastards, they'd stop at nothing. Semantics, diversionary tactics, as if they had a fiat to mock the law. Reducing a trial to a jousting match.

Dilke looked at Leach, his deep-set eyes burning with honesty. "With hindsight, Sergeant, I'd like to apologise. I wish I'd been more forthcoming. I've acted foolishly and I can see that my behaviour probably looks odd to you chaps. Hindsight is a wonderful thing. I should have volunteered all these things to you. I know that now .."

***

Dilke paused, looking around, hands expansive as he searched for the right word.

"My attempt at *discretion* might have left myself open to misunderstanding."

Rosie gave him one of her brightest smiles.

"From where I'm sitting, sir, it looks as if you attempted a cover up which has been rumbled."

Dilke was not to be rattled. He returned her smile.

"Yes, I'm sure it does Miss .. I'm so sorry, I'm afraid I missed your name .."

"Diamond," she said. "Rosie Diamond."

"Yes, of course .. Miss Diamond .. well, all I can do in the circumstances is to once again say how sorry I am and to apologise if I have been a little circumspect about the matter. I realise how foolish I've been. What more can I say?"

Charlotte Clarkson suddenly blurted out "It's all so unfair. I don't know who you think you are. Barging in here at this hour. But I'll tell you one thing. Alistair is the most honourable of men. He'd never do anything untoward. The idea of a cover up is preposterous. You'll be saying next that he killed Charles."

Raven looked at him.

"Did you?"

"Don't be so damn silly."

Raven turned to Mrs. Clarkson.

"You told us your husband used to play snooker with somebody but that the man had died. Was that person Mr. Dilke?"

"Yes, alright .. it was Alistair. I'm sorry I told you what I did. I know it was wrong. But I didn't want Alistair dragged into all this. He's a man of standing. Something of a public figure. I didn't want anybody knowing about our relationship. It's nobody's business but ours. I cherish our life together. Our privacy. There's nothing grubby or soiled about it. But I know that people like you and the newspapers will put some nasty construction on it."

Rosie asked: "Do your children know about you two, Mrs. Clarkson?"

Dilke's face darkened. "You make our friendship sound furtive."

"Isn't it?"

"How dare you?" he said, his face flushed.

Rosie ignored him, pressing on.

"Answer the question Mrs. Clarkson? Do your children know about your relationship?"

"My husband had been away on one of his bird watching jaunts. My daughter arrived back unexpectedly. She caught us .. it's as simple as that .."

"Caught..?"

"Yes .. dammit .. do you want a map? Do you want me to spell it out? We were in bed. OK? Are you satisfied?"

"And that's the reason your daughter doesn't come down very often?" Rosie said "Have it your own way. Think what you like."

"Not because of being involved in Green politics or unable to afford the train fare?"

"I s'pose so .. yes."

Raven said: "You've told us a pack of lies Mrs. Clarkson. Lies from start to finish."

***

Dilke glowered.

"You're over-stepping the mark. This isn't a formal interrogation. We've not been charged. The worst you can claim is that we've told a few fibs for personal reasons to cover our embarrassment."

Raven's voice was as cold as his eyes.

"Don't play the judge with me Mr. Dilke. You're not in court now. Your prevarication and omissions and *fibs*," he spat the word out, "have hindered my investigation. I don't give a toss who you are and I don't give a damn about your *embarrassment*. You'll answer the questions here or we'll go back to the nick and you can answer them there."

The atmosphere was electric.

Charlotte Clarkson began to cry.

"What's the point of all this?" she asked.

"The *point*," Raven said, "is that we're trying to catch the person who murdered your husband, though clearly he was not as high in your affections as you'd led us to believe. We're doing it on your behalf."

"You've a damn fine way of showing it," she said, handkerchief dabbing at her eyes, flouncing towards the door.

"Sit down," Raven said. "We've not finished."

Dilke said: "You can see how fraught Charlotte is. She's been to Hell and back. It's not your fault, of course it isn't. We understand that. I think we should all calm down a little. Charlotte and I both know you're only doing your job."

***

Raven registered the steadiness of Dilke's hands. The guilty sometimes trembled. Though it could be misleading. Some would begin to shake as soon as he said he was a policeman. If Dilke had secrets he'd keep a grip. No giveaway tremble would ever be allowed to betray him. Dilke smiled at Rosie, getting her measure.

"If you don't mind me asking .. what motive could I possibly have for killing these people? Give me one reason."

She returned his smile. "That sir, is what we're here to find out."

He turned to Raven.

"If you don't mind me saying .. I find your combative approach a little alarming and discourteous. A different stance and you might get more out of me."

Raven could feel himself beginning to lose control.

"Such as what?"

"Look here .. there's no need for all this unpleasantness. I'm trying to help you. I've given you honest answers from start to finish, and I've apologised for not volunteering more information earlier on."

"Combative? Discourteous? What planet are you on Dilke? This is a murder investigation. It's not apple scrumping. If you think this is *unpleasant* I could show you what that really means."

Dilke sighed, looking at his watch.

"Please .. don't let's start making threats .."

"Believe me .. it's no threat .."

Dilke stared at him. "Would you mind if we called it a night now? It really is getting awfully late."

"I'll decide when we're finished. Not you. We haven't finished with either of you. But it'll do for now. You'll be around if we want a further word? And we will."

"Of course .. I've nothing to hide. Let me assure you, you're making a mountain out of several mole-hills. I don't know who you're used to dealing with but we're not the sort of low-life who'd do a runner or anything as dramatic as that."

Dilke held open the front door. "Incidentally, are you likely to be asking Grace anymore questions?"

"She told you then?" Raven looked at him.

"Of course. She tells me everything. There's really no need to way lay her in some café. You're always welcome to come and talk to her at my home. Whenever you wish."

"Perhaps she'd feel inhibited," Raven said. "You're her boss. She works for you."

"You're not suggesting she's afraid of me Inspector? This is all getting too silly."

"I'm not suggesting anything."

***

As they stood in the hall, a moment before they left, Raven asked: "Has Grace got all the proper paperwork?"

Dilke was nonplussed: "What's that got to do with anything?"

"Immigration papers .. work visas .. you know the sort of thing?"

"I've really no idea .. I suppose so."

"Well, let's hope so. Questions like that are taken very seriously these days .. has she worked for you long?"

"I don't quite understand what you're driving at ..?"

"It's a simple enough question .."

"About five years I suppose."

"Well you'd better start looking up her documentation .. we couldn't have a former judge employing an illegal immigrant. That would look far worse if it got into the *Herald* than if you were caught up in some petty gambling misdemeanour at *The Imperial*. Goodnight sir."

***

With that the three of them crunched off down the gravel. Raven nodding at a woman neighbour peeping from an upstairs bedroom window.

"Nosy bloody lot round here," Leach said. "What was all that about the maid?"

"Oh nothing," Raven said. "Just thought I'd give him something to worry about."

Rosie laughed. "Bloody Hell Jack. I think he's got enough to worry about already."

"Yeah .. maybe .. but we haven't pinned him. One thing's for sure. He's not the killer. He was downstairs writing up his legal notes when Gleeson was being butchered. I thought we'd just have a bit fun with him about Grace .. a stick in the pond .. waggle it about a bit.. see if anything nasty comes to the surface."

Rosie smiled.

"You'll be doing a Reinfeldt on him next. Asking him about his teeth. If he's got dentures."

Raven glanced at her.

"We'll save that for next time."

***

Luis moored his launch at berth thirty-eight in Belem, as he'd been instructed by Professor Ruiz. Luis had been one of his students. Ruiz knew Luis never had much interest in becoming a philosopher. But the two of them had retained their friendship. Luis was a local boy who'd built up a range of contacts. As a high-speed courier, operating his craft in the mouth of the Amazon, his little business had flourished. Ruiz felt it prudent not to inquire too closely about the precise nature of some of his cargoes.

***

At berth thirty-eight two men stood close to a crane, stepping out of the shadow of a vast warehouse, edging warily towards the launch. Luis gave the eldest a fat brown envelope stuffed with American dollars. The launch looked tiny tucked in among the freighters which loomed above it, stained and blackened. The younger man took Luis and Roberto, crouched in the back of a small van, to a far corner of the sprawling dockyard, halting in a discreet corner screened by a wall of rusting steel containers, a mountain of palettes and a morbid, high-sided hulk awaiting repairs. The men quickly unfurled a small section of the high-wire fence which ran round the perimeter of the yard, making a gap big enough for Roberto and Luis to scramble through.

***

The opening let on to a narrow, unlit road. An elderly drophead coupe was waiting. Rakish lines, a long fluted bonnet, the passenger door ajar. Lights doused, its engine purring. In a moment they had sped off, Luis handing another bulging envelope to the driver. The car raced past the Federal University of Para. Ignoring the newer part of the city, with its gaudy modernism and small forest of skyscrapers. Veering sharp left by the white stone Hall of the Virgin Saints, ornate as a wedding cake. Swinging right, tyres screeching, past the Septuagesima School, founded on the third Sunday before Lent and seventy days before Easter. Where the rich sent their siblings when the rubber boom began to gather pace. Sweeping into the colonial old town. Past the Church of the Blessed Martyrs, a confection of rare fussiness, its heavily gilded steeple pointing to a universe dotted with stars. The break-neck speed had Luis leaning forward from the draughty gloom of the car's rear. Tapping the driver on the shoulder. Chiding him that he was not Ayrton Senna and that they had no wish to attract the attention of the police.

***

The driver was squat and fat. From the back seat he seemed to have no neck. His hair matt black, lank as a wig, his vacant grin as manic as his driving. Elegant homes with blue tiled roofs and tree-filled squares of cobble and mosaic shot by in a blur. Testimony to the sudden wealth the rubber boom had brought to Belem: Cidade das Mangueiras, the city of the mango trees. The car stopped in the square of Santa Domingo, where Luis said his goodbyes. He had to get back to the launch before it was impounded. His confederate would be waiting near the gap in the wire. He pointed to an alley which ran off the square in its far right-hand corner.

"It's on the left," he said, "the eleventh house in the row. It's painted white. It's got a roof of dark blue tiles."

The car roared away, shiny black with a crimson hood: running boards, flared wings, the long bonnet with its mascot, a silver leaping cat. Roberto knew it as a post-war Jaguar SS. His grandfather's affection for cars had been excelled only by his love of motorbikes, and Roberto had been an avid learner. As he set off across the square his grandfather's gleaming motorbike, the Velocette Venom that he'd used to track Gleeson to his cottage in Norfolk, flashed into his mind.

***

In the alley, painted cottages in bright colours, white, pink and creams. Neat and welcoming. Window-boxes with red trailing plants. Like those in the quiet, hushed backwaters of Hampstead, with which he had become familiar. Suddenly, another memory reared up: the dainty houses in Gloria, in Rio, in which he had been made to suffer. He was at his destination. A gentle rain had begun. The eleventh house on the left; its roof of dark-blue tiles, glistening in the moon light. He tapped at the door.

***

Raven and Rosie climbed the steps to Dilke's front door, their distorted reflection mirrored in the high gloss of its black paint, the shrillness of the bell echoing through the house. Raven had said in the Alfa that he wanted to keep Dilke under pressure, to remind him that he was in their thoughts. Such tactics had worked in the past, making suspects nervous, inducing them into a rash move.

Dilke sat by the fireplace. Rosie and Raven on the chesterfield.

"You're becoming regulars," Dilke smiled.

Raven ran his hand along the top of the chesterfield. "I've always wanted one of these. It reminds me of the one in the snooker room where Gleeson met his maker."

Dilke had a languid air. His eyes too deep to gauge if they were as benign as his manner.

"So how can I help today? Or perhaps it's Grace you've come to see?"

Raven glanced around the room. Pale eyes flicking back to Dilke, a minacious stare.

"What else did you and Clarkson share besides snooker and his wife?"

If Dilke was surprised he didn't show it. "Such as?"

"Anything at all. On our first visit you said you had many vices."

"I made a puerile joke about having too many to mention."

"You did."

"Inspector Raven .. please .. it was a throwaway remark, A joke for pity's sake. I was speaking metaphorically."

"Interesting."

"What?"

"Interesting word."

"What word?"

"Pity. The word pity. Not a lot of it around today." Raven's eyes bored into him.

"You've lost me."

"So you can't think of anything which you and Clarkson had a liking for?"

"I'm sorry .. I still don't know what you're driving at."

"Right sir. I understand. I think that'll be it for today. We'll catch up with you again. There's no doubt about that." He got up from the chesterfield.

"Is that all you want?"

"Oh no sir. We want a *lot* more. But it'll do for the moment."

With that he and Rosie made off down the hall.

"We know our way .. we can let ourselves out."

***

When they left Dilke moved to the window, standing to one side, partly hidden by the velvet drapes, watching them get into the Alfa, as upright as a Guards officer, hands clenched behind his back. A vein at the side of his temple had begun to pulse. There could be no mistaking Raven's animus. Raven glanced back at the house, knowing Dilke would be watching, knowing that he'd unsettled him.

Rosie said she'd changed her mind about Dilke.

"He's too fawning. There's a menace."

The Alfa sprang to life. Raven glanced in the mirror. No blue haze.

"We'll let him sweat. He's a liar and he's blethering. Let's see if he makes a move."

***

As they drove away they didn't acknowledge Detective Constable Sean Lake parked further along the road at the wheel of a small dark Vauxhall.

"Lake says he wants a car with more guts. I told him if he keeps complaining I'll have him on a push-bike."

Rosie laughed.

"Fancy a drink later?"

"Why not? We'll have one in that boozer on the heath when we've had a chat with dear old Charlotte. Poor cow."

"Why do you say that?"

"Would you want to be mixed up with him. Supercilious bastard."

"No .. perhaps not .. your mood's improved since you went skiving on your boat."

An endless traffic jam.

"Bugger."

Raven drummed his fingers on the wheel.

***

Wilf pondered the name which Roberto had shared with him. He'd promised him that he'd look after everything. Tie up loose ends. Things had worked as he'd planned. He'd had to imagine scenarios from afar. The success of his plan hinged on the competence and trustworthiness of others. Some of whom he'd never met. He'd received a one-word email from Borges. It said OK. It meant Roberto had been transferred to the speed boat. He now wanted confirmation that Luis had played his part. Luis had recruited the two men at Belem and the driver of the Jaguar. Each had been paid with Roberto's money. Roberto had told him to give money to Ugly George and his mission for seamen. He'd made a large donation to the Beggar's Palace. For a new roof, central heating, a new boiler, cooker and large-screen TV for the clients. He wanted Wilf to buy himself a new bed, a decent sweater, anything else he needed. He'd asked Wilf why he was taking such a risk. What was it that drove him?

"God knows," Wilf had told him. "At least, I hope he does."

***

Charlotte Clarkson was not overjoyed at seeing them.

"You again?"

How long had her husband known Dilkes?

At the mention of her lover's name she was immediately

guarded.

"We told you .. for years."

"And it was just snooker?"

"Can you make yourself clear?"

"Did they share other pleasures."

"What do you mean?"

"Anything .. anything at all."

"No .. not particularly .. I don't understand what you mean."

"Why do you think your husband's head was on the bird table?"

"You've asked me before. I've no idea. They must be sick."

"There's no significance?"

"Not that I know of. It was obviously something to do with his bird-watching."

***

"Did Mr. Dilke and your husband meet when you weren't around?"

"No .. perhaps .. why would they?"

"This might sound odd .. do you think your husband knew about your affair?"

She turned away, looking through the window of the lounge at the snooker room over the garage.

"Since you ask .. he did, yes .."

Rosie: "And he didn't mind?"

With her back to them she said:

"He didn't have much choice. I told him I'd leave him and go to Alistair. We often talked about it."

"Why didn't you?"

She turned back to them, arms folded.

"Look .. it wasn't just me. There was another woman in Charles's life. It was convenient for me .. for us, if you like .. to stay together. But our marriage was a sham. It had been over for a long time. I turned a blind eye to what he was up to and he had learned to live with my relationship with Alistair."

Rosie said it sounded an odd arrangement.

"To you, perhaps. You'd have to be involved to understand."

She'd taken on a resigned, weary air.

"There were the children. You read all these ghastly things about children who suffer when their parents break up. We didn't want to flaunt everything in front of them."

Raven had taken a step closer to her.

"Mrs. Clarkson .. your children are adults, they live away, they're grown ups. Surely they could have come to terms with such a thing? Millions of others have to."

"Perhaps. But it was our decision. It was the way we dealt with things, how we preferred things. It was very difficult for Alistair as well .. with his position."

"But he's retired – he's not in the spotlight to the degree he was. You could have divorced your husband and gone to live with him."

"I told you .. it was the way we wanted things. Alistair didn't really want me to move in with him .. it was very difficult."

"Why not? Why didn't he want you to go and live with him?"

"There was no particular reason .. all the upheaval .. messy legal proceedings, a divorce case .. he was quite happy coming out here. He used to laugh and say it was like coming out to his house in the country."

**

She had begun to cry.

"Charles was often overseas," she said. "So Alistair I were able to spend time together. I'd sometimes go to his place.."

Rosie's voice was soft.

"Look, aspects of your private life might have a bearing on the case. Every time you tell us something .. well, it seems to be different from that which you told us previously. Who was this woman in your husband's life? It's the first time you've mentioned her."

"I honestly don't know. I don't know anything about her."

"You must have heard a name. Something about her."

"He sometimes called her Alison. She doesn't live here. She's overseas."

She had begun to strain Raven's patience.

"You're still keeping things from us," he said. "You must know more about her."

"All I know is her name and that she lives in the Philippines. She isn't English."

"So your husband used to go abroad to meet her?"

She slumped on the sofa.

"Yes .. I suppose so. OK, yes, he went abroad. He used to go regularly. All the time. The children thought it was to do with the business. But it was really to see her."

"But your husband had sold his business. The children must have known that."

"He told them that he'd still got a consultancy role and that he had to go off and meet suppliers and contacts."

Rosie moved to the window.

"Did anybody else come and play snooker with your husband as well as Mr. Dilke?"

"I've told you .. sometimes my son would have a game."

"Nobody else?"

"No."

Raven asked her if her husband ever played at Dilke's house in Regent's Park.

"I don't think so."

"Come on Mrs. Clarkson. There are still too many inconsistencies. You said a moment ago you didn't think your husband and Dilke met up when you weren't around. But you were sleeping with Dilke .. he'd have mentioned if your husband had been in the house playing snooker with him. You'd have known one way or the other."

Rosie asked her how often she'd been to Dilke's house.

"Many times," she said, her voice low.

"And sometimes you slept with him there?"

"Sometimes."

"Have you been in the snooker room?"

"Of course. I've never played. Not there or here or anywhere else. I'm hopeless at it."

"So you must know Grace," Raven asked.

"Of course, she looks after Alistair .. cooks for him, does the cleaning. I know her as well as you'd expect me to know her. She's the maid. We're not sisters."

Rosie sat next to her on the sofa.

"Grace comes from the Philippines doesn't she?"

"I believe so."

"Did Grace know your husband?"

"I've no idea."

"But she must have done. They'd have talked about your husband's girlfriend being there. He must have known the Philippines well .. you said he often went there .. perhaps they talked about places in the Philippines they were familiar with."

"If you say so .. look, she's the maid, she helps Alistair, there's nothing more to it. I can't help it if she comes from the same place that my husband had his tart."

***

They stared at her.

"Is that what she was?" Rose said. "A tart?"

"Yes .. some bar girl."

Raven: "But you just said you didn't know anything about her."

"I suppose I knew that. Her name was Alison. She's a bar girl and she lives in the Philippines. But that's it. I don't know anything else about her and I don't want to know."

She looked at them, silently imploring them to leave.

"Mrs. Clarkson." Raven had picked up a photograph of her husband with the children. "Was Charles a good father .. good with children?"

"He was very good. He had a way with them."

"You didn't, by any chance, know any of the other people who've been murdered."

She dabbed at her eyes with Rosie's handkerchief.

"Of course I don't. I haven't a clue who any of them are. I'd have told you."

"There are a lot of things you didn't tell us. And things you did tell us which weren't true."

"I'm telling you the truth now. I haven't the foggiest idea who they were .. and neither has Alistair."

"Why do you say that? Why would it be in your mind about Alistair knowing them?"

"I don't know."

"Did Alistair tell you he didn't know them?"

"I don't know .. I suppose so. I suppose he must have done."

"Mrs. Clarkson .. don't prevaricate. Did you and Alistair Dilke talk to each other about knowing or not knowing the other victims besides Charles, your husband?"

"I don't know what you're talking about .. Alistair and I have talked about Charles's death so much. You've just got me totally confused. I don't know what you're talking about. You've got me into such a state I don't know what I'm saying."

She had become close to hysteria, begging them to leave.

***

"You didn't go with your husband to a bird of prey centre did you?" Raven asked.

She shook her head, tears rolling down her cheeks.

"It was another lie wasn't it?"

She nodded.

"You went for a weekend but it wasn't with your husband. It was with Alistair Dilke wasn't it?"

"I only told you it was Charles because I didn't want you finding out about our affair. You know all this. Why do you keep on about it?"

"Because you keep telling us lies. It's not true that you explored antique shops in the area is it?"

She bowed her head, looking at the floor.

"We checked with the hotel. The Three Chimneys. The staff told my officers that you and Dilke hardly left your room. You even had all your food in there."

"We wanted some time to ourselves," she said. "A bit of peace and quiet."

"So why the elaborate lies? Bird centres, walks by the River Stour, antique shops, cottages with pin-tile roofs? You saying you'd quite like to live there? That's quite a construction."

"I don't know. I went into panic. I just started inventing things, trying to make it more plausible. I wasn't thinking straight."

"You even told us you listened to Liszt in your husband's Lexus."

"I just didn't want anything about our relationship to leak out. It would have been awful."

"We checked the CD player in Charles's Lexus. There was Beethoven and Chopin and Max Bruch. But there was no Liszt. And there was no Liszt in the CD collection in your house."

"I made a mistake .."

"No, I'm afraid not Mrs. Clarkson. You were thinking of Alistair Dilke. He's the one who likes Liszt isn't he? You'd got Charles and Alistair Dilke mixed up."

She shook her head, wiping at her tears.

"Did Mr. Dilke help you with your story. Did he coach you about what to tell us? Did he tell you to put in plenty of little details to make it that much more convincing?"

"No .."

"Are you sure about that? It's what lawyers do .."

Tears rolled down her cheeks.

Raven told her none of the questioning would have been necessary if she'd told them at the outset everything she knew.

"It's been like trying to get blood out of a stone." he said, closing the door behind him. Leaving Charlotte Clarkson chalk-faced. Crying on the sofa.

In the Star and Compass pub, on Blackheath Common, Raven told Rosie he thought Charlotte Clarkson had probably, finally, told them the truth.

"She'd gone into a panic. She was in shock. She'd pulled back the curtains and seen her old man's head on the bird table. It'd be enough to make anybody talk gibberish. Especially if you're trying to cover up a few dirty secrets."

"What about the Liszt?"

"Oh, she just made a mistake .. my guess is that Dilke tried to school her in what to say .. he's a lawyer. He'd have done it in the past with his clients .. all barristers do it. He'd have told her to say something about listening to classical music in Charles's car, build up a story, make it sound plausible with lots of minutiae and colour. But in her panic she mixed up Dilke's musical tastes with those of her husband. She's besotted with Dilke. Her head's full of him."

"How did you know that Dilke likes Liszt?"

"It was on at his house when we first went there. Don't you remember? He asked the maid to turn it down."

"I remember it was classical. And a piano. I didn't know it was Liszt."

"When we first went there .."

"Yes, I remember that. But you knew it was Liszt?"

"Franz Liszt's Piano Concerto No.1 in E-flat major. It's pretty well known."

"I thought jazz was your thing. Didn't realize you were into classical music."

"I've been around longer than you. You learn stuff along the way. There's a lot you don't know about me."

***

At Roberto's shy knock the door of the house in Belem was flung

211

nearly off its hinges. An ecstatic Flaherty hurled himself on his visitor.

"You're safe! We've been on tenterhooks so we have."

He pressed him to his great chest.

"I wouldn't have believed it."

His black eyes danced.

"You left here a tinker of a boy so you did .. and just look at you now."

He propelled him into the snug.

Bernard's face lit up. His small wiry frame in old jeans and frayed shirt just as Roberto remembered. They hugged one another. The intensity of reunion heightened by the sudden evaporation of duress.

"Wilf's message was so curt we knew there was trouble," Bernard said.

"We learned it like a code years ago in the seminary. It's what the Orders do. If anybody's in danger you make your message brief. Cryptic. You have to try and work it out for yourself."

Flaherty ferreted in an oak chest for a bottle of Bushmills.

"It's from a benefactor. A good old Irish boy who thinks he can drink his way through the Pearly Gates."

"Cheers," Bernard laughed. "As you'd say in England. Cheers to a wee boy who's turned into a big fella. He's nearly as big as you Flaherty so he is."

"Aye .. and twice as handsome."

Roberto said. "How can I ever thank you."

"I've never heard anything like it." Flaherty's black hair and beard were as wild as ever. "Thanking us! Bernie and I sat here in this wee house feeling as helpless as a pig at a barbecue. We were getting worried and there's not a drop of doubt about that."

***

They talked for a long time about Roberto's family. Saying how devasted they were when they learned of the accident. And they talked of many other things. Trying to catch up on the years they'd been apart. Bernard said it had been better in Brazil since the election. But that there was still no justice. And there wouldn't be until the land was more equably divided. Millions of people still lived in squalor. If he had his way he'd parcel up the land and stamp out the corruption. Flaherty cut him off saying he was the one who used to spout politics. Roberto wondered if Flaherty had become less political.

"Not really You get older. You start to run out of energy. You're continually banging your head against a brick wall. It wears you out. You begin to realise that all politicians are bloody mad. Anybody's got to be as daft as O'Reilly's drum to think they're good enough to lead a country. Any country. They're all arrogant bastards. We still need more schools, hospitals, houses, jobs .. there are countless numbers who still haven't got clean running water and proper sanitation. I haven't met a politician who isn't on the make."

And what would Flaherty do with the politicians? Bernard wanted to know.

"Well," Flaherty tugged at his ear. "I'd send 'em to one of your favelas in Rio, Bernard. And I'd tell 'em they've all got to get down on their hands and knees and clean out the lavatories. Not that there are any lavatories in the favela. Well .. there are, sort of .. it's just that you wouldn't recognise them as such."

When they'd finished the Bushmills they moved on to the thick bread and the goats cheese which Bernard had bought earlier from the little shop in the square. Flaherty found bottles of Xingu in a cupboard under the sink.

"This is thanks to a man who owns this wee house," he said. "He's a friend of a man called Ruiz at the university. He left a note saying we should make ourselves at home and have the beer."

"I knew Wilf was in touch with Ruiz," Roberto said. "But I didn't know the detail. Wilf organised everything."

When Roberto started to tell them what he'd done Bernard said the hour was late, that they had drunk too much, and that

213

they were tired. If he really wanted to tell them it could wait until later.

"But we're not going to go round asking you all about it," he said. "Come the day Robbie boy and we'll all be a standin' in the dock about something or other. And that'll be a mightier court than anything down here."

He raised his eyes to the ceiling.

"There's not a man Jack of us who hasn't done wrong. God help the lot of us when the time comes."

With that he threw back his head and downed his Xingu in a gulp.

"We can only worry about the man today," Flaherty said. "Not what he was yesterday, when like as not he was a different person. Now, come on, let's call it a night. You'll be wanting a good sleep after all your exertions."

In the kitchen Bernard turned on the householder's lap top. He called up Wilf's address and typed 'OK.'

***

Wilf knelt at the back of St. Peter and St. Paul. His face partly hidden by a muffler and the raised collar of his jerkin. Old Edith Morgan who was doing the flowers paid him little regard. As long as he wasn't a sniffer, or a drinker, or being sick on the stone floor, or some tearaway wanting to pinch something, she didn't mind who he was. She tried to keep an open mind about what Father Mack called the sinners, while also insisting that his duty and hers was always to try and look after them. But old Mack didn't have to clear up the vomit. Or shoo the meths drinkers off the pews curled up after a skinful. Only last week, God in heaven, there'd even been a lad and a girl going at it hammer and tong on top of somebody's tomb. Wilf knelt down, head in hands, eyes half open. From his reconnoitre he'd learned that the church was open every day, unlike so many others forced by vandalism and pilfering into locking their doors. Old Mack had told Eadie the church couldn't be a sanctuary if its doors were locked.

"It's just a church," he'd say. "It's very beautiful, but that's all. A nice looking heap of old stones. If people doze on the pews it shows how tired they are. It makes you feel guilty that they've nowhere else to go."

Eadie tutted about it being God's house.

"And God'd want me to turn away the needy would he Eadie? Lock his door against them?"

"What about that kid who rifled the donation box?"

"Isn't it terrible that they're so poor they have to do that? Anyway, I caught up with him and gave him a bloody good clip around the ear."

"And the police'll be having you for assault if they find out."

"Well, in that case, you make sure you don't go telling them Eadie."

Mack began confessions at five p.m. Mass started at six. The confession stalls were at the back of the church to the right of the nave. Wilf slipped away as quietly as he'd entered. Eadie had her back to him. Worrying if the chrysanthemums would last another day.

***

Raven returned home in the early hours. There was a note stuck on the fridge from Miriam. She'd left him. She'd gone back to Greenwich. He telephoned. Apologising for the late hour. Saying he was still worried about her being on her own.

"Jack, there's something I haven't told you. I'm not on my own anymore."

They talked for an hour. She'd been as gentle as she could. She wanted to get married and have children. The clock was ticking. He said he hated the phrase but knew what she meant. He wasn't ready for marriage. It was too soon. The conversation was a re-run of one they'd had many times. She told him he was fixated by his job. She felt excluded by his single-mindedness. She couldn't play second fiddle to his work. She said he was in love with a ghost. To that he had no riposte. They finished on a note of sadness more than recrimination. He put on John Coltrane. Keeping the sound low for his neighbours. And reached for the Tanqueray. He hadn't wanted to argue with her. He was too tired to argue with anybody. And he knew she was right. He knelt down. The paper construct snaked across the floor, creeping into the hall.

***

At Heathrow airport, Grace checked in for Manilla, under her real name of Amor Santos. Poised. Expensively dressed. Unrecognisable from the humble maid in the fawn raincoat Rosie and Raven had quizzed in the Italian greasy spoon. Over the years she'd learned to play the part of a meek Filipino. Head bowed, eyes down. She got more out of people by pretending to be servile. After the long flight to Ninoy Aquino International she'd taken a taxi to Ermita. The driver caught in the choking traffic, doubling back along Roxas Boulevard. In the hotel, the Casa Jasmine on the corner of Mabini and Arquiza, she ordered supper in her room. An iced bottle of Chablis and crispy pata. At four in the morning three drunken German tourists from Hanover staggered back to their pension. They'd had too many San Miguels and vodkas in the Furry Kat on MH Del Pilar. Grace was so tired she slept through the racket. It was seven years since she'd been home. She'd forgotten about the non-stop noise and partying in Ermita.

***

The next morning she squeezed aboard a jeepney bound for Santa Cruz. In an upstairs back room of Benjie's Global Bookshop on Rizal Avenue she'd told Dakila Emayo that he must immediately suspend all operations until further notice. Emayo shrugged his shoulders and smiled. It wasn't the end of the world. He'd find

216

other lucrative markets. He had plenty more buyers. Later she'd taken a cab to Angeles City in the province of Pampanga. Arguing with the driver about the fare. She was a local. She knew the score. Not some tourist he thought he could fleece. He'd dropped her at the Asian Moon hotel on Sampaguita Street. Drained by the heat she showered and fell asleep. Blinds pulled low against the sun.

***

In the evening a tricycle took her to Fields Avenue. Running along the perimeter of USAF Clark. Once the biggest air base outside America. She'd passed the Wide Open club. The Meat Market club with its flashing lights. The Ping-Pong where girls did tricks with table-tennis balls. Past the saunas, the Go-Go clubs and karaoke bars. The trike turned right into Raymond Street and left into Real Street. Stopping at the Red Fox. It was owned by Alison. Her real name was Dalisay Garcia. The long-time lover of Charles Clarkson. The Mamasan welcomed Grace and took her through to Garcia's office. One wall was fitted with one-way glass so Garcia could keep an eye on the till and the bar. Where punters pawed the hospitality girls and the nude waitresses serving costly watery wine. A lithe young man, and a pneumatic red-head, performed in a live sex show on a small stage which slowly-revolved in the middle of the audience.

***

Grace and Garcia embraced. Garcia ordered a minion to bring Cristal champagne. Garcia told her that Clarkson had always read too much into their relationship.

"We went to bed, had a lot of fun," she laughed. "But look .." she glanced at the one-way glass. The turning stage. A tangle of flesh.

"I was too old .. he didn't want me. He wanted what they all want. The little girls. The young ones. The *very* young ones. You know how it is. Charlie was lonely. In England his marriage was fucked. He was doing the business for us. And he was enjoying a few perks along the way. It's how it is. He'd been like it for years. You know what the men are like .. little girls, the younger the better. They can't resist them. How could I compete with nine and ten year olds?"

They laughed. Grace sipped the Cristal.

"London's crawling with coppers," she said. "There's a policeman called Raven. The killings are a bastard. We don't know who the fuck's doing them or what's going on."

Garcia understood. She'd catch the shuttle to Bangkok the next day and talk to the Thais. Another link in the chain.

"They've been a good source for us," she said.

"But there are plenty of other places and outlets. Belgium's a good market these days. And Austria. We'll start things up again when everything's cooled down a bit. China's got possibilities. Charlie did some exploratory work there. He was very excited about it. He said there was a big demand for Chinese kids. Some of the Chinese are so dirt poor they'll flog you a kid for a few dollars and a bowl of rice. Families are even having kids just to sell 'em on. That's how poor they are. But it's still China .. tricky sort of place .. very alien. Lots of red tape. Quite difficult getting the kids out. We'll find a way. We always do."

***

The next morning Grace returned to Manilla. At the hotel she showered and slept. Exhausted by the heat. Perspiration soaking the cotton sheet. When the sun began to lose its glare she caught the late shuttle to Calbayog airport at Samar. One of the Visayan islands. She'd grown up in a shack on a plantation with a hundred coconut palms. Her father was a copra farmer. Removing the shell, drying the kernel of the coconut. Crushing the copra to extract the oil. Using the meal as fodder for the livestock. Her father had become wizened with age. His back bent almost double. Ravaged by arthritis. Her mother had died three years before.

***

When Grace was a small child running barefoot on the plantation a group of strangers had arrived. They'd come from Mindanao, another island. They told her mother and father they would be able to find work for her as a domestic in Cebu. Her parents were as impoverished as everybody else. The money would be good. She'd be looked after. She'd live well. She'd be able to send money home.

***

The strangers took Grace away and raped her. She was fortunate to have been spared the forced injections which had become standard practice. When the abusers tired of them the stolen children were given drug injections to seal their fate as addicts. The usual precursor to their initiation into prostitution. But a trafficking boss had taken a particular liking to Grace. She'd been spared the injections and recruited into his circle.

***

For years her parents thought she was dead. She'd been warned by the traffickers that if she contacted her mother or father they'd kill them first, and then her. On this visit her father, Datu, had been overjoyed at her unexpected return. She told him she didn't know how long she'd be staying. Though privately she had determined to lie low in the Philippines until the investigation in England had begun to wind down. As the day cooled, and the clammy dampness of night set in, her two brothers and Bituin, her sister, had come to the family shack and held a celebration. Many years had elapsed since they had all been together. They lit a great bonfire in Grace's honour. On the edge of Datu's plantation, with its one hundred coconut palms which swayed in the warm winds from the sea.

***

They drank San Miguel and dined off gulay, simmering the vegetables in coconut milk. As a special treat Bayani, her elder brother, brought balut. Boiled duck eggs containing the embryo of a chick. Making a tiny incision in the shell at the top of the egg he sucked out the juice before carefully peeling back the shell. They laughed when Grace said she couldn't stomach balut.

"You've come back a Westerner, Amor," Bayani said. Crunching on the feathers and the little beak. "You used to like balut. But you've changed. Now you've got different tastes."

She lied about herself.

"I was in business. Import, export. That sort of thing."

They looked at her clothes and jewellery and thought how profitable her business must be. Datu clutched her to him. His long-lost daughter. Home at last. He'd tell his neighbours of his pride. Her hair was sleek. Her skin fine and her eyes shone. The red and gold sari shouted money. They had seen such clothes in the best shops in Manilla. Those patronised by the Americans and the tourists.

"You've made money," Datu said. "It's the finest silk. I've worked the coconuts all my life and they've given me nothing but a bad back. Giving you away to the strangers was the best thing we could have done. Your mother and I were very upset when they came for you. You were such a pretty little girl, so beautiful. Your mother cried for a week. But now I can die at peace, knowing that you're so well and so rich."

He asked her to twirl round to show off her sari. Her face lit by the flames of the fire. "You have a bearing. You hold your head high. Filipinos don't have presence. It's all in the walk. We Filipinos look at the ground, our eyes downcast. We know our place. We don't look people in the eye. It's because we've been invaded, we've been colonised so many times. Everybody's had a nibble at us. When one lot left, another arrived. The Spanish, the Americanos, the British. We don't know who we are anymore. We're all mongrels. But not you daughter. You've climbed high. You have dignity."

Grace kissed her father and told him she'd been fortunate.

"It was the money, Amor," he said, tears on his cheeks.

"We had no money for food. We couldn't feed you. That's why we had to let you go. Will you forgive me? Can you forgive me and Mama?"

"There's nothing to forgive Papa. You said it yourself. You and Mama had no money, no choice. It's always money Papa. That's what drives everything. It makes us do things we don't want to do. You thought you were doing your best. In rich countries they don't have to give their children away. You had to let me go."

***

Two a.m. Rosie and Raven at his flat. A new paper construct. What links had emerged? Raven was gaunt, haggard.

"We know Gleeson was a paedophile," Rosie said. "There's no evidence the others were."

Her eyes were pressed down with tiredness. "Dilke says he first knew Gleeson in passing. As a member of *The Imperial*. He says he knew Clarkson as his optician. Then to play snooker together. Then as Charlotte Clarkson's lover."

"It's a coincidence too far," Raven said. "Dilke says he didn't know Lockhart or Capes. It's a ring that doesn't quite join up. There are missing parts. Dilke's a liar."

"We don't know the killer," she said. "It wasn't Dilke. That's for certain. The servants vouched for him. Somebody knew them all and hates them."

"Revenge is the only theory we've got."

Rosie spent what was left of the night on Raven's sofa.

"A gentleman would give up his bed for a lady."

"The lady would need to be of a higher rank. You can use the

221

bathroom first in the morning. Bring me tea and toast at six. That's about three hours away."

"Sod off."

***

Wilf had carefully addressed and sealed the parcel. Marking it confidential and urgent. He'd left it next to the kneeler in the Confession Box. Eadie Morgan had gone in to plead for forgiveness for having uncharitable thoughts about a dosser she'd found swathed in newspapers in the sacristy.

"I try to be nice to them," she'd whispered to Old Mack, his face obscured by the lattice grille which divided him from the penitent. Three Hail Mary's would more than suffice, he gently told her, mentioning how nice the flowers looked again today. It was then that she told him somebody had left a parcel in the Confessional.

"It's by my feet Father. Probably one of those people again," she said, a touch irritated. "It wasn't here when I cleaned."

"Please Eadie," Mack murmured, "We've just ironed out those problems."

***

Wilf had judged his courier well. Mack noted the address and the scrawled plea for both confidentiality and urgency written in capitals. After Mass he changed his vestments for his well-worn ankle-length black overcoat, its pile becoming worn and mothy. A black beret and a thick scarf, both of which Eadie had spent hours knitting during the summer, completed his ensemble.

"I look like Father Brown," he said.

"Who?" Eadie asked.

"Chesterton. I'll tell you when I get back."

He rushed from the church. Cutting across the little green. Over the wet cobbles into the foggy damp of a still London evening.

Flagging down a bus to take him to the West End. Clutching Wilf's parcel as if he were the keeper of the Holy Grail.

***

In Brazil, Roberto, Flaherty and Bernard made their way to the dock on Av. Castilla Franca, to buy tickets for a government Enasa boat, the *Santa Catarina*. It would take them upstream to Santarem on the Amazon's southern shore. Midway between Belem and Manaus.

"You'll be safe now Roberto," Bernard said. "Brazil's so big and chaotic that once you're in you can get away with just about anything .. it's the same with so many places in south America. Keep your head down as best you can .. don't go tempting Providence and you'll be just fine. Nobody knows who you are or gives a damn about you here."

At Manoel's travellers' store, on Travessa Dona Leao, Roberto stocked up on essentials. Hammock, lavatory paper, mosquito net, rope, soap, tin knife, fork and spoon.

Flaherty was an expert.

"Buy the cotton hammock. It costs a little more but the others stick to you when you sweat. And whatever you do – don't fall in the river. There are some horrible things in there." He told him about the alligators, Black Caimans, twenty-feet long, with big, heavy heads.

"If the Caimans don't get you .. the Pacu will." It was a species of fish with which Roberto was familiar, with human-looking teeth and a fondness for nuts and fruit.

"Ah yes," Bernard said, laughing, "But if the Pacu can't find any real nuts they've been known to go for the other sort – chewing off your balls."

They all laughed. Flaherty reminded them that the Payara – the Vampire fish – could be pretty nasty too.

"They've got great tusks growing out of their lower jaw," he said. "I saw one once when I was having a morning swim .. it

223

scared the living daylights out of me. You've never seen anybody get out of the water as fast."

"This boat won't be Cunard so it won't," Bernard said. "The ferries get crowded so they do. Find a space for your hammock. And don't even think about the sanitation. You have to learn to hold yourself."

His slight frame was bent beneath the weight of his rucksack.

"I can only look at the ground. If I look up at the sky, I'll topple over backwards so I will. If the food's up to its normal standards we'd best stock up on bananas and lavatory paper. But as I say, it's better to cling on to your guts if you can, until we reach dry land. Try and hitch your hammock outside. It's cooler at night, but not a lot."

***

They found a tiny space at the ship's open stern amid wire-fronted coops holding chickens. After tying his hammock down with the chains, to stop it being stolen, Roberto pushed through the throng to the bow. The Amazon began to narrow. The *Santa Caterina* winding its way through the land of many islands. Yellow-brown water twisting and swirling. Trees reaching down to the river's edge. It became narrower still in the Furo Grande, the ferry at snail's pace, negotiating sharp bends, enclosed by the great trees which loomed above. Branches and fronds scratching at the sides of the ship. Bare-chested children waved from villages which clung to the bank. Roberto smiled, waving back at them, he was coming home.

***

At Santarem the greenish waters of the Tapajos joined the yellowy-brown of the Amazon in a swirling confluence, the different currents running adjacent one to another. A raucous gang of prospectors pushed to the front. Wild beards, mad-eyed with drink, weighed down by rucksacks. Aggressive and excited. Heading south to the lawless gold fields of the Mato Grosso territories. That night they holed up at the Sao Jochim bar on the Praca Rodrigues. Sharing a room over the bar. Small and sweltering with a spasmodic fan. Crowded with three thin beds. A fly-ridden bathroom with a distinct scent at the end of a corridor.

"Like the bowels of Hell," said Bernard.

"Think of it as Beverley Hills," Flaherty said.

Bernard said his imagination wasn't that strong. He ripped the algoa sheet from his bed, sending a hundred cockroaches fleeing, falling to the floor, scurrying for shelter between the boards.

"You have to do it quickly. They've been dozing in the heat. Knocked out by the sun, like the rest of us. When you wake them up they try and make a run for it."

In the past Bernard had helped the son of Angel, the Spanish proprietor of the lodging house. The boy had fallen in with one of the gangs in the Mato Grosso.

"I told the gang bosses that the devil would fry them in flames a thousand feet high if they didn't leave the lad alone," Bernard said.

"Did they believe you?" Roberto asked.

"No, of course they didn't"

"So what did you do?"

"Ran like hell."

***

The next morning Angel refused any payment, telling Bernard: "The gang's still looking for you, but the boy's safe."

"Well, that makes me feel a lot better," Bernard said.

"He's in Manaus," Angel said, "learning the trade in my brother's carniceria. Carving the meat. He sometimes steals it for his mother and me. He's a very good boy."

"If he's a trainee butcher," Flaherty said, "he'll be able to use a knife. It might come in handy. There's not a lot of law and order round here so there's not."

For breakfast Angel fried them a small mountain of churros, long curly fritters in a thick coating of sugar.

"Eat them like this," he said, ladling on spoonfuls of sugar, then dunking them in a steaming mug of thick, dark chocolate. Angel became emotional, his eyes red and watery. "It's my boy and the way you saved him. And it's the churros. They remind me of the old country. You can take the man out of Madrid .. but if you're a Madrileno you can never take Madrid out of the man."

Through Angel they secured the help of Paco, his friend. He was small and tubby with a sad, lugubrious face.

"He's like me, from Madrid," Angel said. "But he doesn't speak much now. He's downcast because his wife went off with the manager of the bauxite works. There's nobody knows the river as well as Paco."

When he was not on the river, Paco laboured at the waterfront before dawn each day, unloading the fish. He'd been proud of his wife. Happy that she was a Madrileno. But when she ran off with the man from the bauxite works he'd bought a launch. It had replaced her in his affections. The craft had a stout diesel engine and was built of mahogany, its brass fastenings glowed with polish.

***

Paco took them on a sweltering four-hour trip. Travelling south on the Tapajos. A pram-like hood did little to shield them from the sun. Eventually he turned into a tributary. Muddy and shallow, turning and twisting. Overhung with fronds and branches, pressed in by trees on either side. As they went deeper the tributary shrank to a stream. Finally, it was so overgrown, the water blocked by roots and weed, and so shallow, that he could go no further. They would have to walk the rest of the way. Paco thought that Paranela would take them two hours if they followed the stream. Though he hadn't been there, so he couldn't be too sure.

Old Mack sat at the small interview table in a bare and windowless room in the nick. It was airless. A stale smell of urine and stilton reminded him of altar wine which had become corked. Opposite him, sat Raven and Rosie. Mack's scarf and beret on the table next to the cardboard box.

"And the woman who found it hadn't seen it before? You're quite sure?" Raven could hardly contain his excitement.

"That's correct. Eadie Morgan," Mackie said. "We'd finished Confession when she said it was at her feet by the kneeler. She'd done the flowers and the cleaning which she'd have finished by about four o'clock. She likes to go home and put on a frock and a bit of make-up if she's going to take Confession and Mass." A gentle, knowing smile. "People are funny like that. They like to dress up. It's a mark of respect .. anyway .. whoever it was that put it there must have been in the church sometime between four and five. They must have waited for Eadie to leave and then made sure the place was empty. If they'd put it there any earlier Eadie would have seen it. She doesn't miss a thing. And there's not a day goes by when she doesn't run a duster round the Confessional."

"So there's nobody in the church between four and five?"

"Maybe a vagrant trying to keep warm. Or one of the drunks or druggies sleeping it off. Eadie usually sends them packing. I've told her about it .." The quiet smile. "But you know how it is. She's a very good old soul."

***

The moment Raven showed Mackie out, thanking him and telling the desk sergeant to have an unmarked car whisk him back to Wapping, he turned to Rosie.

"Got the bastard!"

His tiredness had fallen away. A new vigour surged through him. He'd worn surgeon's gloves to open the shoe box, Rosie

227

at his shoulder. The man with Melody Lockhart in the alpine photograph in the small silver frame was Alistair Dilke. When Roberto had taken it as a keepsake from Lockhart's bedside table he had no idea who the man was. Nor could he have imagined its subsequent significance. The videos were a catalogue of screaming children being raped and tortured. Some of them babies. The cameraman or woman had been meticulous in avoiding the faces of the abusers. The tapes were numbered one, three, four and five.

"Where's two?" Raven said. He cupped the red snooker ball. Rosie flicked at the bird book. "Whoever sent it wants us to link Dilke and Lockhart with paedophilia. He wants us to see what children go through, and perhaps what he endured."

Rosie held the lock of Capes's hair in her gloved fingers.

"So it's as we thought," she said. "Our man was abused as a child? Revenge. Perhaps he'd been filmed like the children on the tapes? Perhaps he's one of them? Maybe we've just watched our killer being hurt ?"

"Doubt it," Raven said. "He'll be on tape two. The one we weren't sent. He obviously doesn't want us to identify him. Get the labs to work on the videos and make the childrens' faces bigger. Try and age them so we can see what they look like as grown-ups. See if we can identify any of them. Let's see what the clever buggers in white coats can find on this box and all the contents. It makes quite a collection. It's a good breakthrough. But apart from the photograph of Dilke and Lockhart tying them together there's not much else. We don't know who did the filming. We can't tell if the abuse took place here or overseas. We don't know the children. Or when they were tortured. And we're still clueless about the abusers."

"No .. but at least it makes the motive pretty clear," she said. "If our boy was abused, like those kids on the videos .. well, that would account for the savagery."

***

228

The bell sliced through the silence of Dilke's house. No response. They ran down the steps. Hammering at Grace's basement door which let into her flat. Raven launched a flying kick. The wood splintered. Rosie said they should get a warrant.

"Screw it," he said, shouldering his way in. A narrow hall ran the length of the flat. Doors to either side. At its conclusion a half-glass door let on to the back garden. Kitchen to the right. Its small barred window facing the small yard. The fridge was empty. Crockery clean and stacked. Raven knew she'd gone.

***

Freshly laundered maids' outfits. White blouses, black skirts, white pinafores. Lace-up black shoes, well polished. The cheap fawn raincoat she wore in the greasy spoon café. Shopping basket, cheap plastic purse, a handful of coins. Tatty pink umbrella, beanie hat. The bathroom, white and clinical. No tooth brush, make-up, wash-bag. Raven cursed that the budget had forced him to take Lake off full-time surveillance. Grace's bedroom. Walls of cream slub silk, carpet white and thick, a king-size bed. Pillows plump, inviting, sheets of fine Egyptian cotton. Above the bed a Metzger abstract in shades of blue. Drawers of silk underwear, silk blouses, sweaters in softest cashmere.

"Bizarre," Rosie said, taking a grey trouser suit from a run of rosewood wardrobes.

"A poor little Filipino maid wearing Armani, Yves St. Laurent, Dolce & Gabbana. And they're not fakes."

In the lounge, a chaise longue in gold velvet. A Jacobean sideboard in black carved oak. Persian rugs. A Queen Anne chair, legs delicately shaped. Silk curtains at French windows giving on to a bricked terrace, the narrowing lawn beyond.

"Quality quarters for a maid." Rosie said."Makes my drum look a tip."

***

Stairs ran up to the ground floor. At the top, a locked door. Raven kicked it in. It let on to the main hall with its black and white floor. The house was on four levels, walls hung with paintings of nymphs and cherubs and thunderous black skies. The chandeliered library. Dilke was on the library committee of *The Imperial*. The study: shelves heavy with certificates and photographs chronicling Dilke's illustrious career. One photo had him in a procession of dignitaries at St. Paul's Cathedral. Wig, stockings, buckled shoes. Another showed him in animated conversation with laughing bankers and financiers, attired in white tie and tails at a glittering banquet in a City livery house. The snooker room: its musty tang. The Riley table laid in readiness for a match. The green baize smooth and ironed. The master bedroom: untidy, cluttered, a scattering of clothes, the bed unmade. The bathroom: an electric shaver flashing green, fully charged. A narrow staircase to the attics. Two rooms with sloped ceilings. Small, barred windows at either end. Markedly spartan, with twin beds and bare mattresses. A chest of drawers in each.

"For unimportant guests," Rosie said. "What happens if he walks in?"

"I don't give a damn. When he knows that we know about his links to Lockhart he'll have other things on his mind. We're wasting time. Let's do it properly."

"Shall we get Phil and the boys?"

"Not yet."

***

The rains came. The muddy stream they had followed for hours had turned into a torrent, brown and swirling.

"The boatman hadn't a clue how far it was," Flaherty said.

Bernard wiped at the rain streaming down his face.

"We'll soon dry out. We'll find somewhere open where the sun can get through the trees. We'll be steaming in the heat."

Roberto knew the ways of the forest as well as his companions.

But while they remained energetic he had become weary, pale and listless.

Flaherty was worried.

"You're taking the medicines?"

Roberto nodded.

Bernard said. "We'll look after you. Don't you be worrying about that."

They found a clearing where loggers had left their burned and blackened stumps. A patch of ground higher than the stream.

Flaherty fixed a hammock between two stumps.

"Have a sleep Robbie boy. The heat drains you. You've been in cold England. You'll soon get used to Brazil again."

He spread a plastic sheet. In his rucksack he had matches, a tiny stove, a tin kettle. A sachet of dried soup. By the time the soup had boiled in the kettle Roberto was asleep. They whispered about HIV and how he would need to look after himself. The sun burst through, Flaherty shielding Roberto's face with his wide-brimmed bushman's hat. When he awoke they boiled him more soup, Bernard tearing bread from the loaf given to him by Angel.

"It's gone stale, but it's not too mouldy. There's no blue stuff on it. Dunk it in your soup. It'll soften it up."

They walked for another two hours. Flaherty leading. Slashing with his knife at fronds blocking the track. Following the course of the water. Quickly, the swollen waters shrank back into a meandering, muddy stream. Suddenly, without warning, there it was. An enclave of grass-roofed huts. Open-sided, each raised a yard above the ground on a wooden platform. Children running barefoot. Elders gathered at the eating hut. Blue smoke from an open fire curling into a cloudless sky. The tang of black bean stew.

***

Rosie had gone back to the snooker room. The table with its rich patina. Squat, bevelled legs. Chinese rugs on the parquet floor at either end of the table. Cues in the rack. A mahogany cupboard with a brass catch: chalk, spare tips, the brush and iron for the baize. She sniffed the mahogany, smelling the polish. Rolling the black down the baize. It sprang silently off the cushion. Clicking into the reds, fragmenting the perfect triangular pattern in which they had been laid. She crawled beneath, tapping the slate bed. She looked down on the back garden. The bench by the tree, the grass carpeted in red leaves. The tradesman's gate at the far end. She shivered. A musty vapour. The house felt cold, unfriendly. She thought of her small, terrace house. Her fat, spoiled cat.

***

Upstairs in an attic, Raven pulled a bed from a wall. A small door, an inspection hatch. Allowing cramped access to the eaves. He squeezed inside. Crawling across rafters. Feeling his way in the dark. Making out the shape of a tank. Lagging, pipes, the soft gurgle of water. He remembered the Leeds killings. The cottage on the moors. The woman's body in a pig-food mincing-machine. Her head covered in maggots in a cardboard box hidden in the eaves. He crawled out, backwards, the dust making him cough. Brushing himself down he stood at the small casement window facing Regent's Park. It was locked. Steel bars on its glass like those in Grace's basement flat. And those on the windows of Lockhart's mews in Knightsbridge. He and Rosie went through each room. Drawers, cupboards, wardrobes. They looked in suits and pockets. Scrutinised photos, mementos, objet d'art. Tapped at walls, lifted carpets, checked behind each painting on every wall. They didn't know what they were looking for. But they'd know when they found it. Raven's instincts were screaming at him. Where was Dilke?

***

The villagers flocked round, laughing and pulling at their clothes.

The chief was old and wizened, his smile warm, black-toothed. Welcoming them with bottles of Xingu. His wife had led them to a clearing in the forest and dug four catfish from the ground. She had buried them previously at the foot a tree whose roots had preservative qualities. She'd scrabbled on her hands and knees throwing the soil up behind her, Flaherty whispering that she looked not unlike a demented rabbit. When she'd dug a hole two feet deep she pulled out the fish. Large, rank and caked in soil. Triumphantly she held them up to the sun, fingers in their eye-sockets. Cackling and grinning, she had fewer, and blacker teeth than her husband. This was the happiest day of her life, she said. The fish were the finest in the universe. And when she'd cooked them over the big fire they'd be the best and saltiest they'd ever tasted. Bernard said he'd certainly give them a try, privately hoping that they would taste better than they smelled. They wound their way back to the village, single-file on a narrow track. The chief's wife leading the way. Flaherty said he hoped they wouldn't be poisoned.

"We must eat every last drop or they'll be offended," he said. "If you want to be sick go into the jungle and hide yourself away. Don't let them see you throwing up. That'd be ruder than leaving the food on the plate so it would."

***

The villagers were joyous when they learned that Roberto would be joining them. Flaherty and Bernard told them he was a trainee priest. That he was as kind and clever, as brave and as lion-hearted as their old priest had been. When the old priest died the villagers had been bereft. He had been their friend and protector. The chief said that after they had eaten the fish and drunk more Xingu the tribe would dance and sing for them. The children would tell stories and recite poems passed down over the generations by their ancestors.

The next day, when light first peeped through the trees, the chief said they would have bad heads from drinking too much Xingu the night before. He was right. When the sun rose they all had blinding hangovers. Later on he took them deeper into the forest. Showing them the old priest's grave and its simple cross. The priest had stood up for them against the loggers and the drunken prospectors and the bullying developers. All had wanted to drive them from the forest. Strangers had come to take the children away. But the old priest had stood his ground and run them off. The chief told them that the priest had made long trips to fight for them in Brasilia. He never minded if their Gods were different to his. When they burned their voodoo dolls and the whole village became inflamed with drink. When there was a full moon he used to smile and say voodoo was all part of their culture, that he had no desire to compete with it. He set up a school and a makeshift clinic. He was good with bandages and ointments. He took those who were more seriously sick to the hospital in his canoe, more than fifty miles away. Villagers filled the canoe with such a quantity of fruit and provisions, it sat so deep in the water it nearly sank, with barely any space for the priest and his patient.

***

The priest had been very old when he died. The chief said he was a hundred and sixty five. But he was not good at counting. So he wouldn't swear to it. When he said this his wife sat behind him, with her black grin. Tapping at the side of her head. Her long, curling nails as black as her teeth. The villagers could remember when the old priest had first arrived among them. He had been young and strong with fair, curly hair. When he died they had mourned him for many months. The chief's wife said they shed so many tears the big river had become swollen. When he lay dying in his shack by the Amazon they had beseeched his God and theirs to spare him. But it had been to no avail. At his death other villagers from the forest walked and canoed great distances to mourn him. Lighting fires and placing voodoo dolls next to his cross. Three seasons had passed. The chief said the Gods would by now have taken his spirit to a secret place where the trees grew so tall that they touched the sky. Where the forest was green and silent and the streams ran clear of poison. Where children lived forever. Free of malaria, tuberculosis, influenza. The settlers' diseases. Where the earth and the forest were unscarred by mineral-hunters, loggers, developers, hoteliers and eco-tourists.

**

They had gone back down the stairs which led to Grace's basement flat. Near the foot of the stairs was a small locked door. Its size suggested a cupboard set into a wall. It shattered at Raven's first kick. Ducking low they could step inside. Groping for a light switch they found themselves in a windowless chamber under the snooker room. It was bare but for a bed, and a child's cot with a broken doll and a scuffed teddy bear, one of its eyes hanging out by a thread. Dilke was dead, sprawled on the bed. His thin, aristocratic face, grey and contorted. A scattering of pills, vomit down his chin. He had left a letter. 'Dear Raven,' it began. 'A warm welcome to the playroom.'

**

"I can't stand the stench in here," Rosie said.

They went back upstairs. Raven clutching the note. He sat on the chesterfield. Rosie settled herself on Dilke's chair by the hearth.

Raven read the letter aloud.

'I have decided to bid you farewell. To use a phrase from the game which has given me so much pleasure I had become, I'm afraid, 'snookered.' Your endeavours and those of the madman you have failed to apprehend left me with no escape.

'Let me confess at the outset to a passion for children. Those poor souls who have been murdered belonged to a group who shared my tastes. You will find scant evidence of our activities. There is no point in stripping homes or computers or looking for photographs; I will deal in a moment with the photograph in Melody's home which doubtless you will have seen by now. Early on we pledged that none of us would indulge in silly or crass behaviour which could betray us. As the group members are now dead I will pay you the courtesy of explaining how we functioned. I know how frustrating it must be for a 'local' copper to try and deal with what is, as you will begin to appreciate when you read this missive, a truly international affair.'

"Sick bastard," Raven glanced at Rosie.

***

"It's as if he's summing up a case before he passes judgement," Raven said, looking down at the letter. "He's taunting me, having fun, reminding me that I've failed. You can tell he's enjoying the mockery. He'd have been merciless with the children."

Raven imagined him. His Mont Blanc poised, crouched over the desk in his study, among the photos that showed him hobnobbing with the great and the good, with the grandees of the City and the Law, deliberating over each cruel, silken phrase.

***

'Firstly, let me deal with Capes. She played a crucial, international role. It was her task to find children around the world. There's a network for stealing children and spiriting them away. Passports, visas, documents, all are available. Plastic surgery is employed. Surgeons will do anything for money, and many of them shared our interests. A group such as ours needs intellect, discretion and funding. It's not all expenses. There can be good returns in the second-hand market. Young, exceptionally pretty children, can achieve high prices. As they mature and are used – well, as with any commodity, their value tends to fall in the market place. Rather like second-hand cars; if used extensively, they depreciate, and there are always new models to supersede them.'

"I knew he was arrogant," Raven said. "But I never realised what a sicko he was."

***

'Capes worked for Melody Lockhart with whom I had a long relationship. You will be gratified to know that Melody's death, above all the others, has caused me the greatest pain, even anguish. Charlotte Clarkson did not share my tastes nor had she knowledge of them. She is a pleasant woman, though astonishingly naïve. Being somewhat unworldly and ingenuous, Charlotte was entirely unaware that I was also sleeping with Melody, of whom she has never heard. Since very young, my particular passions have never wavered. They always belonged first, and primarily, to children. Melody would have said precisely the same. Though she cared for me, and showed me an unbounded affection, there was no question that I came second to her intense passion for children.'

"What a freak," Rosie said.

'Sleeping with Charlotte brought an extra piquancy. The danger of being caught out by her added to the excitement. It was enormous fun sleeping with the wife of one of my closest friends, Charles, knowing that she was unaware of my proclivities, and those of her husband, and the real purpose of his overseas' visits. It was, if you like, the ultimate betrayal. I freely confess that it gave me an extra charge.'

***

"Manipulative sod," Raven said. "There's not a sliver of remorse."

Rosie looked at him: "It's the controlling thing – the deliberate cruelty .. the cheating. He clearly didn't give a damn for Charlotte."

"Nor for anybody else." Raven looked again at the letter.

'Charles Clarkson helped set up the network through which we could acquire children – and dispose of them once we had tired of them. A child's novelty can quickly pall. It then becomes necessary to dispose of them and to acquire new specimens. You must remember, Inspector, there are many thousands of private little coteries such as ours. They're in every corner of the world. In towns and villages and remote hamlets. Lawyers, doctors, academics. Professional men and women. Cultured, clever, polished. They are certainly in the police, though I'd hardly call that a 'profession' in the truest sense. It goes without saying that we have politicians and civil servants both here, and overseas; they are, of course, wonderfully helpful in keeping things under wraps. Once the Establishment feels impinged upon by the lower orders, whether it's in the United Kingdom or wherever else, it is marvellously competent at closing ranks, protecting itself, keeping out the light, smothering all attempts at rigorous inquiry. We've been pleased, though always surprised, that some scandal involving children has never engulfed the very highest levels at Westminster and government. Perhaps one day it will happen. Politicians are so inane; terribly mediocre and such a crafty lot, pumped up with self-importance and humbug. No wonder they are held in such low esteem! Each of these different groups, which I have outlined, has the requisite nerve, connections, influence and funding. Few members of these alliances, I suspect, are in reality the low level 'nonces' which most people – and no doubt you – imagine them to be. Rings such as ours blur one into another. They help each other if they possibly can, though the really successful groups operate with a Masonic secrecy. In a lifetime of pursuing our hobby one would never know more than a handful of people who shared our enthusiasms. In this way security can be effectively maintained and people like you, and your rather irritating cohorts, can be kept successfully at bay.'

238

Rosie had moved to the window. She stood staring out at Regent's Park.

"Shame he did himself in. Got off too lightly. And we still don't have the identity of the killer."

"He'd have got life in prison," Raven said. "We'd cornered him. He had no way out."

He continued reading the letter.

'Our troubles began with Gleeson. Gleeson relished excess. He never knew when to stop. His energies endangered our circle. He was always keen to introduce our little guests to more extreme pleasures. It was stupendous fun but I always felt it could prove costly. To be inelegant, we didn't want dead kids on our hands. As well as the inconvenience and difficulty in trying to dispose of a corpse there were monetary considerations. With our contacts we could be confident of a good price for specimens when the time came to trade them in. It surprises me not one iota that Gleeson was the first to be dispatched by the madman whose presence has brought me to this state. The downfall of our circle is largely due to Gleeson.'

"I never thought I'd say thanks to Gleeson," Raven said. "But without him Dilke and the rest of his cronies would still be alive."

"I'm beginning to think we owe quite a lot to the murderer who we haven't caught," Rosie said.

***

'I return now to the question of security. Many times, Melody and I said we ought to destroy a photograph taken in Chamonix, the only link between us. We'd enjoyed a wonderful break in a remote mountain lodge with a little girl brought across from Geneva. She had provided us with three days of pure heaven. She was eventually taken away by her Swiss handler to fulfil another assignation with a group similar to ours in Berne. They were such marvellous memories we simply couldn't bear to get rid of the photograph. We were foolish, of course, breaking our own rules about vigilance. What I can't understand is why you didn't broach my relationship with Melody earlier. You must have found the photograph at the Mews. It was next to her bed. Every time you came to my house I thought this is it, they've found it. But there was never a mention. All I can imagine is that Melody had destroyed it without telling me, which seems unlikely given that we were so close – or, perhaps, the killer took it. For all I know, you still haven't seen the photograph. Or perhaps, Jack, you were being clever with me, just stringing me along, hoping that I'd volunteer some of the things I'm telling you now.'

***

"If only," said Jack. "Without the intervention of whoever it was that sent us the photo and the rest of the stuff – it must have been the killer – we'd still be floundering. We didn't even manage to find the ruddy photo ourselves, and without it we wouldn't have known anything about his relationship with Lockhart."

They moved from the drawing room to the snooker room.

Raven said: "Chamonix .. might have known .. confirms what I've always thought of the Swiss. Cuckoo clocks and yodelling and secret bloody bank accounts. It's a will and testament. He wants it off his conscience. He's worried about meeting his Maker."

"He should be."

The familiar, musty smell, filled the room. They knew now that it was drifting up from the small, windowless cavern below, Dilke's 'playroom,' where his body lay, with the cot, the scattering of pills, the forsaken doll and the ragged teddy bear.

***

'Now what of Grace, my Filipino friend? A mistress of deception.

240

Perhaps you imagined she was an ingénue, a vassal Filipino made subordinate to the cruel whims of a former judge. Grace – not her real name, of course – ensured that our group could tap into the most productive 'farming' areas. The parallel with the livestock industry always entertained us. Grace has fled the nest, so to speak. Given your somewhat limited resources you have absolutely no hope of ever finding her. One could scour the globe without finding a trace. She is travelling to distant corners, settling unfinished business, in search of new 'farming' opportunities with other groups. She had different names and passports and visas, a veritable feast of entirely bogus documentation, all counterfeit but of a magnificent standard. It will add to your annoyance to discover that her real identity, her genuine name, passed into oblivion aeons ago.'

"We'll read the rest outside," Raven said. "I can't stand the smell in here."

***

They went down the stairs to Grace's basement flat. Past the shattered door of the playroom, Dilke's vault, letting themselves out into the garden.

"It's disgusting," Rosie said. "The whole edifice. Dilke and his perverts. This house. The children who suffered. How many children passed through here?"

"And who were they?" Raven looked at her. "Where did they come from? Where were they taken? What happened to them after they left here?"

"They were all somebody's children." Rosie looked up at the sky. More grey clouds. Rain on the way. "All those lives," she said. "All those families. All those wrecked lives."

She looked up at the house. "It makes me vomit. They should knock it down. Turn it into a garden."

They sat on the wrought iron bench beneath the tree. Kicking at the dead leaves turning from red to rust. Raven thought of

Clarkson's pond. The pink lilies stained crimson.

"You read the rest of it," he said. "I'm sick of it."

***

'Grace and I were far more than master and maid. She tended the house and cooked the food. But she also catered for my more personal needs. She preferred this house to her flat and my bed to her own. To outsiders she was the poor Asian maid scuttling around in the basement. However, Grace had gone up in the world a long time ago, and she had made a great deal of money en route. Through her exertions with Capes, sometimes assisted by Charles Clarkson, our group had access to the busiest child trafficking routes in the world. Children are moved around the globe quite easily, in spite of the huffing and puffing of local police forces. There is no way these activities will ever be curbed. The networks are vast and international. They are impeccably concealed, scrupulously organised and handsomely resourced, often with the customary slew of narcotics money behind them. Grace had a further function. She enjoyed the children with the rest of us, but she also carefully monitored them during their stay. She fed, bathed, calmed, drugged and restrained them when it was necessary. One thinks of keeping an animal or pet. One broke them in as one would a puppy or a kitten. Check back on my judgements in court and you'll find that I was notably harsh when sentencing so-called child abusers. This enhanced what you chaps would call my 'cover.' The children were usually only passing through, on their way to other groups. So the starkness of their attic quarters was unimportant. They didn't spend much time there, being usually too busy entertaining the grown-ups downstairs. We held many of our parties in the room in which you have found me. Sometimes members preferred private sessions and wished to be alone with our small visitors. Then we'd move upstairs for a frame of snooker.'

***

242

Rosie walked to the gate at the end of the lawn, looking back down the garden at the graceful curving terrace of houses.

"It's astonishing they could get away with such evil here. In the middle of London. In an area like this. With so many people and tourists around. It all looks so refined, so cultured and elegant."

Raven was on the bench, staring at the ground.

"It's happening all over the place – at this very moment. It just makes you feel so bloody useless."

She continued reading.

'Let me explain why I'm confessing. I am seventy-one. In the natural course of things I do not have much time left. Three score years and ten the Bible insists, that's the standard allocation. Some weeks ago I was pronounced HIV. It must be a loving gift from one of our small friends. One little blighter has kindly infected me. If I was able to get my hands on the kid responsible I would show them just how severe a former judge could be. When I discovered the news I had to curb my physical feelings for Melody. Grace took the news in good part. She and I restricted our activities to matters of a strictly oral nature, an art in which she is wonderfully versed. However, here I encountered a minor problem. Charlotte Clarkson was another matter. She always insisted on a robust physical life. Being a gentleman, how could I refuse? I do hope I have not infected her. But, hey ho! C'est la vie. That's life. I really had very little choice. In what way could I explain to her how on earth I had contracted the wretched plague? News of my contagion, in addition to the worries these murders brought into our lives, caused us considerable anxiety. You'll be pleased to know, Inspector, that we felt your net was closing in. This for us was not a happy scenario. I have had more than my biblical three score years and ten. My HIV would eventually turn into full-blown AIDS. We were likely to be slaughtered by a madman, anyway, and you were rather doggedly on my tail. There was no escape. If I gave myself up, and confessed, then my incarceration as a former judge and so-called abuser would have meant a fate in prison far crueller than death itself. Can you imagine what the inmates would do to a former leading member of the Bar?'

***

'No member of our little group had any idea who was responsible for the killings or if they were next in line. We speculated that he was an avenging child, now a man or woman, whose company we had kept but who had clearly not enjoyed the experience. Children can be such ungrateful little wretches. Why the killings were ritualistic is quite baffling. Gleeson did on occasion make veiled reference to some adventure he had during his years in South America. He had talked about some kid in Brazil being initiated into the more unusual aspects of snooker. It sounded wonderfully imaginative, though we did wonder, for a while, if it could be connected to the murders. So, as you will appreciate, I was faced with a difficult scenario. I could have slipped abroad, had plastic surgery. Passports are easily come by – and then I might, supposedly, simply disappear, in the way that Grace has done. Frankly, however, I really couldn't be bothered. A life on the run, fearful of a knock on the door, with some irritating fellow like you standing there .. I don't think so. I've had a good run, thoroughly enjoyed it, and the thought of scrabbling around in Paraguay or some unspeakably awful place simply didn't appeal. Even if I changed my appearance and went missing, so to speak, the Plague would have done for me.'

***

'The playroom has limited ventilation which accounted for the rheumy trace you noticed in the snooker room. Had our plans not been so rudely interrupted we would have attended to such imperfections. When visitors came to the house discretion was paramount. They came and went quite frequently, generally at night, sometimes by the garden entrance. Now and again a man and a woman would arrive with a child in broad daylight, holding the kid's hand, pretending to be its loving mother and father. They would linger on the front porch, laughing, picking the child up, hugging and kissing it. To anybody watching it would have seemed like an idyllic family group. Privacy was a problem, but not insurmountable. If you have the nerve, and the money, nothing is. London is a city of strangers. In this wealthy corner the residents spend longer at their country retreats, or at their homes abroad, than they do here. Some householders originate from other lands, making them less familiar with London's social and cultural patterns. So many of the once-grand houses in this area are commonly divided into flats. Tenants come and go, as birds on the wing, rarely noticing anything about their temporary abode. People fail to observe that which is beneath their nose. You know, Inspector, as do I from years sitting in judgement on the Bench, how blind are those who should be the perfect witness'

***

"I hate his sneering tone," Raven said. "So bloody unctuous. He's right about witnesses. It was happening right in front of us. We're only a mile or two from the nick."

Rosie looked at her boss. He looked exhausted, eyes black-ringed by tiredness, skin sallow. She put her hand on his arm.

"He's a total bastard, Jack. I'm sorry to say it but I'm glad he's dead, and his scumbag friends. Thank God for the killer. He did a better job than we could ever have done. There's no need for regret. You caught him. We caught him. We forced him into this corner. He says himself he had no way out."

She knew he was unconvinced.

"No .. he knew he was going to die of AIDS. He felt more trapped by that, than by us."

"I don't really agree. But there's no point in me arguing. I know I'll never persuade you. Do you want me to finish reading the letter?"

Raven nodded, holding his head in hands, looking at the ground, at the fallen leaves.

"How many more children are out there, being held by people like Dilke?"

***

'I feel better for my unburdening. I doubt you'll ever get your man Inspector. How shall I put this? You've been on a wild goose chase. Apart from the delicious Grace this unknown assailant has murdered each member of the circle. I too am about to die. So he's effectively killed me as well. As your consolation prize, and it's a pretty big one, you have managed, nevertheless, to ensnare a former High Court judge. Such a catch will enhance your credentials. My demise will assuage concerns about the time and the cost of the investigation which your chiefs will have undoubtedly raised with you. My guess is that they will bury the case, arguing that its pursuance would be indefensibly expensive and ultimately fruitless. In common parlance, Jack – I think I know you well enough by now to employ your first name – you'll be seen as having nailed your man: a former judge, a pillar of the community, a knight of the realm. You'll be hailed as a hero who broke a ring of perverts – which, sadly, will be our epitaph. You'll be seen as the master policeman who secured a memorable coup. Your promotion will be assured. They might even give you an honour. The case will be quietly wound down and when details of the group's activities are released into the public domain the hoi polloi will feed on them as do all swine when faced with the trough.'

***

The Herald and its ilk will work themselves into a lather of self-righteousness. There will be a welter of articles which will demand to know why society has become so poisoned. There will be indignant essays about the pit-props of the community, the professional, chattering classes, and their immersion in demonic activities. Some will say we've received our just desserts. Others will claim that the anonymous killer was entirely justified and doing the job that the police, the courts and the State should have done. Our ring has come to an end. But across the world others will continue to flourish and an endless supply of children will provide them with their nourishment. Try not to fret about their existence, Jack, or that you have failed to find the killer. By the time the Yard and its public relations team has massaged the press releases such considerations will appear trivial. Please convey my affection to your lovely assistant, the delightful Miss Rosie Diamond. I would like to have known her better, to have spent a little private time with her. Though she is quite ravishing, and still young, she is, alas, already too old for my more childish tastes. Goodbye, Jack. Yours etc. etc. Dilke'

***

Raven turned to Rosie: "Didn't you say at one point you liked him?"

"Give me a break Jack. We all make mistakes. It makes my skin crawl."

***

Wilf worried that he had not dealt with the remaining name which Roberto had shared with him, that of Judge Dilke. When the newspapers carried pictures of Dilke and stories about his suicide he had suddenly realised that he had been the unknown person in the Alpine snapshot, one of the gruesome keepsakes which Roberto had garnered and which he had parcelled up and sent to Raven via old Frank Mack. He shook his head in wonderment, and thought of it as confirmation that God worked in mysterious ways.

***

Wilf would eventually grow tired of Kilburn. After a year had passed he quietly slipped away, leaving the Beggars Palace in the care of Stephen Mwenepembe. Mwenepembe would finally move on, back to Kenya to run an orphanage. The Beggars Palace today is in good shape. It's now run by a former colleague of Wilf, an elderly former missionary who had been looking forward to his retirement. But the Order, like all of them, has had such difficulties in attracting people to its ranks that even those who should have been pensioned off years ago are still out in the field. The Beggar's Palace now has a new roof, an excellent heating system and an efficient range on which to cook for its ever growing numbers of clients, the ranks of the homeless and displaced having been greatly swollen by the severity of the world slump. The new television set with its giant screen is already in need of repair, thumped and abused too often.

***

Wilfred went to Brazil, following Roberto, though choosing to make his journey in a more conventional way. To Roberto's astonishment and delight, and quite without warning, Wilf had materialised in the village, declaring that he had come to help in any way that he could, and that there was no way he had ever intended to permit his passing in darkest Kilburn in north London.

***

Flaherty had returned to his patch in Candela in the Amazon. But after a few months he quit his Order and took a job with a charity, the Indigenous Indian Association. He had often warned Roberto and Bernard about his intentions and had said that he could no longer stomach the restrictions placed on him by the Church.

"I am giving up the Order but you don't give up your beliefs," he told them.

He had always wanted to be married and to have children. Subsequently, he married a Brazilian school-teacher from Manaus.

She bore him two children, a boy and a girl. They had thick black hair and eyes like his, as dark and as fiery as coal. He called his daughter Alice and his son Roberto Bernard Wilfred Flaherty.

"Not particularly Irish. But they're the best names I know so they are."

He and his family still live and work in Candela.

**

Bernard still labours at his favela in Rio, coping with the corruption, the narcotics and the gangsters. He thought of 'doing a Flaherty.' Quitting the Order and taking a wife.

"But, as Micheal says, who'd have me? I'm knocking on now. Not as young as I was. I'm a wee little fella and I'm going bald. I live in a shack and get bitten by mad dogs. Whichever way you look at it my prospects aren't good. I'm not exactly a great catch. Anyway, I've already got a family. I've always thought of Roberto as my son."

**

Roberto's grandparents eventually moved from Ealing in London to a cottage in Dorset. They deliberated for a long time before choosing their new home. Fresh horizons and the distractions and challenge of renovating the house and taming its overgrown garden had helped in their healing process. To their huge joy and surprise Roberto had sent them airline tickets. He had booked them in at the Copocabana Palace, a legendary watering hole in Rio de Janeiro which faced the Atlantic Ocean. It would be the first stage of a South American tour in which Roberto would act, for a few happy weeks, as their guide and mentor. They would never learn of his past. Only that he had found some form of solace and salvation back in the land of his birth.

In the village, Roberto had been a whirlwind of energy, leading a team which re-roofed houses, repaired a faulty generator and drilled bore-holes in the ceaseless quest for fresh water. He had renovated the basic clinic which his predecessor, the old priest, had started, and which after his death had become rundown, its stock depleted. With his own money he had bought essential medicines. He had also resuscitated the old priest's notion of an agricultural cooperative. The school flourished. Roberto helped with the teaching, and the elders instilled the traditional knowledge and cultural history of the tribe. As well as assisting with their Portuguese, Roberto also gave lessons in English.

"It will help you in dealing with the white man," he told them.

"Everybody now speaks English and one day you might want to leave here and seek work somewhere else. If that happens then your English could be vital."

He worked round the clock and fought many battles on their behalf. A German pharmaceuticals company had offered the villagers money to act as guinea-pigs for untried elixirs. Roberto had sought legal advice in Brasilia and at his hectoring a posse of civil rights lawyers had successfully railed against the proposition. A Canadian logging company and a South African mining combine had connived to strip the trees from a swath of the forest and then to mine the land for minerals. Roberto had galvanised an effective lobby and the plans had been ditched. He had toured other remote settlements warning inhabitants to be on their guard against strangers. Telling them to protect their children, not to be gulled into letting them be lured away by the promise of a better life. When he was tired he lay on his mattress and through the open door of his shack watched the vultures, black as witches, circling high in the sky.

***

Much of that which Dilke had predicted would transpire. The case had been quietly shelved. Weeks after the sensation had vanished from the newspapers Raven and Rosie had a drink in the Feathers.

"Mother's ruin," he told her, his mood morose, staring into his gin. "I said you'd get to like it."

"You don't look like somebody who's just been promoted."

"Promoted for failure. It's how they try and stop you rocking the boat."

"You're too hard on yourself Jack. Dilke was malignant. Without the intervention of the man we didn't get those animals would still be operating and we wouldn't have known a damn thing about them."

Raven was not to be cheered.

"It's twisted logic. Once we start deciding who deserves to die and who doesn't the whole bloody edifice comes crashing down. We're supposed to catch the wrongdoers. What happens to them afterwards is not our job. That's for magistrates and judges and perverted bastards like Dilke to decide. We didn't get Grace and we didn't get the killer. We still don't have a clue who he was or what he's called. You can argue that Dilke and his pals got what they deserved – but it's not what we're supposed to be about. If we ever got the budget .. well, we'll see. I'll probably have jacked the whole bloody thing in by then. There's got to be a better way of spending your life."

"I gather you're taking time off."

"Toe Rag tell you?"

"Sort of .. going somewhere?"

"Sailing .. probably never come back."

"You'll be back. It's a drug. You know you can't leave it alone."

EPILOGUE

Charlotte Clarkson had a nervous breakdown and is today HIV. After nearly eleven years Roberto died of AIDS. There are three crosses deep in the rainforest where the trees grow tall and sylvan streams run clear and unpolluted. The villagers buried Roberto next to his predecessor the old priest, his grave marked by a second simple cross. Wilf died soon after, of old age and exhaustion. His was the third cross. He was buried next to Roberto, with the small battered crucifix his mother had given him, and which was formerly on the wall at his cell in the Beggars Palace. Rosie is still in the police force and her career is flourishing. Raven is uncomfortable in his new job and the amount of desk work it entails. He talks frequently of quitting. He has never had sufficient budget or the sanction of his superiors to pursue Grace or Roberto. Not that he had ever heard of Roberto. Grace was never seen again. The ring which had snatched Roberto as a child from his favela in Rio de Janeiro all those years before, of which Gleeson had been a member and which was led by a man called Lascelle, was never broken. Nor were any of its members ever brought to trial.

About the Author

John Swinfield has an MA in maritime history and is an ex-Fleet Street journalist, broadcaster and historian. A former Industrial Journalist of the Year, he was an on-screen reporter with Nationwide (BBC1) and The Money Programme (BBC2). For ITV/C4 he made the Enterprise series, an award-winning documentary strand where he travelled the globe, producing and directing myriad films about the rich and influential, such as David Rockefeller, Robert Maxwell, Richard Branson and Gloria Vanderbildt.

He has three Royal Television Society awards. He won the Sandford St. Martin Premier Award for his film Beggars in Paradise (ITV) shot in Peru, one of several documentaries he made about dispossessed peoples in the teeming slums of Latin America and south-east Asia. John Swinfield was also previously the executive producer of Arts & Features for Anglia Television and is a well-known public speaker.

His published works include two world histories *Airship: Design, Development & Disaster*; and the daring saga of early submariners, from Da Vinci's earliest imaginings to the underwater warriors of WW1, *Sea Devils: Pioneer Submariners*.